I0795809

AUTOKILL

Autokill

Sam Schwartz & Cary Pepper

OPEN ROAD
INTEGRATED MEDIA
NEW YORK

All rights reserved, including without limitation the right to reproduce this book or any portion thereof in any form or by any means, whether electronic or mechanical, now known or hereinafter invented, without the express written permission of the publisher.

This is a work of fiction. Names, characters, places, events, and incidents either are the product of the author's imagination or are used fictitiously. Any resemblance to actual persons, living or dead, businesses, companies, events, or locales is entirely coincidental.

Copyright © 2026 by Sam Schwartz & Cary Pepper

ISBN: 979-8-3372-0840-4

Published in 2026 by Open Road Integrated Media, Inc.
180 Maiden Lane
New York, NY 10038
www.openroadmedia.com

Dedicated to the memory of Naibel Benavides (1996–2019)
whose life was cut short after being struck by a Tesla on Autopilot.

AUTOKILL

Prologue

FUNCTIONING PERFECTLY ON EVERY TRIP

October 10, 2036

California's San Joaquin Valley encompasses seven counties, crisscrossed by dozens of two-lane blacktops that connect small farming towns and highway intersections.

Just south of Bakersfield, State Highway 58 runs from Bakersfield through Green Acres and Rosedale; it zigs to the right at SR 43, then zags to the left and runs arrow-straight to Buttonwillow.

As late afternoon slid into sunset, a CAV (connected autonomous vehicle) carrying pharmaceutical cargo was travelling west along 58 on its usual route. Some of its stops included homes where people would be waiting outside, having been notified their order was arriving. Other stops were chain drugstores where robots would transfer inventory from the vehicle to the store's shelves. The CAV slowed if it had to when its camera detected a vehicle directly ahead, or adjusted its speed or lane position when its sensors were alerted to changing conditions by transponders mounted on the countless utility poles along the road. But for the most part, it was cruising at a steady 50 mph, the posted speed limit.

Approaching Green Acres, it dropped its speed to 30 as it passed the first sign advising a slow-down. Forty seconds later, it decelerated to 25 when it entered the town limits. Coming to a stop sign, it glided to a smooth halt, waited seven seconds while its cameras and sensors scanned right, left, and dead ahead, then, seeing nothing, kicked back into gear and proceeded through the intersection. A human driver would have noticed the early (still three weeks away) Halloween decorations in the store windows and on the porches of the houses it passed. But the CAV had no interest in that. Its only concern (though it had no concerns in the true sense of the word) was doing what it was programmed to. It had traveled this route more than a hundred times, functioning perfectly on every trip.

It decelerated again as it approached the remaining stop sign before it would leave town. As it idled at the corner, its cameras and scanners "saw" a pickup truck on the cross-street to the right, data confirmed by communicating with the transponder on top of the stop sign. The CAV "knew" that the truck, having arrived at the intersection three seconds earlier (confirmed by the stop-sign transponder), had the right of way. It remained motionless while the truck crossed in front of it, then waited another three seconds. Had it been able to, it might have mused on the fact that the truck had a human driver. But the CAV's attention was on the millions of messages it was receiving and processing nonstop as it made its way toward Buttonwillow. After the prescribed three-second wait, its cameras and sensors said it was safe to move on, and it proceeded out of town.

On its way to Rosedale and receiving a stream of "all clear" messages, it picked up speed and was soon back to 50 miles an hour, instruments continuously scanning front, rear, left, and right, seeking new information that might lead to an adjustment. Two minutes out, in response to a message from its front camera, it glided left to avoid a pothole. Five minutes later, it decelerated as it came up on an RV that was slowing down to turn. When the RV was out of its path, it returned to its 50-mph cruising speed.

Sixty seconds later, there was a warning from both the rear camera and sensor: a Porsche was coming up fast from behind. The AV slowed and smoothly slid a foot to the right to give the Porsche, travelling well above the speed limit, room to safely pass. As the Porsche increased the distance between the two vehicles, the CAV returned to the center of its lane and accelerated to fifty.

Coming to the intersection with SR 43, it stopped, scanned left and right, and receiving the "all clear" code, made a right onto 43. Within a few minutes it decelerated to make the left that put it back on 58. According to its computer, it was now fifteen minutes from Buttonwillow.

Fourteen and half minutes later, just outside town, it neared the T-intersection where SR 58 met a small local road. Signs at the intersection, and the CAV's computer, told it that Tupman was 10 miles to the left. If it turned right, it could pick up Interstate 5.

Straight ahead, set back 50 feet back from the road, was a small park with a playground and several benches. On one of the benches sat Koresha Reynolds, taking a break from her job at the front desk of the small motel half a block away. She worked a 12-hour day and spent her afternoon breaks here. But now it was time to go back to work.

Still travelling at 50 mph, the AV saw the T intersection.

It read the signs showing the directions and distances to Tupman and Interstate 5. It saw the stop sign on the corner to its right. It should have come to a halt, checked that there was no cross traffic, and made the right turn that would take it to Buttonwillow. Instead, it blew through the stop sign and drove straight into the park, closing the distance to Koresha Reynolds in five seconds. She would later be declared dead at the scene.

The cybermarshal assigned to investigate the incident would eventually discover what went wrong and why Koresha Reynolds died. But that discovery would give her no inkling of what was really about to happen.

1

ONE OF A KIND

Richard Corby looked up as Melissa walked into his office. The corner of his eye caught the clock and he couldn't help but smile. Of course it was three on the button. If there were other students of her caliber at the school, he hadn't met them. Smart, perceptive, unrelentingly curious, and at times ferociously tenacious (and always punctual), she really was one of a kind.

Settling into the chair across from his desk, she dropped what appeared to be her student ID in front of him. When he picked it up, he found himself looking at a blonde woman with shoulder-length hair and blue eyes. Not Melissa—whose burnt sienna hair was cropped close, and whose eyes were a dark brown.

"You found someone's ID?" he asked.

"Nope!" He could hear the pleasure in her voice. "Read the name."

"Melissa Scalo. So, you . . . what? Managed to make yourself a fake ID?"

"Since TruFile, you can't do that," she reminded him.

"If anyone could, it'd be you."

"And I did!" The pleasure had turned to triumph.

"You're saying you found a way to hack TruFile?"

Five years ago, in response to the mass shootings on college campuses that had quadrupled during the '20s, the university instituted triple-tier security measures. Sensors located throughout the campus scanned ID cards that had to be carried by every student, faculty, and staff member.

The scanners would not recognize a card unless it had been issued by an authorized campus safety officer and double checked by another, a process that took place in a secure control room with leaded walls to prevent remote hacking. Identity-checked visitors to the campus were issued temporary cards that expired after 12 hours. Strategically placed facial-recognition cameras triggered a silent alarm if the face and card didn't match, and all cards had embedded chips created by a no-fault secure protocol.

Since then, it was impossible to create a fake ID card because it was impossible to hack the chip protocol. It was also not possible to create a fake ID by creating an entirely new card with a counterfeit chip because the cards were printed on campus, using proprietary watermarked plastic, and fake chips were detected by the scanners.

"You found a way around TruFile?" he asked again.

"Hacked the crap out of it!" Her self-satisfied grin resembled the Cheshire cat.

"Have a little free time last night? If you really did this . . ."

"I *did* really do it!" She gestured to the card.

"Even if you could hack the chip protocol . . . This looks like a real ID."

"It *is*. I know someone who works in the office where they generate the cards. Called in a favor."

"Must have been some favor."

picture that looked nothing like him. Instead of a full head of dark hair, the man he was looking at was bald. Instead of his green eyes, these were a ghoulish yellow. Instead of being six feet tall, his would-be doppelganger was 5'5". With thick glasses (which he never wore). And his age had been changed from 50 to 65.

"What'd you *do* to me!?"

"Wanted to see if I could input anything, or if there were parameters to what it would accept."

"So if I ever need a replacement card, *this* is what I'm gonna get?"

"No," she almost sneered, as if being insulted. "After I made the cards, I zapped everything from the system. These don't exist anymore. No fingerprints."

He shook his head. "You put yourself out there, they're gonna snap you up. If some foreign government doesn't kidnap you first."

"We won't tell them I'm here."

"They probably already know exactly where you are. And they're looking for you."

"OK," she shifted in the chair as she changed gears. "Didn't mean to hijack the afternoon. What has to be done?"

He almost laughed at realizing her question surprised him, pulling him from one context to another. She was here to help *him*, and he'd gotten caught up in what *she* was working on. He wished he had a dozen students like her, knowing how lucky he'd be to have just one more in her league.

"You do *this*," he said, waving the false ID she'd just given him, "and you want to pretend it's an ordinary Friday?"

"It *is* an ordinary Friday," she shrugged. "If I hacked the NSA, it'd be a big deal. This . . . wasn't that hard."

"Be sure you tell them that."

"First item on the list."

"And try to say it without the shit-eating grin."

"Of course," she answered, shit-eating grin stretching ear-to-ear. "What's on the agenda today? Need anything for the *Register* op-ed?"

"Already know what I'm gonna say." Corby rattled it off. "Autonomous vehicles offer a potentially-rich future, but that future will be realized only if we act wisely now. We can have cities with group rides offered by fleets of driverless electric cars and microbuses seamlessly integrated with mass transit, and a greatly-reduced carbon footprint. Or we can repeat the past pattern of decision-making that put cars over people at the turn of the 20th century."

Melissa's voice took on a jaunty lilt as she interrupted him to recite the rest. "Washington seems determined to choose cars over people. As we stand poised to allow private ownership of CAVs again, the federal government is updating its regulations regarding autonomous vehicles. But these policies are being crafted by the industry, not environmentalists and experienced urban planners."

She paused, and he took over. "The new rules will eliminate the power of local governments to implement any control of autonomous vehicles, and if the AV Industrial Complex gets its way, the benefits of CAVs will go the way of so many other well-intentioned but poorly-executed technological revolutions."

Melissa couldn't stop the corners of her mouth from turning down at the AV-Industrial-Complex reference. She decided against pointing out yet again it was reminiscent of Eisenhower '50's rhetoric.

"You've got that middle section down word for word," Corby grinned. "Didn't know you were *that* big a fan. Or have I used it before?"

"Only in the *Post*, *Herald*, and *Informer*." Melissa hoped she'd kept her voice as level as she'd wanted it to be.

"Those words, other words . . . Not sure it's going to matter much. This . . ." He held up one hand, waggling his fingers ". . . is all it takes to count the people who are listening. To me. Washington is listening to the industry."

"OK," he abruptly changed the subject. "Time for *this*!" He opened a drawer, plucked out the Blue Binder, and tapped it three times.

"But you just keep that in the drawer. Are you ever going to—"

Corby held up an admonishing finger. "Never disrespect the Blue Binder."

"No. It's *The Blue Binder*."

"Consider it my hobby. I've evolved from stamps and vintage calendars to collecting Zach Rood weirdness."

"Kind of one-note, isn't it?"

"Only to the untrained eye and mind. In here we have . . ." Corby counted off the categories: "wrong ideas; exaggerated statements; 'facts' not supported by the evidence he says support them; statements not supported by *any* evidence; claims supported by evidence discredited years ago; and a category I just call 'Bizarre.' I'm thinking of color-coding them."

"Yeah, it's fun. But are you gonna *do* anything with this?" She tapped the binder three times.

Corby might have bristled had that come from anyone else. From Melissa, it was everyday conversation. Her beyond-her-years confidence wasn't the false wisdom of young-adulthood "you can't teach me anything," or the arrogance of egoists who believe they're the smartest person in the room. She may have been all of 26, but she could back up anything she said. It was one of the things he liked most about her, yet another reason he was glad she'd asked him to mentor her, and why he'd made her his TA. And she'd proved herself worthy, holding her own in any discussion, never meekly deferring to him like his other students did.

He already knew about her when she arrived at the University of Portland two years ago, having gotten a heads-up from a colleague at Berkeley who suggested Corby keep an eye out for her because "she has a mind you'll love."

So he was pleased when she showed up in his class on Social Justice in Urban Planning, and not all that surprised when she was the only one in the class who'd read his latest book on the subject before it was assigned. She was everything the Berkeley professor had said.

But for Corby, she was more—the first student to seek him out as a mentor since That Day in the dean's office.

"I *have* it," he told her, referring to the binder. "That's enough."

"So it's a labor of love? Must be great to have a hobby that's so . . . gratuitous."

"I think by definition all hobbies are gratuitous. And if *I* don't do this, who will?"

"Does anyone *have* to? The man wants a Right-To-Drive Amendment added to the Constitution! He's a joke."

"That's what they said about Donald Trump in '16. The candidate who couldn't win, the Joke, wound up in the White House. Then he did it *again,* in '24!"

"But the people who listen to Rood—"

"Believe every word he says."

"You're talking about 20% of the country."

"21.3%. New poll out this week."

"Make it 24% Or 29. It's still not enough to pass an amendment."

"That's what they said about Prohibition in 1919. Passed in

13 months." Corby was off and running, and there was no stopping him. "Took the Women's Rights Amendment 48 years to be ratified by enough states, and by then it was too late. The deadline for ratification had come and gone. So even when the ERA was finally ratified by 38 states, it took another five years of lawsuits—all the way to the Supreme Court—before it became part of the Constitution."

"The Right-To-Drive Amendment will never pass." She was just as determined to defend her position.

"*That's* what they said about Prohibition!" Corby threw up his hands. "And that's *why* it passed. People believed it never would, so they didn't bother to oppose it.

"You have any idea how much damage Prohibition caused?" Now he was really going. "Got the Mafia up and running. And it was the law of the land for 13 years. Because of Wayne B. Wheeler, who was *not* a joke, and who, unlike Zach Rood, really did have power, and . . . I'm lecturing again." He finally reeled it in.

"That's what they pay you for." The mischievous grin was back.

"Not enough to do it on my own time. Lecture's over."

There was a knock at the door and Doug Stuart stuck his head in. "Professor, you said to see you about my paper."

Uncoiling from his chair, Corby quickly covered the six steps to the next room. He scooped up a paper from a stack on a table and turned to page four to read the troublesome paragraph one more time. As he did, he heard Doug and Melissa in the other room.

"You and Corby are getting along great. As usual." It was a simple statement, but the innuendo was clear.

"Yeah," Melissa shrugged it off.

"I'd get along with him great too, if I had what you had."

Corby strode back to his desk. "What does she have?"

"Nothing, Professor. Sorry. I was just . . . fooling around."

But Corby wouldn't let it go. "Well, since you can't answer that, I'll tell you what she 'has.' Two years ago she won the DARPA Grand Challenge. Know *how* she won it? By demonstrating the hacking vulnerabilities of robotaxi fleets. Her work transformed that industry when it made her software-fix a standard element in all robocabs. *That's* what she has."

Doug had nothing to offer but a contrite nod.

"Oh, and one more thing. She doesn't make careless mistakes like the one you did on page four." Corby waved Doug's paper. "That's what I wanted to talk to you about. I've circled the paragraph. See me again when you've reworked it."

Doug took the paper, mumbled "Sorry," and slunk out.

Melissa waited a few seconds before speaking. "Could you have slammed him harder?"

"He deserved to be slammed."

"But I wish you'd let me handle it."

"I had to give him a hard time for the mistake in his paper. What he said to you decided how hard a time it would be."

"But when you step in like that it looks like I can't speak for myself."

"Anyone who knows you, *knows* you have no trouble whatsoever speaking for yourself," Corby snorted.

"Anyone who says something like that, doesn't know me."

"*That* still goes on?"

"Richard, when do you think it stopped?" They'd long ago, at Corby's insistence, dropped the formality of Professor or Doctor Corby. He was Richard; she was Melissa. Official and officious titles always made him uncomfortable.

"Why didn't you tell me?"

"Why?"

"So I could—"

"I don't want you to. That's what I'm saying. I can't go running to you every time some idiot says something stupid."

"It's not running to me. It's—"

"That's what it'd look like. That's what they'd say it was. I appreciated you wanting to protect me, but—"

"Protect you? I'm just . . . I can put a stop to it."

"No, you can't. So please, next time—"

"Next time? How often does it happen?"

She rolled her eyes. "If I bothered to keep track . . . If I collected them . . . I'd have a Blue Binder, too."

2

TRUE FACTS

Jason Bartel turned the ignition key and, as he always did, listened carefully as the engine spun to life. One of the burdens of owning a vintage car was the need to catch potential warning signs before they turned into real trouble. He learned that the hard way with his '68 Firebird. He'd been hearing "that sound" every time he started the car, but attributed it to the eccentricities of an older engine. It was only when his mechanic told him the timing belt was shot and he'd never be able to replace it, that he realized he'd been too cavalier about the car and needed to pay attention to every sound and sign. Well, never again.

And it was paying off. He'd had this '60 Chevy Impala for 25 years and the few times it had given him any trouble he had it in the shop within hours. It'd been months since his last repair, the car was running like new, and he was going to keep it that way. So the ever-vigilant listening wasn't really a burden. It was more an obligation, a responsibility any smart owner of a vintage car shouldered willingly.

The Impala was a fire-engine-red first-generation 348-cubic-inch big-block V-8, with triple carburetion and hydraulic lifters, all authentic from the factory. There were times he wished he'd been able to get the high-performance solid lifter tri-power engine, which would have boosted the horse power from 280 to 315, but when he was on the open road, putting the car through its paces as he ran the gears of the four-on-the-floor Muncie transmission, he felt an ecstatic oneness with the machine that surpassed everything else in his life.

He loved the way people admired the vehicle, pointing to all the chrome (the grille, the edges of the fins, the rear-lights panel) that contemporary cars just didn't have any more; he was especially fond of the chrome-and-enamel side sweeps and molding that ran from the doors to the rear lights, starting with the likeness of a sleek jet, crossed racing flags for contrails sprouting from its tail. He'd done some serious work on the Impala, and the hardest part to get was that piece of chrome. But he'd finally chased it down and made sure to lavish it with extra attention every time he polished the car.

The huge fins extending from the center of the trunk to an inch or so out over the sides gave the car a swept look that, seen from the rear, made him feel it *was* a jet waiting to fly. Sometimes he swore he felt the airlift when he hit 100+ mph on near-empty (and occasionally not-so-empty) late-night desert highways. Together, they'd topped 100 in all 48 continental states, thanks to the cross-country Rally Raids he regularly participated in. And he never tired of telling anyone who'd listen about his 2032 third-place finish.

An American variation on the endurance races that began in the 1970s in France, these competitions didn't arrive in the United States until 2029. Bartel loved the cross-country races because they were throwbacks to the past. No car newer than 1975 was permitted to enter, and no navigation tools (especially GPS) were allowed. A paper map was provided at the start, listing the 25–30 cities, towns, or landmarks each participant had to hit. Competitors had no clue until fifteen minutes before the start of the race, when they were given their list. The race went from ocean to ocean (Atlantic to Pacific or vice versa), and the first driver to reach the final location was declared the winner. In the '28 race, Bartel finished in 43 hours, 56 minutes, and 11 seconds, just 4 minutes out of second place and 54 minutes out of first. He averaged 83.7 mph over the approximately 3,600-mile run with a peak speed of 161.3 mph through the Mojave Desert. Jason reveled in the event because it pushed to the max both automotive machine and the person at the wheel.

With the Impala started and running smoothly, he took his special moment to appreciate how new the interior felt, with its original red-and-white striped vinyl seats. He'd added a Chevy 44-watt AM-FM radio to the dashboard (no fancy RainbowTooth wireless connections) and installed two authentic Mecca '60s vintage stereo speakers. He'd very reluctantly put in seat belts (red, to match the seats), but only after he'd been stopped by overzealous cops who didn't care that the car had been manufactured before seat belts were mandated by an overreaching government.

Jason turned on the radio, already set to KXLO, to catch what he could of *True Facts* before Hector arrived.

"Washington loves telling us what to do. Like prayer in public schools. But should the government be deciding for you what's best for your kids? If you want them to be able to pray every morning, what's the harm in that? No one's telling the kids *who* to pray to, just that they *can* pray. Because that's America! And as Americans, you're entitled to every right in the Constitution!"

As usual, Zach Rood was in good form.

"Last year the Virus came back, like it does every year. And they wanted to ban public gatherings. *Again.* Is that fair to the rest of us? Some state governors thought it wasn't. They preferred to allow the public—people like you and me—to meet wherever, whenever they wanted. I believe that's in the Constitution, too. Maybe half of Congress doesn't care what's in the Constitution, but I do. And I think *you* do!

"Now they want to come for our cars. They want you to sit inside a robot. Is that what driving is? Not the way I remember it. And let's talk a little more about that secret plan to outlaw human driving on public highways.

"It's only a matter of time until AVs exceed 50% of all cars on our roads. And when that happens, believe-you-me the Federal government is going to make it a criminal offense—that's right, a *criminal* offense—to drive . . . Wait, let me correct that . . . for *people* to drive, on federal highways. AV's, which we all know are basically robots, will have all the freedom they want. But you, my human friends, will be forced off the very roads your tax dollars pay for. Isn't *that* something to look forward to?

"It's already happened in Europe. What I want to know is, while they're protecting all things robo, where's the protection for *people*? Where are our Constitutional guarantees, that's right, *guarantees* like life, liberty, and the pursuit of happiness. Which, for me, certainly includes driving my own car.

"Now, some people say the right to drive isn't in the Constitution. I say it was omitted only because cars didn't exist yet. But that doesn't mean it's not part of my very American right to happiness. Washington does a lot of things, but it can *not* tell *me* what makes me happy!

"Don't let them tell *you*. Do not let yourself be disenfranchised. Do not let them push you to the margins! Make yourself heard!

"OK, before we take a quick break, I want to remind our Phoenix listeners there's another PARD rally in town today, and it's starting soon, so drive over there—while you still can—and sign some petitions. That's one way to make yourself heard.

"And let's all give a big shout-out to Phoenix chapter chairman Jason Bartel, for his second rally this month. Way to do it, Jason!"

Bartel smiled. That beer he'd bought for the guy who suggested sending Rood an e-mail whenever he held a rally had paid for itself many times over.

"I'm gonna end today's segment with this: If your town doesn't already have its own PARD chapter—and it should!—for God's sake, start one! I've said it before, and I'll keep saying it as long as I have a voice—Make yourself heard!"

Jason started listening to Rood's show four years ago, when work was steady and he spent hours in the truck, crisscrossing the country with full loads in both directions. At first, he tuned in as a way to have company, to fill the cab with sound and have another presence. When the work dried up and Sheila left, he started listening at home, too.

Little by little he found himself agreeing with Rood more and more, finding not only a presence, but also comfort and a kindred spirit. He began to look forward to the broadcasts.

Then he started listening to the podcasts as well as the radio show. The segments that focused on trade deficits or public prayer didn't interest Jason. But Rood began to zero in on something that did—AVs. That's when Jason really started listening. And became a hardcore fan.

Rood had it right. He knew the score. As the title of the show said, he was giving you True Facts. Jason knew better than anyone that AVs were a threat. Rood was sounding an alarm that everyone should be listening to.

He gave Jason a foundation. Before Rood, Jason knew he was angry, but it was a wild, flailing turmoil. He was angry at

Sheila. He was angry at losing his livelihood. Listening to Rood brought things into focus. AVs were why Sheila left him. *They* had destroyed his livelihood. Fueled by his newfound clarity, he formed the Phoenix chapter of PARD—Protect Americans' Right to Drive.

Jason glanced in the rear-view mirror and saw Hector approaching, laptop carelessly slung over his shoulder. Even from here he could see that Hector was still wearing the same shirt (with the same brown stain [gravy? soy sauce? tomato sauce?]) he'd been wearing for the last five days. Tracking Hector's progress toward the car, and his odd gait that was one part shamble, one part shuffle (there was nothing physically wrong with Hector, it seemed he just couldn't be bothered to move with anything approaching easy balance or grace), Jason was about to shout his usual warning, but was distracted by a passing vehicle.

As Hector slid into the car, Jason heard the thump.

"You hit the car again."

"I did?" Hector asked. As Jason knew he would.

"With your laptop. As usual." It wasn't the end of the world—the laptop was snug in a padded carrying bag, so Jason knew there'd be no damage to the Impala. But it was the principle of the thing. He'd asked him countless times to be more careful.

Hector slumped back in his seat, casually propping his feet against the glove compartment.

"Feet!" Jason growled from between clenched teeth as he turned off the radio.

"Sorry," Hector mumbled, sitting up straight.

Jason checked to make sure there were no marks on the dash.

"It's not usual," Hector pointed out. "I hit the car 6 times the last 57 I got into the car. That's only 10.5%. 'As usual' would be at least 50.1%. Which would be 28.557 times. So that's not—"

"Yeah, yeah, not accurate. Why is it so hard to look out for the car when you get in?"

"It's not hard. I just don't do it."

Jason rolled his eyes. "Why do I bother?"

"Because it's important to you."

"And *you* keep doing it, because?"

Hector didn't answer. Jason waited for several seconds, then: "You gonna answer that?"

"Answer what?"

"I asked why you keep doing it."

"No, you didn't. You said, 'you keep doing it because.' That's not a complete sentence. And it isn't a question. And even if it is, it's not a complete thought. So I was waiting for you to finish."

"OK, I'm finished. Just don't do it again."

"I—"

"There goes another one!" Jason jerked his head toward the vehicle that had distracted him a minute ago. "Everywhere you look." He was gazing at the autonomous cab that had just dropped off someone across the street. Now, having turned around, it was headed back toward them. "Watch this."

As the cab approached, Jason edged away from the curb. Seeing another vehicle in close proximity, the cab immediately came to a halt. Jason waited until the cab, sensing no movement from his vehicle, started forward again.

He eased his foot off the brake and the cab stopped. Then Jason did it again, waiting for the cab to start forward, taking his foot off the brake, and watching the taxi instantly defer.

"I could do this all day," he laughed. "And it would just stay there. Can't see I'm screwing with it."

"The sensors can't detect or decipher emotions," Hector pointed out.

"Exactly! A driver would see we're at a standstill here and do something. And he'd know that if he kept coming, I'd back off and let him pass, or I'd start forward, and he'd respond."

"It *is* responding."

"Yeah, but you keep doing this to a person, he's either going to barrel past you, or turn around and go the other way to get rid of you. Maybe jump out of his car and want to beat the shit out of you. But this? If we didn't have to get to the rally, I'd stay here and play with it all day."

Jason took his foot off the brake and rolled into the street. After he passed the motionless cab, he glanced in his mirror and saw it resuming its journey in the opposite direction. "Stupid moron," he muttered.

"That's not only a redundancy, it's a misplaced redundancy," Hector commented. "A moron *is* stupid. Or at least not as intelligent, by comparison, as others, and certainly deficient in what's considered a desirable degree of intelligence. But that's in relation to people. So you can't apply it to a machine."

"Thanks. I didn't know that."

"It just requires an understanding of knowledge and the ability to apply logic."

Jason knew Hector would say that. Feeling less satisfaction from playing with the robo-cab, he was now playing with Hector. But that, too, wasn't as satisfying as he wanted it to be, so he changed the subject.

"What's the count on the site?"

"Yesterday there were 150 followers. This morning it was 153. An increase of almost 2%."

"Could be more, but as long as it's going up."

"By almost 2%."

"Gotta say, I've heard it a million times, but I'm still blown away by how you can do that."

"Do what?"

Jason didn't answer, his attention drawn by another passing car—one with a driver. "Look at that!" he pointed toward the car's bumper sticker: *Protect Americans' Right to Drive*. "One of ours!" He gave the horn two quick raps and shouted "Hey Pard!" The driver tooted back.

"See? You don't get that kind of give-and-take with robos. You get nothing from them."

"Technically, not true. That robo stopped for you. So you did get something from it."

"What? Respect?"

"Not possible, since it's an insentient entity. You got an acknowledgement of Newton's Third Law. For every action there's an equal and opposite reaction."

"I'd rather have respect."

"But that acknowledgement can save lives."

"So can respect. Were the boxes picked up?" Jason asked before Hector could expound on the difference between human and insentient entities, or the advantages of an acknowledgment of Newton's Third Law over respect.

"Yes. They were picked up this morning."

"Good mix?"

"A box of each."

"Oughta do it. And they picked up the petitions, and everything else we're gonna need?"

"The petitions, the pens, the signs, and the hats."

"How many of those have we sold?"

"As of this morning, 173. An increase of 5, or almost 3%."

"As long as it's going up."

"By almost 3%."

Jason shifted his attention to a car that had pulled to the curb 100 feet ahead. Another robo-cab. Glancing around, he saw there were no buildings from which a perspective fare might emerge, which meant the cab wasn't needed at the moment and had pulled to the side to conserve resources. Cruising cabs were a thing of the past. When robos had no fares, they found a safe place to stop and shut down until they were summoned by the Dispatch-Bot.

Jason shook his head. "I swear, sometimes I think they plan their routes just to annoy me."

"I don't think they'd—"

"Joke, Hector!"

"I got the job," Hector revealed, off on his own track.

"Which one?"

"The coding job."

"They're *all* coding jobs. That's what you do."

"The one with TeKeX. Reconfiguring their intranet."

"That's great." Jason had no idea which job Hector was talking about. "This one from home, too?"

"They're all from home."

That, Jason did know. Hector didn't do well interacting with people.

Hector turned to gaze out the window, and Jason's thoughts were taken over by the feel of the Impala's steering wheel under his hands. It was a part of him, a natural extension. The sensation conjured visions of Rally Raids, but rather than giving him the usual pleasure, today they turned dark.

Two, three years ago, he was doing well behind the wheel of his own semi. Then he and just about every other trucker he knew started losing business to AV trucks. For a while he was able to hold on to his most profitable route—Boston/San Diego. Last year he lost it to Auto-Truck America.

He'd busted his ass to do the run in, first, six days, then five, and finally four-and-a-half. To do that, he'd remodeled his cab, installing a refrigerator, coffee maker, portable urinal, and bed. But he was only human, he needed to rest sometime. Meanwhile, the robos were doing the run in three days because they didn't sleep, didn't eat, and never needed a bathroom. The last year, when it was all falling apart, he'd patented his cab and sold a few to other desperate drivers. Then more robos were put on the road as ATA expanded its reach, gobbling up one route after another, and that, too, came to an end. Why buy a cab custom-made for long hauls when you weren't getting long-haul contracts?

Jason made ends meet with the short hops he managed to scrape together. But just making ends meet wasn't good enough for Sheila. As his income diminished, his wife's anger at him for "not holding up his end" increased, until she finally moved out. Now the evenings he wasn't at The Restless Rustler were spent rattling around an empty house, still missing her. Sometimes he looked her up on social media, partly as a way of maintaining at least that much contact, partly to see if she were involved with someone else.

When he wasn't grieving the loss of Sheila or drinking at The Rustler, he replayed Rood's warnings that robos were a menace to an entire way of life—not just to truckers like him, but to everyone.

And Rood had the facts to prove it. Uber bought Lyft in 2028, then UberLyft went robo in '30, and lowered their prices in every major city so much that it was cheaper to take a robo than travel by public transportation. Unable to compete, cab companies went out of business, and many urban mass transportation systems were reduced to bare-bones service. UL won the war. But doing it meant the company was hemorrhaging money. Then the virus of '31 hit, and with millions sheltering in place it didn't matter how low UL's fares were. By '32, its investors abandoned the company, sending it into bankruptcy. Which sent the economy into a recession because, after UL had virtually strangled transit systems out of existence, people couldn't get to work.

But that wasn't all. With fewer people buying cars because it was easier to travel by robo, dealerships went out of business. Repair facilities followed. He knew two mechanics, nice guys always ready to buy a round for the table, who had to close their shops. And with many robos (*all* the new ones) going electric, fewer gas stations were needed. More jobs lost. Three of his favorite truck stops shut down.

Then Washington helped robocabs make a spectacular comeback with its Emergency Auto Transit Act, which authorized the federal government to insure AV businesses. Venture capitalists swarmed in to fund new robocab companies, and now they were everywhere.

Economics aside, AVs were infringements on the individuality that was part of the American psyche. America had invented the automobile. Owning a car was a right, buying your first car a rite of passage, like getting your driver's license.

Thank God for Rood, who was getting the word out and keeping the fight alive. And thank God for the Internet, where people could find one another, come together, and exchange information.

Jason started posting in the chat rooms last year, at first just an occasional inspired thought or pro-human-driver argument. Then he began sharing pro-human-driver information.

One day he realized people were listening to him. Reposting and spreading *his* ideas. He had followers. Initially, a dozen or so. Then Rood mentioned him on the air, and suddenly he had hundreds. Fired up, Jason started the Phoenix chapter of PARD. It was the country's first local chapter, and Jason was proud that Rood often held it up as an example of what could be done when you make yourself heard. If Rood was the voice of the Right-to-Drive movement, Jason had become its most vocal and enthusiastic cheering section. He didn't have the platform Rood did, but he was no less committed to campaigning for the amendment.

Part of that commitment was defiance through language. They might now be called CAVs, but, following Rood's lead, Jason didn't care if a robo was "connected" or not, nor what it might be connected to. They'd started out as AVs, and he wasn't going to dignify or even acknowledge the "progress" they claimed they were making. PARD's unyielding position was: This technology must be opposed.

It was the PARD-Phoenix website that led him to Hector. One night at the Restless Rustler, Jason overheard someone he'd seen at the bar a few times mention that he'd started a web site (Strong Border, Strong Country). Darnel was a little sketchy, but Rood had said each local chapter should have its own site, so Jason asked him about his designer. "Guy lives around here," Darnel told him. "He's kind of weird, but knows his stuff."

When Jason met Hector, he immediately saw the weirdness but had a hard time believing he knew any "stuff." All doubt vanished when he saw the site Hector created for him.

Jason was running PARD-Phoenix out of his apartment, and soon Hector was dropping by to "check on the site" (which he didn't need to do in person); then offering to do other things, first for PARD-Phoenix, then for Jason. Jason gradually came to see that Hector was doing it not so much out of the goodness of his heart or belief in the cause (he didn't think Hector believed in any cause), but because he had nothing else to do. And living in the same neighborhood made it easy for Hector to just "pop in." He eventually learned Hector had no friends, no social life, and no skills to get either one. The more he learned about Hector, the more he thought he was his only friend, which turned out to be true.

By now, Jason knew that if Hector wasn't with him, and wasn't busy with some coding project, he had nothing. It worked for Jason because, though Hector often drove him up the wall, he'd become Jason's *de facto* personal assistant, willing to do anything Jason asked. All he seemed to want in return was someone to be with. Jason suspected that anyone else would serve just as well.

Hector was maintaining the PARD-Phoenix site for nothing, and refusing to take money for other things if Jason offered it, which was less and less as he'd come to expect "things" from Hector. When Jason started planning the rallies, Hector agreed to store the t-shirts, hats, and bumper stickers in his over-a-garage apartment. When Jason began holding the rallies, Hector tagged along, and now it was a given that he'd help out, part assistant, part lap dog. Like a dog, he was always there, always ready to serve, always ready to obey, asking in return simply a little attention.

They reached the mall where the rally would take place. Jason eyed the Saturday-afternoon crowd assembled in a back corner of the parking lot and asked, "How many you think that is?"

Hector scanned the lot for five seconds, then said, "Ninety-three."

"Not bad. You clear on everything?"

"Set up the table. And get the names and contact details for anyone who wants to volunteer."

Getting out of the car, Jason stripped off his shirt and put on a blue tee with three lines of red and white lettering. He was a big man, easily topping six feet, with broad shoulders and a solid midsection that had slowly grown bigger from years of sitting at the wheel. But he was still in good shape, and though 44, he could still hold his own in a bar fight against some punk kid if he had to.

Hector, standing next to him with slightly stopped shoulders, looked like a clumsy heap in comparison. His ball of thick curly hair, which gave him a slightly gnome-like appearance, did nothing to add to his stature. Jason liked how standing next to Hector made him feel. He figured Hector to be about 30. Someday he'd have to ask.

As Jason slid the t-shirt down his chest, the lettering unrolled with the material. The first line was red, the second line was white, the third was red.

He watched as Hector started to set up the table, first laying out the petitions, pens, and signs people would need when they took to the streets to gather signatures for the Right-To-Drive Amendment, then arraying the merchandise for sale: PARD hats, t-shirts, and bumper stickers. *Drivers, Not Robots!; Cars don't cause accidents, robots do!; They're coming for our cars!; Protect Americans' Right To Drive.* And the most popular, which was how people often greeted one another at rallies: *Hey, Pard!*

"Shirt," Jason reminded Hector, who grabbed a t-shirt like Jason's and pulled it over his head. *You can have my car when you pry my cold dead hands off the steering wheel.*

3

WHAT WAS WRONG?

After staring at the computer screen for several minutes, Dana Grant sat back and slowly shook her head. She wasn't happy and she didn't know why.

The case seemed simple enough. Last week a CAV killed a 35-year-old woman in California. She was sitting in a park, set back from the road some 50 feet, when she was struck by the vehicle. According to local police, the car ignored a stop sign, which was one reason the case landed on Dana's desk. That, and of course, the fatality.

Dana Grant was a federal cybermarshal assigned to the National Transportation Safety Board's Portland-based CAV unit, Western Sector. With thousands of robo-cabs, trucks, and buses on the nation's roads and streets, the NTSB had created a new branch to investigate CAV-related accidents. It was similar to the division that investigated aviation incidents, but only two offices had been opened so far (Eastern Sector was headquartered in Boston), its operating budget was smaller, its staff had not been provided with the in-depth training that allowed agents in the aviation division to effectively probe air-transport events, and, unlike the aviation division, the CAV unit had no NTSB Training Center. The marshals had been promised such expertise, but the agency, despite being in existence for six years, was still getting "up to speed" and Congress (swayed by the powerful CAV lobby) had repeatedly failed to adequately fund it, leaving many marshals to obtain any special training they felt they needed on their own, at their own expense. Dana had overheard several of her colleagues proudly vowing not to "go all tech" as long as they had to pay for it themselves.

Not Dana. If she were doing the job, she wanted to be as good at it as she could be. Just as she'd gone the extra distance as a cop in Phoenix. Since joining the unit, she'd been taking workshops and reading as much as she could to educate herself on the intricacies of CAVs. When she needed help, she didn't hesitate to reach out to the small network of advisors and consultants she'd slowly assembled around her during the five years she'd been on the job.

Influenced by those advisors and consultants, Dana had stopped using the word *accident* when talking about her cases. She investigated crashes.

An accident is an unfortunate incident that happens unexpectedly and unintentionally, an event that happens by chance or that is without apparent or deliberate cause. But CAVs, obeying algorithms designed for maximum safety and free of road-rage-inducing ego, didn't do things unexpectedly or take potentially-dangerous risks. So when a CAV collided with anything, it wasn't an accident. It was a crash.

Dana also quickly learned that crucial to investigating and understanding any incident involving a CAV meant knowing how to read and interpret the information gleaned from its black box, which included every decision, maneuver, and change the vehicle made during a trip. It included interactions with passengers. It included everything the car did, saw, and heard. And because this data was all in computer code, it required knowing how to understand what you were looking at.

Even with all the time Dana had spent learning about this arcane corner of the universe, she still had large gaps in her knowledge of it. But she was light years ahead of every other agent in her office, and she knew it.

Now Dana sat pondering why the CAV ignored the stop sign. Programming error? Software failure? Faulty sensing equipment? If any of those were the issue, did the problem lie with Relyable, the company that manufactured the car? Or was it a matter of a repair, similar to fixing the brakes on a human-driven car? And if *that* were so, was the root cause a failure by the company that operated the vehicle to properly maintain it?

Or, if it was a programming or software error, did that signal a failure by the engineers at the company that made the car? Which would mean Dana had to see if the same company created both the computer code and the software, because it was possible that correct computer code had been negated by faulty software.

A third possibility was that someone tampered with the stop sign, which happened often in the 2020s, when kids defaced traffic signs or anti-AVers tried to demonstrate the weakness of autonomous infrastructure. Then came the '29 Topeka School AV bus crash. A couple of teenagers out for kicks turned a 30-mph sign in to one reading 80 mph by making the three an eight. The bus raced around a sharp curve doing 80, left the road, and plunged 35 feet down an embankment, killing 21 children and the bus attendant.

For the next three years, all AV school buses had to have a human driver. Meanwhile, every inch of roadway in the United

States was minutely mapped: every traffic sign, signal, lane marking, and channelization. And the federal government required any change, no matter how small, to be immediately entered in the central Geographic Information System (GIS) Command file, the huge database where all this information lived. Failure to do so resulted in states and cities losing as much as billions in federal highway dollars. Now, any discrepancy between what an AV saw and what was in the GIS database, was detected by the CAV's Command Center (all the companies that operated CAVs had command centers that controlled their fleet) in a nanosecond, and the GIS Command Center threw the vehicle into fail-safe mode, choosing the safest available option for its next action.

If a vehicle saw "80 mph" but the database listed "30 mph," the GISCC would send an alert, slow or stop the vehicle, and a remote driver would take over the CAV. In addition, all other vehicles from that company would be alerted and a post-mortem would be conducted.

The system worked almost flawlessly in cities and on state roads; the only gaps now were the small towns and rural areas that didn't have the ability to update the GIS files, or the few places where locals believed that routinely updating their files was an infringement by an overbearing government. Since '33, there had been only nine instances of minor crashes due to un-updated traffic devices, and none due to vandalism. Could this be the first?

Maybe. Yet Dana had a gut feeling it was something else. There were thousands of Relyable delivery robos operating in the county and there hadn't been similar incidents. Which suggested that the computer code, the software, and pretty much everything else in the vehicle was operating properly. So what else could it be?

Relyable had already responded to the police-finding that the car went through the stop sign. Company spokespeople maintained that the sign had been defaced with both a hole and graffiti, so the fault lay not with the vehicle and its sensing equipment, but with the town for not repairing the sign. Relyable also noted that the town had been cited four times for not complying with GIS Command. The company could not be held responsible, it reasoned, for signage or traffic signals that were not repaired or replaced in a timely manner.

Dana studied pictures of the sign; there was no question that it had been vandalized. A tagger had gone to work on it, and there was a hole dead center in the middle of the *O*. If it was a bullet hole, someone was quite a shot.

Did that mean the CAV had not seen the sign? Or had it seen the sign but was no longer able to identify it as a signal to stop, perhaps interpreting it as nothing more than a lamppost or structure designating street parking? Why did the Topeka failsafe protocol fail?

"Oh, you caught that California thing."

She hadn't heard Kyle coming up behind her. But now there was that soft wheezing through his seemingly-always-clogged nasal passages. Perhaps if he lost some weight . . . The thought ran through her head almost every time she saw Kyle. He wasn't obese. Just unnecessarily overweight, all in his belly, which hung over his belt in a loose fold.

Kyle Beaumont would always be overweight, always breathe heavily through his nose, always be, in Dana's mind, one nasal breath away from a heart attack. Which of course she hoped would never happen. She didn't hate Kyle or wish any bad would come to him. She just wished he wasn't her boss.

Not because he was overweight and breathed through his nose. Because he was always hovering, and he wasn't thorough.

He'd been with the NTSB 20 years to her 5, and was more interested in clearing cases than conducting competent, thorough investigations.

So, rather than encourage his people to spend as much time as they needed to properly run a case, he'd be satisfied with a preliminary finding, even one still open to questions, if it added to the "Case Closed" log he submitted weekly to the head of the Portland bureau.

As a result, Dana's unit had a high closure rate, which Kyle was determined to maintain. But given how they were achieving it, she wasn't sure that was something to be proud of.

Their findings tended to hold the vehicles or companies blameless, and Dana sometimes wondered about that. But the truth was, in crashes involving CAVs and human drivers, it was almost always the human driver at fault. CAVs had proven themselves to be more consistent, more stable, and less erratic than human drivers. They were not distracted as easily or as often, never tried to beat a changing traffic light or speed past an approaching train, and had no interest in pushing themselves to test their power, speed, or endurance.

So the fact that Kyle's long list of closed cases often found in favor of the CAV wasn't surprising. Nevertheless, Dana often found herself wishing he didn't reach that conclusion quite so fast.

Standing behind her looking over her shoulder, he'd moved closer. She knew, without turning, because the heavy breathing was now only inches from her ear.

"New perfume?" he asked.

"Nope."

"You smell different. New shampoo?"

"Nope."

"Different soap, maybe?"

She pictured him sniffing the air around her. Or, worse, sniffing her.

"Same soap."

"Something about you is different. Are you. . . ?"

It was time to end this. She shifted in her chair, sending it backward into his foot, then turned around and was "surprised" to see the wheel of the chair pressing on his shoe and the edge of her seat against his leg.

"Oh, sorry! I didn't realize you were that close."

"No harm done," he assured her, reaching down to lightly rub his knee. "You still working on that?" he nodded toward her computer.

"Hmm-hmm," she muttered, studying the screen again to indicate she was too distracted to talk.

"Stop sign was vandalized. The town didn't update its GIS records. Like the company says, it's their fault. Can't you close it?"

"I'm not sure yet," she started. "I—"

"You have 'a *feeling*,'" he finished for her. "Here we go."

She hated when he did that. But it had been years since she took him seriously when he said those things in that tone of voice. That had stopped after working with him for two months, when she almost caved in the wake of his response to her first "feeling."

That first time, still new to the unit and trying to find her way, she'd almost let him intimidate her because she was half-doubting herself: Had she really been on to something, or was it more an attempt to prove she could do the job?

But she stuck with it, and it paid off. Driver vs. CAV, and the driver swore the robo had swerved into his lane. There *was* activity to the right of the CAV that might have made it swerve toward the driver, but a check of the black box showed it swerved no more than a foot and did not cross the double yellow line that separated the vehicles.

On a hunch, Dana checked the driver's cell-phone records and found that he'd been on the phone at the time of the accident. It was him, not the robo, that had swerved across the double yellow line.

Two lessons learned: Always trust her gut, and never listen to Kyle about such matters.

It took her a while to stop railing at herself for letting him come as close as he did to shutting her down, but she finally landed in place of self-understanding: she was navigating new territory with insufficient training. She was allowed a few missteps; she could forgive herself. Afterward, she did more than that, using the episode to redefine their relationship.

Never one to be intimidated (easily or otherwise), not even as a child, she would never again be bullied by a bureaucrat now that she was 35, carried a badge, and believed *(knew)* that she was better suited for this work than he was.

"Here *I* go," she corrected him. "It's not gonna affect your life much."

"Except what it's gonna do to our clearance rate."

"You mean *my* clearance rate?"

"Ours includes yours. You slow up, we slow up."

"I'll work this extra fast."

"Work what? The cops confirmed the CAV went through the stop sign. No one's contesting that. The cops confirmed the stop sign was vandalized. No one's contesting *that*. The town didn't update its GIS file. You wanna blame the robo? It's like, someone blindfolds you, then blames you for walking into something. How much more open-shut can you get?"

"Looks that way."

"Except you know better."

"I just want to leave it open a little longer so I can—"

"You can have a *little* more time on this. But don't take too long. And don't neglect your other cases."

"I never do," she answered, fingers busy on her keyboard, focusing on her screen, as a way to end the conversation.

Finally sensing their talk was over, Kyle walked away, triggering a new train of thought for Dana: What kind of ratings was he getting on his quarterly evaluations? But why go there? For years he'd been part of a federal bureaucracy that valued meeting quotas and demonstrating its own skewered sense of "efficiency." She knew exactly the kind of evaluations he was getting. And he knew exactly how to keep getting them. And keep his job.

She peered at the screen for real now, hoping to find something new. Kyle was right about one thing: It did seem like an open-and-shut case. The CAV had functioned perfectly until it encountered the vandalized stop sign.

So what was bothering her? What was wrong?

4

WHAT WOULD IT TAKE?

As soon as Corby saw the 202 Washington area code on the phone's screen he knew it was Doris. He'd been both eagerly awaiting and pessimistically dreading her call. The fact that it was Friday, the end of the weekly news cycle, made him settle on dread. Friday's news wouldn't get real media attention until Monday. By that time, there'd be other news. Whatever development Doris was about to share with him wasn't going to make headlines any time soon. His greeting reflected his frustration.

"I'm not gonna like this, am I?"

"Neither of us is going to like it. And hello to you, too."

"Sorry. Hi, Doris."

Doris Richmond was the freshman Representative from Colorado. They'd met a few years ago at an urban-planning conference, and their mutual environmental concerns motivated them to stay in touch. When she was elected to Congress, they'd both hoped she'd be able to do more than just attend conferences. Now they were watching many of those hopes fade.

"The updated regs will be completed by December 12th, she told him.

Corby flipped the page on his wall calendar a month forward, and immediately registered that the 12th was another Friday. How convenient. "Conway and the boys deliver as promised."

Greg Conway was the head of the National Autonomous Vehicle Association (NAVA), the trade alliance that had grown so powerful that virtually no one in Congress was willing to stand up to it for fear of losing their seat when NAVA poured money into an opponent's next campaign. NAVA could afford an army of lobbyists, but Conway didn't need an army—just the cadre that had been crafting the new federal CAV regulations. Corby had taken to calling them "the boys" but that was disingenuous. These "boys" knew exactly what they were doing. Now they were one step closer to a future Corby had been trying to prevent—prioritizing CAVs over people.

It had happened before, when Herbert Hoover's 1926 Panel of 100 drafted a Model Municipal Traffic Ordinance codifying the principle of "streets for cars" that relegated people to sidewalks and gave vehicles their between-the-curbs fiefdom that pedestrians safely entered only when allowed by traffic signs and timed lights. Corby's argument against it was how it changed American culture and people's moment-to-moment interactions with cars. Instead of a well-considered long-range plan that balanced the needs of people with those of vehicles, it enacted measures designed to promote and expand the automobile industry, with no public input. Exactly what Corby was arguing was about to happen again.

He might as well have been shouting into a bottomless canyon. The only person in Congress who was listening was Doris, who had no leverage. And since the last election, defying NAVA also meant opposing President Boyle. Pro-industry and anti-environment, he was not only under NAVA's sway, but had made a campaign promise to support its agenda.

Within a month of Boyle taking office, his Transportation Secretary, Leonard Paulson, issued "guidelines;" but they, too, had been crafted by NAVA. Now the final regulations were about to be released, and NAVA would decide how CAVs would be integrated into American culture.

Doris had been keeping Corby apprised of the situation in Washington, and was the bearer of bad news every time they'd spoken for the last three months. She'd tried to muster support among her colleagues, but every conversation ended with some variation on the same theme: "I sympathize with your position, but we all have to get re-elected in order to accomplish anything, don't we?" There was no need to say anything else. NAVA's shadow hung over every colleague she spoke with.

Melissa knew something was wrong the moment she walked into Corby's office. When he told her, all she did was nod.

They seamlessly fell into a conversation about what could be done, but it was just an academic exercise. They knew the central question: What would make Congress consider another approach? And they knew the answer: The threat of having to give up power. Faced with losing their seat, most Senators and Representatives would change a position no matter how often they'd supported it. They'd argue they were listening to their constituents (and on one level that would be true), but the truth was, they wanted to stay in office.

"If only people weren't so passive," she mused.

"This isn't people being passive," he countered. "It's people not being informed. NAVA has this whole thing flying under the radar. They're vocal and loud when they want to fire up the base, but they're suddenly struck dumb when there's any news about the regs. And no wonder, with what's at stake. The CAV industry is on track to be worth $8.5 trillion. With a *t*. That's a lot of incentive to do it their way."

"And it's not sexy," she added. "Kind of hard for people to get fired up about connected autonomous vehicles. Talk about a soft issue. Nothing to see here, folks!"

He nodded. "I brought it up at a party the other night. After five minutes, someone changed the subject. This is gonna play out just how NAVA wants it, and people won't even realize it's happened for five to ten years. How the hell do you stop it?"

"You just made it sound like it can't be stopped."

"Maybe if people demanded—"

"You just said people don't even know this is happening."

"But what if they *did*? And told Congress what *they* wanted? What would it take to make people want to change the minds of 100 senators and 435 representatives? Put it on the front page, make it so it can't *not* be an issue. And *keep* it on the front page."

"So how does that happen? You've been trying—"

"Maybe I should try something else."

There was a half-pause, then Corby ended the conversation. "OK, enough of this!" he declared, segueing into their usual Friday activity, pulling out the Blue Binder.

One of Melissa's tasks was to gather Rood's tweets and statements, and have a list ready for Corby on Friday. It was easy enough, but also meant enduring the dull ache of his rhetoric, always pitched to arouse fear, suspicion, and anger.

As he activated the speech-to-text function on his computer, she fished her phone out of her pocket and began scrolling through this week's catch.

"'Compared to real cars, five times as many people die in AV crashes per 100 million miles traveled.'"

"Half-truth, with distortion." Corby was in 'the game' now, and part of that game was immediately classifying each statement she'd culled. "We'll let the 'real cars' part go. What does he, think CAVs are animation? Does he . . ."

"That's not letting it go," she pointed out.

He conceded her point with a hastily-raised hand. "A grain of truth, a lot of distortion. 'Five times as many' is Rood's fantasy. You can go as high as three times as many if you include the one spectacular crash in 2033 when a school bus rammed a robo-cab from behind and lost control, killing 5 children and the driver. Of course, Rood is conveniently ignoring the fact that a big chunk of those crashes are caused by people smashing into CAVs, usually because CAVs are more cautious than people, and a lot of people take more risks when they're around CAVs. He's also leaving out—probably doesn't know—that those fatality rates are trending downward. With more CAVs on the road by 2040, the prediction is a 25% reduction in fatalities. 60% by 2050. Next."

"'There's a secret plan to outlaw human driving on public roads once AVs exceed 50% of all cars," she read. "'In five years, the Federal government is going to make it a criminal offense to drive on federal highways.'"

"I can't believe he still refuses to call them CAVs! He's got one foot in the past, the other trying to hold back the future. He wants to make this his go-to issue, he should at least stay up to date. We've been calling them CAVs since—"

"Let it go," she reminded him.

"Gone. That one's a flat-out lie. The Department of Transportation just said—again!—that driving will *always* be allowed on federal roads. Rood wants to make *that* argument, he should move to Switzerland. In Zurich they plan to phase out human driving by the middle of the century. Finland's talking about it, too. And his math's off. CAVs are at 25% now. Fast as it's increasing, we're not gonna hit 50% in five years.

"Then there's the 2030 provision, conveniently forgotten

by Rood, that prohibits, until 2040, *privately-owned* fully-autonomous CAVs, so the vehicles out there are mostly cabs and buses, which use mostly local, not federal roads. Robo-trucks use federal roads, but unless the private ownership cap's lifted there's no way we're gonna be at 50% in five years. But mentioning all that would be inconvenient, so why bother?"

"Last one," she began to wrap it up. "AV parts are manufactured mostly in China, North Korea, and Iran, and our trade deficit with these countries exceeds $1 trillion.'"

"Tired old argument that was never true to begin with. Only 6% of CAV parts come from China. *Nothing* from Iran. North Korea supplies *Europe* with about 20%."

"You want to look up any of those statistics?"

"Why?"

"Because how do you keep all that in your head?"

"It's going into the Blue Binder. If it's in the Blue Binder, it's committed to memory."

She jabbed a finger toward the binder. "Not just a hobby."

Corby smiled as he returned the binder to the drawer.

5

THE RIGHT TO DRIVE

Jason had to read it again, to make sure he'd gotten it right. But first, he needed to calm down. Because he knew he'd read it correctly. Now he was going to give it a chance to read differently, as if, by doing so, the words would change.

Fed to Formalize CAV Regs by Middle of Next Month said the press-release headline. *The Congressional Committee on Connected Autonomous Vehicles (CCCAVs) announced today that it will formally codify updated federal regulations by December 12th, establishing a framework of rules, laws, and policies governing connected autonomous vehicles (CAVs). Addressing the widespread call for a homogenous plan established by Washington rather than states, cities, and other local governing bodies, the CCCAV will locate the authority governing CAVs at the federal level. According to committee chair Byron Jordell (R-AL), "This will create a consistent set of laws, eliminating a chaotic jumble of local ordinances that vary from state to state and city to city."*

Jordell added, "The committee has been working closely with industry leaders and has been careful to address the concerns of all stakeholders in its efforts to create the best future for the industry, the country, and the public. We've taken all viewpoints into account, and are crafting a set of rules that will guarantee everyone is treated fairly, in line with their best interests, to reap the most benefits from this cutting-edge technology."

Jordell predicts that the committee will be able to finish its work in five weeks and send it to Congress for approval. President Boyle has indicated numerous times that he will approve the committee's recommendations.

They were really going to do it. The part of him that hoped it could be stopped had been at odds with the part that feared it wouldn't be.

He'd been over it and over it. Sometimes it was a quiet voice whispering lone, random, unsettling visions of an impossible future. Other times it was a screaming argument, raging at him from all four corners of a room whose walls were closing in.

Even with all the robo-cabs and trucks on the road, so many businesses shut down, people thrown out of work and losing their livelihoods—somehow AVs had felt like a dark tomorrow, coming, but not yet irrevocably here. There was still time to, if not stop it, at least reshape it.

That was the point of the Right-To-Drive Amendment, the rallies, the petitions. And there was always the hope that people would pay attention to the alarm Zach Rood was sounding.

But now it was so close that they were announcing it to the public. It was coming on like an 18-wheeler chewing up the road as it barreled toward him. With federal regulations in place, AVs would be an institution. For Jason, that would be literally hell on wheels.

How could the decision makers, who answered to the people, be made to understand this *wasn't* what people wanted? They hadn't listened when they enacted tougher background checks on weapons; now people had to go through a week-long process before they were allowed to exercise a right guaranteed by the Constitution. They hadn't listened with abortion, which Jason had nothing against, but there were plenty of people who didn't want it to be a federal law. Now they weren't listening to people fighting for their right to drive. They were overreaching and mismanaging it all.

Zach Rood had said it perfectly on this morning's show. "It's an egregious, politically-motivated violation of every American's fundamental, God-given right to drive, which was inadvertently omitted from the Constitution, but clearly folded into every citizen's right to happiness. What's happening here is that you're being ignored. You are being left out. You're being disenfranchised. No one is considering *your* happiness or *your* rights.

"The question is, what can you do about it? You can speak out. You can stop them from pushing you to the margins of your own country. You can make them listen to you. You can make yourself heard!

"But you have to do more than that. Someone has to step up and show them that these robots on wheels are more of a danger than anyone knows. Someone has to . . . *Do Something.* I don't know who you are, but I know you're out there."

As always, Zach Rood was saying what needed to be said. The longer Jason thought about it, the more he felt the truth behind Rood's words.

Every one of them.

6

NEW INFORMATION

Dana's eyes kept darting back and forth between her computer screen and the notes she was making on the legal pad next to the keyboard. She was slowly discovering there *was* more to "the California case." Each time she looked at it from another angle, something new revealed itself. She'd been right to want to dig deeper.

Today's tidbit: at the time of the crash the sun sat at not-quite eight degrees above the horizon. The topography around Buttonwillow and the site of the crash was low and flat. And it had been a cloudless day. With the sun at that angle, the CAV heading west, and no cloud cover between the sun and the road, the sun would have been shining straight toward the front of the car.

The vehicle's sensors would respond to and adjust for glare, but an angle of eight degrees creates conditions that would make a human driver squint, curse, and tug the visor down in a futile attempt to see better. (Dozens of years ago she was a passenger in her father's car in the same situation, when he suddenly stopped the car in the middle of a city street, shouting "I can't see a thing!")

So, did the setting sun interfere with the car's detection system? Was that why it blew past the stop sign? And, having done that, did it then think it was on an open road? Or perhaps couldn't see where it was, or where it was going?

If that were true, did it make the case more straightforward because the crash could be attributed to mechanical error? Or did it make it more labyrinthine because it potentially pointed to a failure by the car manufacturer or software engineers to foresee and address this issue?

If *that* were so, did it indicate a software vulnerability that needed to be eliminated? Or negligence on the part of the software's creators, for not considering it before putting the car on the road? The permutations were beginning to seem endless, and she . . .

"What'd you turn up *today*?" Kyle asked from just behind her, derision thick in his voice.

She'd caught the case last Wednesday and he'd given her "a little more time" to work it. End of day Friday, he'd asked about her progress, clearly expecting she'd be ready to wrap it up, only to hear that she'd found new information she wanted to look at. Another boss might have praised her diligence and tenacity. Kyle accused her of clouding up her investigation just to do it. Now she braced herself for another round of their clumsy dance.

He didn't wait for her reply. Leaning closer to her shoulder than she wanted him to be (forcing her to yet again ignore his labored breathing), he scanned her notes and landed in the most obvious, simplest place.

"There it is!" he said triumphantly. "The car was headed into the sun. It couldn't see the stop sign or the woman. Same as if it couldn't stop because its brakes failed. Tragedy, but it happens. So there's no 'great mystery.' We can close the case and move on."

"Maybe. But—"

"What's maybe?" he demanded. "You say right here," he tapped her notes, 'possible cause.' I say it's more than *possible.* It's what happened."

"Maybe," she repeated, firmer this time. "But in your own scenario, if the car's owner *knew* the brakes were failing, and did nothing to repair them, there's the possibility of negligence."

"So?"

"So we should look further, to see if there's anything related to the sun blinding the car's detection system."

"Like what? Look at the sun, it blinds you. Driving west at sunset is dangerous. Ask anyone who's done it."

She forced herself to stay calm, and instead of saying what she really wanted to, went with "That might be what happened. But maybe there's more to it."

"Like?"

She didn't know what "more" she was looking for. But she was determined not to settle for Kyle's quick fix that would keep his unit's closed-case stats high. Something was still bothering her about this. There was still new information to unravel. There was still Kyle's troubled breathing inches from the back of her head.

"It's still too soon," she tried, hoping that being vague would stop him from immediately negating anything definite she might offer. "I want more time."

"How much more time?" he sighed.

"I don't know."

"I'll give you more time. Because *maybe* you're on to something. But I want a hard number. Make a guess. What does your *feeling* say?"

"Two weeks."

"You have *one*," he decreed. Then added, "Try to do it faster."

He turned on his heel and walked away before she could argue, muttering "Them and their feelings!" as he put distance between him and her desk.

Alone again, Dana let a half-smile crease her lips, happy with the week she'd just bought herself. Which was what she really wanted.

She'd known full well when Kyle asked the question, that whatever number she came up with, he'd halve it.

7

SOMETHING HAS TO MAKE IT HAPPEN

Melissa had already read the piece at home. Now she sat in Corby's office, giving it a final glance. It was just for a small local paper, and no different from the other op-eds he'd recently written. Except for the part she'd circled. Was that why he'd said, "We can talk about it tomorrow," as she left yesterday?

Or had he gotten overly-cautious about going into print because he rarely got the opportunity these days and knew (or believed) that when he did publish something it received extra scrutiny, because *he'd* written it?

She was still amazed that some people could easily bounce back from a transgression that would ruin someone else, quickly forgiven multiple trespasses and sins, while others made one mistake and never recovered. Perhaps someday she'd do a study of who did and who didn't recover and regain admission into the fold. And why. But now her attention was on Corby's op-ed.

It's long been acknowledged that we can better understand the present by studying the past. Similarly, we can gain a better sense of our near-future by carefully considering what we do in the present. This is especially true in the realm of the automobile.

In the late 1800s "horseless carriages" arrived, launching the car-pedestrian battles of the first quarter of the 20th century. By the 1920s, pedestrians (who were rarely killed by horses) were being killed by the tens of thousands annually. The largest number of casualties were children, who often played in the street, and cities erected monuments to the hundreds of kids killed by cars. Cincinnati (among other cities) tried to stop the carnage by forcing cars to have speed governors that limited them to a maximum of 25 mph. The auto industry fought these efforts with a scorched-earth approach, enlisting "modernists"—city planners who believed a fast city was a successful city.

Many of today's "modernists" argue that decision-makers in the 1920s could have put people first, which would have resulted in a society where we were safer, the air cleaner, and there would be better, more efficient mass-transportation options, especially in cities.

Today we're at an analogous turning point—the coming federal decisions regarding CAVs will inform the next hundred years.

We got a lot of it wrong the first time around, and society has been paying the price: As far back as 2018, statistics showed that vehicles were responsible for killing and maiming more people than all the wars of the twentieth century combined.

Now came the part that had stopped her when she first read the piece. Just as she touched pen to paper to underline the words she wanted to talk about, Corby walked through the door.

He pointed to the stack of papers she'd placed on his side of the desk. "I almost called you back to remind you to bring those, then decided I didn't have to." He glanced over her shoulder and his eyes darted to the red circle she'd drawn last night. "Problem?"

"Just want to discuss the ending." She read the words quickly. "'Will we get it right this time? What will it take for the AV industry to accept outside regulation created for the greater good? A different government? A mass public protest? A tragedy?'"

"What about it?"

"It's . . . pretty dramatic. Really different from what you've been saying."

"What I've been saying hasn't been having much of an impact."

"Is this," she pointed to the circled passage, "the 'something else' you were talking about last week?"

"What 'something else'?"

"Getting people to demand what they wanted from Congress. Putting it on the front page. Keeping it there. Is this a way to try to make that happen? Ratcheting up the rhetoric?"

"It's one way." He scanned the circled words. "If this doesn't work, I'll try something else. But *something* has to make it happen. And soon. We're running of time."

8

WE WON'T LET THEM

As he walked up the three steps to the makeshift stage, Jason quickly adjusted the t-shirt he'd chosen for this rally, smoothing it out so his audience could easily read the message: *I Won't Give Up My Right to Drive.* The words, in white, were laid out underneath an American flag. The shirts came in three designs (red except for the flag and text; blue except for the flag and text; and white, with the words beneath the text alternating red and blue) and were selling well.

He also adjusted his baseball cap, so the words over the visor, *Help America Drive Again*, would show up clearly in the pictures Hector was taking for the web site.

Now in front of the microphone, Jason surveyed the crowd as he waited for it to settle down. Estimating there were about 100 people (later he'd ask Hector for the exact number), he was pleased to see it was one of their biggest rallies yet. If this kept up, an all-day festival might be something to think about.

Seeing him at the mic, the crowd grew quiet. His eyes swept the lot for Hector; when he found him at the merchandise table, he gave him a quick nod, signaling he was ready to speak.

"Glad to see so many of you out here today!" he began, met with a cheer and applause.

"I won't ask how you got here, because I already know!" He paused for dramatic effect, then shouted, "YOU DROVE!!"

Hoots and whistles joined the cheers and applause.

"Of course you drove. Why wouldn't you? Until they take that right away from you, and replace people with robot cars on *your roads*!" The hoots and cheers turned to boos and hisses.

"But that's not gonna happen!"

"Damn right!" someone shouted.

"And why won't it happen?"

On cue, the crowd roared back: "We won't let them!"

Jason upped it a notch. "What was that? I can't hear you!"

"We won't let them!" the crowd yelled back.

"I still can't hear you!"

"WE WON'T LET THEM!"

"Damn right we won't! Not if we make ourselves heard!"

A chant filled the air: "No Ro-Bos! No Ro-Bos! No Ro-Bos! NO RO-BOS! NO RO-BOS!! NO RO-BOS!!!"

He let it go on for several seconds, allowing it to fade on its own. "The idea that one government, thousands of miles away, knows what's right for everyone, just doesn't work. Anything important—and the right to drive is as important as it gets—must be decided locally, where *local* leaders, *your* leaders, the people *you* elect, know what *you* need!"

Applause . . . cheers . . . whistles . . .

"Take praying at school. You want government saying how you should raise your kids? They want to pray in school, why shouldn't they? Your kids should be able to pray, any time, any place. Because we live in America! And we have a Constitution!

"Take the Virus. People get it every year, just like a cold. And when that happens, *they* say, you can't go out in public.

Well, here it is, October 25th, just before virus season, and we're doing it right now. And I don't see anyone getting sick! So if you're willing to do it, isn't that your right?"

"Hell yeah!" answered a voice in the crowd.

"Some state governors, who know what their people want because they live with them, thought so. Where does the Constitution say the government can tell you what germs you can inhale? It's your state, it's your town, and it's your home! And if you don't invite them into your home, they can't come in. *That's* in the Constitution, too!"

The cheers and applause were coming faster, more frequently.

"Maybe they don't care what's in the Constitution. But I'm an American, and I do! And I'll bet *you* do! They want to grab for power they're not entitled to, they're gonna have to come through us first! And what's our answer to that?"

"WE WON'T LET THEM! WE WON'T LET THEM! WE WON'T LET THEM!"

"You bet we won't! Now they're after our cars. They want us to sit inside robots! With no steering wheel and no brakes! Nothing for you to do but talk on the phone. Or write e-mails. Or, I don't know . . . maybe read a book? Is that what driving is? Not for me, it isn't! And not the way I'll let them make me do it in the future! What about you?"

"WE WON'T LET THEM! WE WON'T LET THEM! WE WON'T LET THEM!"

"It gets worse. Since the government owns the highways, what'll they do next? *Only* AVs allowed on the road? That's what they're doing in Europe. But where's *our* protection? They can do what they want over there. But this is our country! And our Constitution guarantees life, liberty, and happiness. That includes sitting in *my* car, behind *my* steering wheel, looking through *my* windshield, with my foot on *my* gas pedal, on roads paid for with *my* taxes! And guess what? I don't see a robo anywhere in there! So what do we say to Washington?"

"No Ro-Bos! No Ro-Bos! No Ro-Bos! NO RO-BOS! NO RO-BOS!1 NO RO-BOS!!"

"I'm gonna say one more thing, and see if you don't agree with me here. Every American has a God-given right to drive. It's not in the Constitution because cars didn't exist. But horses did, and horse owners had rights. What happened to someone who stole a horse? They got hung! And what did they call a car at first? Horseless carriages! Now, I'm no constitutional scholar . . ." he made sure to sneer at the word *scholar* . . . "*but* I know that Thomas Jefferson, the father of our constitution, owned more than 100 horses and drove a carriage. I say *drove* because *he* said drove! Not rode in! And if Jefferson were alive today, he'd say driving a *horseless* carriage is a God-given and constitutional-given right! And he should know. He wrote the damned thing! Know what else Jefferson included in the Constitution? The Pursuit of Happiness! Well, driving makes *me* happy! What about *you*!?"

Applause . . . cheers . . .

"Which means, you don't want to be told by Washington, or anyone else, what you can and can't do behind the wheel of your own car. And I don't know about you, but it does not make me happy to look into the car next to me at some stop light, and see there is . . . and I really do mean this . . . NO ONE AT THE WHEEL!"

They could feel him winding down. The cheers grew louder.

"Don't let them push you to the edge of the margins! Make yourself heard!"

On the ride home, Jason was so revved up he could barely sit still. It was one of his best rallies. They'd sold half-a-dozen t-shirts and hats, and collected more signatures for the petition. Best of all, he'd turned a corner in his thinking.

Listening to the crowd chant "We won't let them!" felt like a personal call to action.

It's easy to chant "We won't let them." But how do you make that happen? How do you *not* let them? He'd barely spoken a word to Hector since they got in the car. He was working it out.

It helped that Hector, after reporting a 5% increase in t-shirt sales and a 3% increase for baseball caps, was content to quietly stare out the window.

When they'd gone about a mile and a half, it was Jason who broke the silence. "That wasn't just talk. I've figured out a way to do something."

"About what?" Hector asked. He'd left the content, concepts, and conceits of the rally back in the parking lot. Jason knew that for Hector, it could have been a rally to save a local ballpark, a demonstration against renaming a state, a convention to declare war on Canada. Hector was there because he had no other place to be. The issues were of no concern to him. He just wanted to be with Jason.

Which, though he would have preferred having a kindred spirit beside him, Jason had no objection to. Hector's loyalty would serve Jason far better than any commitment to a cause. He could always find someone who was in it for the politics. What Jason needed was an attack dog. And while *attack* would be the last word one would associate with Hector, Jason knew the ability was there. If it were the right kind of attack.

"About what?" he answered Hector. "About AVs."

"You should be calling them CAVs," Hector proposed. "AV stands for Autonomous Vehicle. CAV stands for Connected

Autonomous Vehicles, which are connected to one another and millions of transponders, data towers, cables—"

"AV, CAV, it's still the same goddamned robot on wheels."

"But a CAV is a much more advanced robot than an AV because—"

"I don't care which is more advanced. The only good one is one that doesn't exist."

"That's a contradiction, because—"

"OK, how's this. I don't use CAV because to me there's no difference. Everyone knows what I mean when I say AV. I've been saying it for years, and I'm not gonna change it just because the government says, 'We've got a different name for it.' No matter what they call the sons of bitches, they're still trying to take away my right to drive. Now they're gonna tell me how to talk? I don't think so!"

"Technically—"

"Never mind! Robos suck. That's all there is to it. And if the feds can't see it, we'll prove it to them."

"That might be hard. They've conducted thousands of studies that show—"

"I'm not talking about studies. I'm gonna prove it to them with cold hard facts they won't be able to ignore."

"It might be hard to find facts they don't already—"

"I'm not gonna *find* facts. I'm gonna *present* facts."

"I suppose that with some detailed research—"

"No research. Just cold hard facts. True facts. They're convinced AVs are safe. We're gonna show them they're *not*."

"Actually, they are."

"And it's not gonna be as hard as you think. I don't know why I didn't see this sooner. Gonna show them these robots on wheels are more a menace than anyone knows."

"How are you going to—"

"Accidents."

"Their accident rate is currently only .005%. According to the most recent study—"

"Forget *studies.* These accidents haven't happened yet. But they will."

"But how are you going to—"

"I'm not. You are."

After a short silence, Hector said, "That wouldn't be right."

"Oh yeah? What about the means justify the ends? We cause a few accidents, they won't put robos on every goddamned road in the country. They won't cancel a right we're all born with. And they won't put thousands of more people out of work. Why isn't that right?"

"People could get hurt."

"No one has to get hurt. They don't have to be serious accidents. Just enough to change how they see AVs. Look . . . We're getting nice crowds at the rallies, and signatures on petitions, but people aren't really getting out there to stop it because they're swallowing the line of crap they're being fed by the government. But what if people knew the real truth about how dangerous robos really are? That'd get them off their asses. Behind the Right-To-Drive Amendment. It's that simple. I don't know why it took me so long to see it."

"What are you going to do?"

"Look, the goddamn things are run by . . . what d'ya call it . . . all that computer shit you do."

"Coding. Algorithms."

"Yeah. So if you give them different shit, you can make 'em do whatever you want them to, right?"

"Yes. CAVs are programmed to follow the instructions that—"

"So we instruct them to have accidents. Can that be done?"

"And no one would get hurt?"

"No one would even know you did it."

Jason sensed something shift in Hector. "That *would* be an interesting experiment. If someone wrote the right code—"

"Not someone. You. Hector, my friend, if anyone can do it, it's *you*."

9

THEY HAVEN'T FIXED IT

Dana waited in Kyle's office, trying to decide if he was taking this long to join her because he really did have to take a call from Washington, or he was punishing her for first, spending too much time on what he was now calling "that California thing," and second, because she'd just told him it was going to take even more time to close it out. He'd barely bothered to contain his frustration fifteen minutes ago when she'd stopped him in the hall and said she needed to talk.

"What about?" he demanded, making it clear he already didn't like where this was going. "Don't tell me it's that California thing."

She nodded. "Something's come up."

"Of course it did. Wouldn't have, if anyone else caught it. But I've got Miss Sherlock Holmes working on it. Last Tuesday, you said you'd have it wrapped up in a week. Well, it's been a week. Now 'something's come up.' So you're gonna ask for *more* time. I can see, this isn't gonna clear until Christmas."

"I think I can get it finished by Thanksgiving," she smiled.

"I don't want it in two weeks. Get it done *this* week!"

"All I need right now is five, maybe ten minutes of your time."

"That's all you're getting. Wait in my office. Washington's on the line." He emphasized *Washington* to show how important he was, then quickly brushed past her as if he couldn't get away fast enough, leaving barely an inch between them. Was he hoping to knock her aside? Or did he just like being barely an inch from her?

Now she was sitting here doing nothing. She could already hear him berating her for wasting time. And it wasn't time he was really concerned with. It was his precious clearance rate. His favorite running joke on any new case was, "Take all the time you need. As long as you do it fast."

She'd once responded, "How about I do it right?" He'd glared at her, then dismissed her by making a call.

Some cases just didn't clear fast, and she was becoming convinced this was one of them. The irony of it was, she'd clear it a lot faster if she didn't have to fight him every step of the way.

She heard his heavy steps coming down the hall; entering the office, he made his way to his desk and muttered "Clock's ticking," as he sat back to hear what she had to say.

"I'll get right to it," she began, ignoring that fact that he seemed more interested in picking at something on the arm of his chair than whatever it was she thought was so important. "The CAV that killed the woman outside Buttonwillow had always used its vision detection system correctly in clear dry conditions."

"I can see why you're concerned."

She held up a hand. "The car can be blinded by sun. When that happens, its failsafe systems, which include radar and lidar, both good at detecting objects but not as good at figuring out what those objects are, kick in."

"So far, everything is in fine working condition. I don't see a problem. But of course, you do."

"*This* is the problem." She presented a folder. "I've found complaints and supporting documents that the car's failsafe system sometimes takes up to a half-second to activate."

"There's a whole lifetime."

"For us, sitting here, no. But a vehicle moving at 50 mph, the speed of this one, travels about 37 feet in a half-second."

"Good to know."

"So this car was effectively sightless for those 37 feet."

"And. . . ?"

"And, Stratto, the company that built the car, knows it. *And* they know the standard is 1/100 of a second, not half-a-second."

"Then they have a chance to fix it."

"They've known it for six months. They've had that chance. They haven't fixed it."

"Well, then they—"

"*And* they've been covering it up."

Kyle's face darkened. "How do you know that? How do you know 'they're covering it up'?"

"This isn't the first time I've dealt with something like this."

For once he paused before reaching for the first dismissal that came to mind. "Oh. That's different. We'll have to do something about that."

Could he have said that with less conviction? She wondered. What she said out loud was, "Do what?"

"Above my pay grade. I'll pass the information on. They can decide what."

"They" were the people in Washington who ran her department. Who were firmly in the pocket of the AV industry. "Doing something" would be merely telling Stratto what she'd uncovered and giving them a chance to release the information as they wanted to, so they wouldn't face consequences for hiding it in the first place. She was beginning to feel like a hamster on a running wheel; it was turning into a dream in which she was trying to reach an ever-moving destination.

"If Stratto's hiding this, what else might they be hiding?" she pressed.

"Don't you already know?" He was back to sarcasm.

"Give me some time and I'll find out."

"Because you *know* that's what it has to be. You *know* if they haven't come forward with this, which maybe, just maybe, is an innocent mistake rather than an evil dark cover-up, there's a vast corporate conspiracy that's going to destroy the world."

"What I *know* is, I've seen it before. Companies concealing . . ."

"Who hasn't seen it before? All right, maybe they are concealing something. They conceal, eventually it comes out. Then it gets fixed."

"But—"

"You caught the case because the woman died. Work on *that*. Finish your report, clear the case, and make a note of . . . whatever else you *think* might be happening."

"But if they're covering up—"

"You gonna take that on, too? Take who-knows-how-long on a simple case while you find and solve every problem you *think* may be out there?"

"I'd like to."

"I *wouldn't* like you to. Have your report on my desk—case cleared—by EOD today."

"And you'll—"

"I'll . . . do whatever I decide to."

Dana knew exactly what *that* would be.

10

IT'S LIKE THEY'RE TAKING A MEETING

Two days later, Denver Police Sergeant Phillip Delgado was cruising Market Street when the alert from Central came in. "We just got a call there's something strange happening at Sixth and Foster. Something about a group of cabs acting strangely. Can you go take a look?"

"A group of what?" Delgado wanted to know.

"Robo-cabs."

"Doing what?"

"Acting strangely."

"They're robos," Delgado clarified. "How can they be acting strangely?"

"Caller didn't say."

"What are they doing?"

"Nothing. Just sitting there in the middle of the street."

"They're stalled?"

"Nope. Just idling. Delgado, don't give me hard time. Just—"

"How many are there?"

"Six. No, make that seven. Now eight."

"More are coming?"

"That's what I'm getting now."

"So we've got eight—"

"Nine."

"And *what* are they doing?"

"Delgado, you could have been there by now!"

"OK. On my way. Sixth and Foster?"

"Yeah. Burns is on his way, too. So's Layton."

No way this could be as nuts as it sounded. Even so, he was glad Burns would be there. Burns never got ruffled and had good judgment. Layton wasn't the sharpest knife in the shed, but he was big and didn't back down from a fight. Based on what he'd just heard, Delgado didn't expect a fight, but he thought maybe . . . Oh hell, he didn't know what to think.

Sixth and Foster were wide streets, each with 3 lanes of traffic in both directions, making their confluence a huge, very busy intersection. By the time Delgado arrived, the 9 robos had grown to 12 and had formed a circle around the intersection's perimeter, blocking all 12 lanes of roadway feeding into the intersection. The cabs' noses were pointed toward the center, as if they were waiting for someone. Or something.

Burns was standing outside his cruiser.

"What the hell is this?" Delgado asked.

"Damned if I know."

"What are they doing?"

"Nothing. They just seem to be . . . waiting."

"For what?"

"Don't ask me."

Layton pulled up behind them, talking as he got out of his car. "I hear that right? A bunch of robos?"

Delgado nodded to the circle of cabs about fifty feet away.

"What the fuck?" Layton exhaled.

"People are calling this in?" asked Burns.

"Wouldn't you?" Layton responded.

"We have to figure this out," Delgado told them. "Traffic's already backed up, and that crowd," he gestured to the three dozen people gathered on the nearby sidewalks, "is going to get a lot bigger. Cams on," he ordered. "'Cause no one is gonna believe this, and I sure as shit can't describe it."

"Cams on" was standard procedure, but Delgado knew how easy it was for officers to forget to do it because they were dealing with a sudden life-or-death situation or simply distracted by something . . . like this.

"What are we supposed to do?" Layton wanted to know.

"I don't think there's a protocol for this," Delgado muttered, staring at the cabs.

"It's like . . . They're taking a meeting or something," Burns observed.

"They got a leader?" wondered Layton.

"Layton . . ." Delgado was trying to keep this from getting really nuts. "You're talking about a bunch of cabs."

"Who formed a circle. Someone's telling them what to do. Hey Sarge . . . Tomorrow's Halloween. You think that has anything to do with this?"

Burns playfully nudged Delgado as he turned to Layton. "Which one you think it is? The leader. 3466 or 4218?"

"4218," Layton declared with confidence. "Nicer paint job."

Delgado peered at Layton to see if he was serious. He decided he was.

"What about 9966?" Burns couldn't resist. "That one looks like the type to pull something like this."

"4218 has shiftier headlights," Layton doubled down.

"But 9966 has—"

"Hey, guys . . ." Delgado interrupted. "Can we focus on what we're we gonna do?"

"About what?" Burns wanted to know. "They're just sitting there."

"In a *circle*," Layton reminded them, emphasizing the gravity of the situation.

"They breaking any laws?" Burns wondered.

"Good point," Layton nodded. "They're not—"

"They're blocking traffic," Delgado pointed out.

"And that crowd looks like it's doubled," observed Burns. "So . . . Disturbing the peace?"

"How about assembling without a permit?" That was Layton. "Or unlawful circle on a public street?"

"Who do we even talk to about this?" Delgado wanted to know.

"I say we start with 4218. I don't like his looks." Burns wanted to see how far he could push Layton.

And of course Layton took the bait. "That sounds like profiling."

But Delgado was determined to . . . He wasn't sure what they should do. "We gonna stand here and make jokes, or we gonna do something?"

"Hey, Layton . . ." Burns was going for it. "Go over to 4218 and tap on the window."

"Then what?" Layton wanted to know.

"Ask them to step out of the vehicle." Somehow Burns was keeping a straight face.

"Ask who? It's a freaking robo!"

"You think it's a stand-off?" Burns suggested. "Should we call for back-up?"

"Maybe." Layton turned to Delgado. "What d'ya think, Sarge?"

"I think this is getting way out of hand." He glared at Burns, who responded with a wicked grin and the tiniest nod toward Layton. Delgado couldn't really blame him. Layton made it too easy.

"OK, when in doubt, pass it on to somebody else." Delgado spoke into the radio on his shoulder: "Central, Delgado, Burns, and Layton at Sixth and Foster. We've got a dozen robos in a circle here."

"Doing what?"

"Nothing."

"Who put them in a circle?"

"No one. They did."

"What are they doing?"

"Nothing. They're just . . . sitting here. Please advise."

"Is there a leader?"

"They're robos. They're machines."

"Is there someone you can talk to?"

"Just Burns and Layton. The cabs are empty."

"And they're just sitting in a circle?"

"Yeah."

"Why?"

"I have no idea. But traffic's at a stand-still, and the crowd's getting bigger by the minute."

"Well get them out of there!"

"Yeah, but how do we get them moving again?"

There was a long pause, and for a moment Delgado thought he'd lost Central. Then: "Let me get back to you on that."

As Delgado took his hand off the radio, the stopped traffic, politely silent until now, sent up a chorus of toots and honks. And the crowd, now one-hundred-strong, started coming closer for a better look.

"There's gotta be someone we can talk to, like at the cab company or something." Burns was finally trying to figure it out.

"Dispatch is looking into that," Delgado told him. "I hope."

"Can we break into one of them?" Burns offered. "Maybe drive it away."

"Might piss the others off," Layton countered. Delgado thought it was a joke, but Layton appeared genuinely concerned. "And they outnumber us four to one."

"Layton, you're talking like they're alive or something." Delgado was beginning to wish it was just him and Burns.

"Well, they did *this*!" Layton held his ground. "Who knows what else they might do if we piss 'em off. You know how many movies there are, where it starts like this? And before you know it—"

Delgado was glad when Central cut in. "You guys still there? We have a Central Control number for a cab company. Maybe they can—"

"Hold on. Something's happening," Delgado interrupted. "They're starting to move."

"What are they doing?"

"They're . . . leaving."

The cabs, which had shut down after forming the circle, started up and shifted into gear. One by one, they began gliding away at a very-legal 30 mph. Within minutes, whatever it was that had just happened was over. All twelve cabs drove off, leaving the street free for other cars, and the cops staring after them.

"Looks like the meeting is over," Layton said softly as he watched them make their way down the street. "Wonder what they decided."

Delgado rolled his eyes, but Burns wasn't through yet. "We'll never know. You should have frisked 4218 while you had the chance."

"Might have pissed the others off," Layton repeated, shading his eyes as he stared up at the news helicopters circling overhead.

"And they outnumbered us four to one," Burns took his final shot.

"Should've called for back-up," Layton said almost wistfully.

That might have been the end of it. And "it" might have been little more than a human-interest story, the kind of quirky item news broadcasts like to end with to leave the viewers they've depressed with the news feeling a little better about the state of the world.

Except for what happened later that day.

11

IT KEPT GOING

Having just dropped its passenger at a downtown Chicago office building, the orange robo-cab might have shut down where it was and stood idle until engaged by its next fare.

But the cab company's Dispatch saw the robo was in a loading zone and there was a cabstand outside the hotel on the next block. So Dispatch told the robo to make its way to the line of waiting cabs a street away.

Once there, it would remain motionless until someone got in, or the cab in front of it left the line and it moved up to take its place, or it received notice of a new fare somewhere else. Whatever the next notification might be, it was one of the megabillion messages passed between CAVs (vehicle-to-vehicle communication, or V2V) or between CAVs and the objects around them (vehicle-to-infrastructure, or V2I communication) as part of the moment-to-moment back-and-forth digital chatter that made it possible for CAVs to navigate safely. Everything from traffic lights, stop signs, and other road signs, to lampposts, telephones, overpasses, and billboards were fitted with sensors that let the CAVs see and talk to their environment, providing them with the guidance and instructions they needed to negotiate road conditions and reach their destinations without crashing. To do all this, each CAV used 300,000,000 lines of code, more than six times the 45,000,000 in a passenger jet.

Left turn-signal blinking, the robo scanned the street to its left, saw there were no vehicles approaching, and eased away from the curb. It cruised to the corner, registered the red light, and glided to a stop. Ten seconds later, the light turned green, the cab's sensors reported cross traffic was stopped in both directions, and the cab proceeded through the intersection, now only 50 feet from its destination—the space behind the last cab in line outside the hotel.

As it approached the space, the robo activated its right-turn signal and arced out of traffic, coming in perfectly aligned with the cab in front of it. But instead of rolling to a stop, it kept going, crashing into the parked robo in its path. Its front bumper crumpled and its hood creased on impact; the rear bumper of the cab it hit popped free and dangled an inch above the pavement. The collision was loud, and later nearby pedestrians would wonder which startled them more: the sound of the crash, or the fact that it happened.

More startling was the evening news and the next morning's headlines. There were eleven other crashes just like it all over the country.

12

START WATCHING THE STREETS

Jason sat back in his recliner, popped the cap on his first Corona of the evening, and turned on the TV, which was always set to US-News. He had plenty of time to catch Rood's entire broadcast—the last one of the day—live. He never missed a show, but when it was recorded instead of live, he couldn't help but feel he might be missing part of the story. Seeing it in real time made him feel like he was plugged in to everything that was happening.

"I'm going to begin with this late-breaking story," Rood intoned. "I'm not quite sure what to make of it yet, but I can make a good guess. We'll see what *you* think after you hear all the facts. And as always, these are *true* facts. We don't deal in lies or misinformation here.

"I'm talking about the outbreak of strange, dangerous behavior by a roving group of robo-cabs in Denver. We've already reported on all the chaos and confusion they caused when a . . . I guess the best word to use here is *gang* . . . When a roving gang of robo-cabs stopped traffic and terrified people by massing on the street.

"You heard that right. There might have been many more,

but there were at least twelve of them, out of control on the streets of one or our most important cities. They massed in one of its biggest, busiest intersections and formed a circle, stopping at least twelve lanes of traffic, in two directions, terrorizing everyone who happened to be nearby.

"Know what they did? They just sat there. Doing nothing. While everyone around them wondered why they were doing it. And, even scarier, what they were going to do next.

"The police department has released video from the body cams of the heroic officers trying to deal with this bizarre, terrifying incident, and we have that video.

"Now, these are police officers, trained to deal with any emergency. When shots are fired, they run toward them, not away. When someone's drowning, they jump into the water. When someone's kidnapped, they go out looking for them. And these veteran officers, according to this official police video, believed those robo-cabs, that formed that circle, were . . . Alive.

"Don't take my word for it. Listen to what the police themselves actually said. One said 'It's like they're taking a meeting.' Another wondered if they had a leader because, and I quote, 'Someone's telling them what to do.'

"The situation quickly turned into a stand-off. Those aren't my words, they're the words of the officers at the scene, who then feared that they might need back-up.

"For some unknown reason, that back-up never arrived. Meanwhile, the cops who were there stood by helplessly, wondering what was going to happen next, concerned that if they approached one of these silent, ominous vehicles, and here again I'm quoting, they 'might piss the others off.'

"Then came the scariest part of all, as one cop, and this is another quote, realized . . . and you can imagine how terrifying this must have been . . . 'They outnumber us four to one.'

"I don't know about you, but I can't help but wonder just why that desperately-needed back-up never arrived.

"So how does this weird, frightening story end? Fortunately, after holding police at bay for as long as they wanted to while they held their ground on that city street . . . the robos disbanded on their own, for reasons that still remain a mystery.

"That's right. We still don't know why they did it, what they wanted, or what they plan to do next. And I guarantee you, and I've never been wrong, they *are* going to do more of this.

"The only answer we have . . . And this might be the only answer we'll ever get . . . Are the final words the police exchanged among themselves as they watched the cabs escape. And I quote: 'Looks like the meeting is over. I wonder what they decided.'

"Now, what I want to know is this: What the hell is going on out there? Know what I think? This is the beginning, just the *beginning*, mind you, of a much bigger problem. Now hold onto your seats here . . . I have to agree with that officer who thinks driverless vehicles . . . these robots on wheels who are supposed to do what *we* tell them to . . . I have to wonder: Are these machines beginning to think for themselves?

"That's not a new idea. It's been predicted for decades that as machines and robots got more advanced, they'd start thinking. That's what artificial intelligence is. Now, is it possible we've developed such advanced machines . . . we've *let* them become so advanced . . . that they've started to think for themselves?

"Sounds fantastic, doesn't it? And maybe just last week . . . just two days ago . . . I might have said the same thing. It's too fantastic. It's too unbelievable. But after this, what are we supposed to think now?

"While you think about that, think about this: Something else happened.

"They keep telling us robos are safe. That they crash much

less than cars driven by people. Well, maybe that's just not true anymore. Because at four o'clock this afternoon—the same day that gang of robos terrified Denver . . . Within the space of 15 minutes, there were 12 . . . *12* incidents of robo-cabs rear-ending each other.

"So, first we have 12 of them having a meeting . . . . Remember, those are the recorded, official words of a heroic police officer . . . And we still don't know what those dozen dangerous vehicles wanted, or decided at that meeting. Then we have 12 robos smashing in to each other.

"And if you haven't already thought of what I'm about to say next, I'll say it for you. What's the common thread here? The number 12.

"You think it's coincidence that 12 robos went rogue and called a meeting in broad daylight? You think it's coincidence that the very same day 12 robos crashed into each other? You want to think that, I'll let you. But you put those two things together, and we've got more than coincidence here. There's no way these machines can arrive at that same number and have it be coincidence. No way.

"I say we've reached a very dangerous tipping point. I think these robots on wheels are no longer taking orders from us, and instead they're beginning to . . . fantastic as it sounds . . . think for themselves.

"Don't take my word for it. Listen to the police recordings for yourself. And if it scares you as much as it does me, think about what you're going to do about it.

"Here's a suggestion . . . Start watching the streets. Keep a sharp eye out for robos behaving strangely . . . acting suspiciously . . . Doing things they're not supposed to. Because you never know when they might be planning something. Or doing something.

"Keep an eye out for these things, and keep an eye *on* these things. And if you see something, *do* something. Say something. Make yourself heard.

"That's all I have for today. I'll see you all tomorrow for more True Facts."

Jason drained the last of his beer as Rood closed the show. As always, he was right on the money, calling it like it is, trying to make people aware of what was going on out there. And thank god for that.

His story about the robo meeting was some strange shit.

But the story about the 12 robo crashes was great news. If it meant what Jason hoped it meant. He rose from the recliner, and went to find out.

13

I CAN DO IT

The Restless Rustler was Jason's neighborhood bar. He liked the neon cowboy above the entrance outside, and the smell of beer he could almost feel permeating the air as soon as he stepped through the front door. He liked the old-wood décor, and the downhome welcome he got from the long-time waitresses who knew him. The prices were reasonable, the bartenders generous with their pours, and as raucous as the place could get on a Saturday night, you never had to look over your shoulder or jump in to a brawl to help a friend. He was ready enough to mix it up if it came to that in another bar, but at the Rustler everybody got along. Tonight it was festooned with pumpkins and swaths of toilet paper. On the mirror behind the bar, in deliberately-askew lipsticked capital letters, someone (must've been Denise) had written "Life's A Witch!"

Jason arrived a good fifteen minutes before Hector and ordered a Corona. No fancy IPA beers here! The glass was half-empty by the time Hector slid into the booth, bumping the table with his laptop as he maneuvered into the seat.

"You even take that to a bar?" Jason asked, nodding to the computer that was now sitting safely to Hector's left.

"I take it everywhere."

"Want a beer?"

"I don't drink alcohol."

Jason knew that, just as he knew Hector took his laptop everywhere. He just felt chatty tonight.

He nodded to Beryl, who was taking care of this section tonight. "Another Corona, and, I got it . . ." he stopped Hector from ordering . . . "a ginger ale for my friend. With ice. Thanks darlin'."

"You had a good day today, my friend!" Jason tilted his glass toward Hector.

"Yes! I broke my record for the number of coding lines in a day."

"I'll bet you did. But I'm not talking about that. I'm talking about Chicago."

"Chicago?"

"Not the time for modesty, buddy. You did good and we're gonna celebrate!"

"What are we celebrating?"

Jason saw that Hector really didn't know. "You stopped working and came straight here, didn't you?"

"Yes. You said to be here at 7:00, and I didn't finish working until 6:53, so I—"

"You didn't listen to the news."

"I hardly ever do."

"And you didn't listen to True Facts."

"True Facts is a redundancy. If something is a fact—"

"Nah, I'm talking about Zach Rood. *True Facts*."

"I never listen to him. He's—"

"He's one of the few people telling it like it is."

"But if the name of his show is—"

"Never mind all that. We are here to celebrate, pal!"

Beryl brought their drinks. Jason quickly finished his first Corona as she placed the new order on the table.

"First thing, which we're among the first to know, 'cause I'm on Bobby Landry's mailing list, is he's getting ready to introduce the Right-To-Drive Amendment in Congress. It's not even in the news yet. Got the e-mail ping on the way over here. So that alone'd be reason to raise a glass. But what we're really celebrating is you!" He again raised his glass to Hector, who lifted his an inch in Jason's direction.

"How'd you do it?"

"Do what?"

"The accident in Chicago. And the other eleven, everywhere from . . . I don't know, Miami up to Boston, San Diego to Portland, and just about everywhere in between!"

"They happened?"

"Damn right they happened! Twelve happened! Four times three! Boom, boom, boom, boom!" Jason's finger travelled across an invisible map hanging in front of him, targeting one city after another. "C'mon, tell me. Was it easy or hard?"

"On a scale of one to ten, one being the easiest, ten being the hardest, it was an easy two. Although that's redundant, since the construction of the scale indicates that two is very easy. I should have said—"

"You said it was easy, and that's good enough for me. Any reason you picked Chicago first?"

"I didn't pick Chicago. Or any of the other places. I didn't pick anywhere. I just temporarily altered the V2V algorithm for one-tenth of a second."

"A tenth of a second? Is that enough time?"

"As little as a nanosecond would do it. The odds are overwhelmingly on your side that there'll be several accidents. Not always twelve. One day there might be ten, another day there might be seventeen. Or twenty, or even thirty. It depends on—"

"But you're still leaving it to chance. Why do it that way?"

"It's the easiest way to do it. Change one line of code and let technology do the rest."

Jason zeroed in on the "leaving it to chance" part, which he didn't want to hear. Even with the odds "overwhelmingly" on their side, he wanted something more reassuring. What if it didn't work out as well next time?

"But will it always work?" he pressed.

"It would be more unusual if it *didn't* work. There are ten million robo-cabs on the road at any given moment, driving about one billion miles a day. Change the V2V algorithm—"

"OK, Got it. Even though I have no idea what V2V means."

"Vehicle to Vehicle. Temporarily altering the V2V algorithm will always lead to random results. The way it works is—"

"Don't need to know how it works. As long as it does. What about the circle? The 'meeting' everyone's talking about. Was that chance, too? And I still say, is leaving everything to chance the best way to do it?"

"It's not really leaving everything to chance. When you alter the V2V algorithm there'll almost always be an accident. There almost has to be, if your alteration stays in place. I just don't know where and when it will happen. It's the Law of Big Numbers, which states—"

"Right," Jason said, not really understanding but not really caring. Results were all that mattered. "Now, raise your goddamn glass high because you are the man of the hour! Or should I say nanosecond? Or tenth-o-second?"

"Tenth-o-second doesn't make sense. It—"

"Hector!"

Jason hoisted his glass. This time, Hector met the gesture all the way. But in his enthusiasm, he hit Jason's glass too hard, sloshing beer on the table.

"Sorry," he mumbled.

In other circumstances, Jason would have been annoyed. But all he wanted tonight was to make Hector happy. "No worries, buddy. Accidents happen."

"They can happen in a nanosecond!"

"Hey, you made a joke! You really are having a good day!"

Hector grinned, not used to praise, especially from Jason. And Jason grinned back, pleased to see how much it mattered to him.

"Lemme get back to this V2V shit for a minute. If you don't know where and when things are gonna happen—"

"It's impossible to predict."

"That's what I'm saying. So they could happen in the middle of nowhere instead of cities."

"They will."

"But that could mean they might not make the news."

"They might not."

"So people might not hear about them."

"Maybe."

"But we want them to know. That's the whole . . . Wait! I just got a brilliant idea! How about, we add a feature to the web site. We can call it . . . 'Unsafe At Any Speed.' It'll be for people to report robo accidents, so we don't have to rely on the news. And anyone who adds to the list gets a PARD t-shirt, or hat, or something! We play this right, there'll be accidents reported every goddamn day!" Jason could already see it. The next big-deal feature on the PARD website.

"We can't do that," Hector stopped him. "Ralph Nader wrote

a book with the title *Unsafe At Any Speed* in 1965. The publisher called it 'a scathing indictment that lambasted the auto industry for producing unsafe vehicles' and said 'the book led to congressional hearings and automobile safety laws passed in 1966, including the National Traffic and Motor Vehicle Safety Act.' The rest of the jacket copy said—"

"I get it. Don't need to hear every word."

"There are only a few more. It went on to say—"

"OK, I don't care what we call the web page. We can call it . . . 'Unsafe On Any Road.' You OK with *that*?"

"It doesn't matter what I'm OK with. It's a matter of following the law when it comes to—"

"We'll follow the goddamn law! Call it any freaking thing you want. As long as all the other accidents get reported."

"There'll be more?"

"Damn right there'll be more. You'll make sure of that."

"I thought this was a one-time experiment. To see if we could—"

"Can't be a one-time thing. It's got to keep happening."

"But that wouldn't be right. Accidents consume resources and—"

"Lots of things consume resources. Hector, you've got to think in terms of the bigger good. Causing a few accidents now is going to change things for the better down the line. Which will . . . *save* resources. And you said yourself how easy it is."

"But someone could get hurt."

"Not if you do it right."

"But what if someone were walking between two of those cabs when they crashed?"

"But no one was."

"But they could have."

"Well you can prevent that, can't you?"

"No. When you alter the V2V algorithm—"

"Yeah, you never know what's gonna happen. But no one getting hurt this time shows how good you are. Just keep doing more of the same."

"But the randomness creates a variable that—"

"Hector, am I hearing some doubts here?"

"It's not a doubt, it's a fact. That variable—"

"I mean doubt that maybe you can't do it. I'm sensing you thinking maybe you're not up to this."

"I'm just saying—"

"I know what you're saying. So I'll tell you what. If it's more than you can handle . . . like it's beyond your capabilities . . . I wouldn't want you to embarrass yourself."

Jason watched Hector almost wince each time he called his ability into question. He'd just won high praise from his best—his only—friend, and now it was being withdrawn because that friend doubted him. So Jason went a step further.

"It's all right. Shame, though. I thought we'd be celebrating a lot more together. But if you can't do this . . . And I know you're busy with your other projects . . . And not doing this will give you more time to spend with your other friends, so that's another thing to consider."

Jason stopped there to let his reference to "other friends" sink in. And inwardly grinned as Hector squared his shoulders. "I can do it," he said confidently.

"You sure?"

"Yes. I can do it."

"OK, then."

Jason took a satisfying pull on his beer, then made sure he sounded neutral to the point of disinterest as he said, "Next time, let's be celebrating something a little more . . . creative."

Hector's brow creased. "What would that be?"

Jason "searched for an answer" and came up with, "How

about, we . . . take out a truck or two. Maybe operated by Auto-Truck America."

"Why them?" Hector wanted to know.

"They're the biggest robo-trucking company in the nation. Hitting them will show that anyone's vulnerable."

"Why should we show that one company is more vulnerable than any other?"

Hector didn't ask questions like these. Caught up short, Jason had to made a quick recovery. "Not necessarily *that* company. Robo-trucks in general. Anyway, we couldn't target *them*, because you said you never know what's going to happen when you alter the . . . what are they called again? Cargorithms?"

"Algorithms." Hector corrected, as Jason knew he would. His deliberate mistake sidetracked Hector; then, to make sure he stayed distracted, Jason added, "So tell me, any new coding projects coming up?"

"Yes! I've landed two more, both work from home!" Hector launched into a detailed description of both projects, filling Jason in on details he wouldn't have cared about under any circumstances. But Jason had immediately stopped listening for reasons of his own.

He was making a mental note to remember that Hector could be more perceptive than he'd been giving him credit for. From now on, he'd have to take that into account.

14

I'M CLOSING THE CASE

Dana had no choice but to keep her word to Kyle and close out "the California thing" by the end of the week. Today. But closing the case for him and keeping it open for her were two different things. By now she was sure there was more to it than Kyle would ever permit himself to imagine.

Wrapping up the case didn't seem to please Kyle. "Well, at least that's done," he groused. "I'll get back to you on what it's done to our clearance rate. Meanwhile, you have another. Chicago cab thing. This one's so cut-and-dried even you won't have trouble closing it by Wednesday."

"Are you *telling* me to close it by then?" she couldn't help asking.

"Yeah. To make up for the one you just turned into a marathon."

As she left Kyle's office, she ran into Jeff, who she'd already decided to track down for a few minutes of light conversation as a welcome change from her boss.

Seeing the door she'd just walked out of, and the look on her face, he asked, "How'd it go in there?"

"Same as it always does," she rolled her eyes as she fell into step beside him. "He climbed up my ass over the case I just cleared, then gave me a new one with a deadline attached."

"Sounds about normal. I got one, too. Robo-cab fender bender in San Antonio. But no deadline. Maybe I'm the one doing something right around here."

"If it means doing *his* right, I'd rather be wrong."

But this time, Kyle had been right. The new case *was* so cut-and-dried that she wondered why they'd gotten it. One robo-cab rear-ended another as it was pulling into a cab stand. Both cabs were put out of service but fixable, no one hurt, and no other property damage. Seeing that both cabs were made by the same manufacturer (Launch), she checked the incident logs for past crashes involving their vehicles, only to find the company had an exemplary record.

In the end, she couldn't land on anything other than a rogue software glitch or vehicle-equipment issue (camera or sensor malfunction?). Why had this been forwarded to her unit? Quick investigations by the local police and the cab company should have put it to rest.

She was about to sign off on it when a new thought struck her: Jeff had referred to his San Antonio case as a fender bender. Three minutes later she was at his desk, just as he was clearing the case.

"Finished!" he proclaimed when he saw her. "And don't tell me you haven't already done the same."

"You're smarter than you look." Dana enjoyed their rag-on-each-other banter. It was a respite from her Kyle-battles, and he was able to match her shot for shot.

"And you're sorry you're not gonna mess up Kyle's CR this week. Though not for lack of trying."

"I do what I can. Tell me about yours." She indicated the new case, which was still on his screen.

"Nothing to tell," he shrugged. "Just one robocab bonking another."

"Both cabs out of service for repairs, no injuries, no other property damage?"

"Yeah."

"Both made by Launch?"

"You working your case or mine?"

"Let me see something." She reached for his keyboard.

"I *was* using that!"

"Only be a minute," she said absent-mindedly as she called up yesterday's incident log. Then: "I'll be damned."

"What?"

"There were twelve of these yesterday."

"Of *these*? You mean the same kind?"

"I mean the *exact* same." She hit different keys. "And all of them Launch cabs."

"Launch is gonna have some explaining to do."

"Launch has a perfect safety record."

Jeff knew where this was headed. "OK, listen . . . This could be anything. An issue with V2V. A problem with I2V. Or just about any other algo."

"I know that."

"Then why do you look like this?" He did an exaggerated imitation of her.

She knew she probably did look like that, but she couldn't help it. And she knew Kyle would give her no end of shit for "crapping up" such an uncomplicated situation. But she was getting a red flag here, and just as Kyle couldn't *not* want her to leave it alone, she couldn't *not* do her job haphazardly to make his life easier.

"Why didn't Kyle tell us about the other crashes?" she asked Jeff.

"Maybe he didn't know about them."

"He knew. He assigns cases. And I'll bet he assigned one of these to each of us. Lemme see something else." She called up the unit's case assignments "Uh-huh. We got six. So Eastern probably got six. Bet you lunch each of us here pulled one of these today."

"OK, one . . . No bet. And two, before you go pissing Kyle off, which you're gonna do no matter what I say, consider this: Shit happens."

"But it's never happened to Launch before. So why now?"

"Why are we even having this conversation! You're gonna go to him with this anyway."

"Relax. I'm not gonna ask you to come with me."

"Good. Then I won't have to turn you down."

"C'mon, Jeff. We never get fender-benders. Now we get these, and Kyle goes all stealth about how he assigns them? You really don't see something wrong here? Launch has the technology down, and now twelve crashes in one day. Really?"

"They have rubber tires down too. But track blow-outs or flats for a day, and you'll find dozens. Kyle's just gonna say it's the law of big numbers. Then get pissed at you all over again. You really want that?"

"What I want is to find out why he didn't tell us."

"I didn't *want* to tell you!" Kyle was struggling not to scream.

"And I'm asking why."

"I don't have to tell you that! But I will. I didn't tell you because I knew this is *exactly* what you'd do!"

"What I'm doing, is my job."

"Which is, no matter what *you* think it is, to do what I tell you to. Which is clear your cases. Quickly and efficiently. Not make everything more complicated and drag the unit down with you!"

I just want to find out what this really is. Or what it might—"

"I'll tell you what it is. The law of big numbers. Flip a coin a million times, there's a high probability you'll get a stretch of ten heads in a row, maybe more. CAVs travel, what, 1.3 trillion miles a year? How can there *not* be a few crashes. It's just ten heads in a row."

"I know what the law of big numbers is. And I think—"

"How about, you *don't* think. I gave out six cases this morning, to six people, and every one of them has been closed. Except guess whose?"

"I want to keep mine open until I'm satisfied."

"But that doesn't satisfy *me*. Know what? Never mind. I'll take care of it."

"I haven't signed off on it."

"You don't have to. I will. I'm closing the case. Keep this up, and maybe I'll close you, too."

"Is that a threat?"

"Of course not. I'm just doing my job. Which is making sure my department runs smoothly and efficiently. Which means identifying anything that gets in the way of that. And eliminating it."

15

THE GUY WHO WAS ALWAYS IN THE TIMES

"Richard, this is Bill Preston, from KPRW. We're doing a story on the recent spate of CAV crashes and I was hoping to get a statement from you. I'm sure you know about those 12 accidents last Thursday."

Of course he knew about that. And what happened in Denver. He was tracking it all. And he was profoundly aware that with Preston's call the media was coming to him instead of his having to seek out a new venue to run something he'd written.

"Of course I'll give you a statement."

"Hang on, I've got a better idea. Would you be willing to do an on-camera interview? In the studio, or we can come to you."

"An interview? Yeah, sure."

"Terrific. I think I can get my producer to go for it. I'll call you back in an hour."

Two hours later, Preston called back to say the interview was a go, and six hours later Corby was sitting on the news set of KPRW, a local station, about to go on-air.

"Hey, Richard," Preston turned to him. "Aren't you the guy who was always in the *Times* a few years back? And CNN? How come you don't do that anymore?"

Corby was considering how to respond, when Preston waved him off. "Never mind. If you were doing them, you'd be too busy to talk to us."

Before Corby could respond to *that*, the floor manager signaled they were live.

After answering Preston's questions on the recent "spate of crashes" (not much to say about the crashes themselves because not much was known yet), Corby worked the conversation to what he really wanted to talk about: "The federal government is crafting its new regulations according to NAVA and industry leaders, rather than what the public needs."

When Preston commented that there didn't seem to be much public input, Corby countered with the fact that people were being told only what NAVA wanted them to know.

Not eager to pursue that, Preston returned to the hotter topic of CAV crashes, asking if Corby was concerned that they showed the technology wasn't perfected. Corby replied, "The real danger is more from—"

"Are you saying that CAVs are dangerous?" Preston jumped in, sensing there might be some heat in this exchange. "That sounds like—"

"I'm saying that there are other reasons to be concerned. One is that CAV manufacturers keep their technologies secret. Years ago, before CAVs, Volvo engineers invented the three-point seat belt shoulder harness and made it available to anyone, at no cost, so all vehicles could have it. The companies making CAVs today lack that kind of benevolence and public interest. Each has different technologies, and those tasked with making sure CAVs are safe have to navigate a labyrinth of proprietary coding they're often denied access to.

"The other concern is what I said before: We need more public input, more involvement from traffic engineers and urban planners, before Washington finalizes its regulations."

"How will that stop CAVs from crashing?" Preston wanted to know.

"*That* won't," Corby conceded. "What we *can* stop, is CAV technology 'crashing' into society. We deserve a future in which CAVs co-exist with people in a beneficial way that doesn't sacrifice the needs of the public for the convenience and profit of the industry."

"I thought that went well," Preston said when the interview was done and they were off-camera.

"Any time. Glad to do it."

"I'm gonna hold you to that. You're my new go-to source for all things CAV."

"Works for me. But do me a favor . . . I know you can't include everything we talked about when you air this. I know you have to edit. But can you please not take things out of context?"

"Absolutely. This stuff is pure gold!"

When the interview ran on the evening news, it was pared down to two neat sound bites: "The federal government is crafting its new regulations according to NAVA and industry leaders." Corby had said that, but it was meant as a warning. Omitting the crucial six words that ended his sentence made it sound like an endorsement.

The other sound bite was positioned to reflect his concern about "CAV technology crashing into society." Which made *that* Corby's main thought on the subject.

Taken together, they gave Bill Preston his Big Finish: "So, according to one expert, we're at a crossroads. Is the government planning a safe future by listening to industry leaders? Or a future in which CAVs crash headlong into society? This week, they already started crashing into each other. Maybe it's still to be determined just who is—and who isn't—in the driver's seat."

It almost made Corby glad he was being asked to do so few interviews.

16

LOCAL STATIONS HAD A FIELD DAY

Cabbo, Philadelphia's biggest cab company, was proud of its five-year record of serving the city successfully and efficiently. Its fleet of 300 cabs was all electric, cutting down on greenhouse-gas emissions, and consisted almost entirely of Relyable 4000s, which had just been cited as one of the safest robos on the road. The company had four garages strategically located around the city, making it easier and faster for cabs to be deployed or recalled, reducing traffic around each garage. And its new volume algorithm had been performing flawlessly for the last six months, putting the highest concentration of vehicles on the streets during the morning and evening rush hours, making cabs available when people needed them most, shutting them down or bringing them back to the garages during off-hours when demand was at its lowest.

The industry's leading trade magazine had just lauded Cabbo as an example of "How To Do Robo Right."

But on November 5th Cabbo's unblemished record was

stained. It was 5:00 p.m. Wednesday, the middle of the workweek, the end of the workday, and as the city's workforce left downtown, many looking for cabs, there wasn't a single robo in sight because every one of Cabbo's vehicles had returned to the garage. However, instead of going to the nearest garage, as they should have, all three-hundred cabs descended on the downtown facility on South Street just off the Schuylkill River.

The result was chaos. First came the congestion, snarling traffic in all directions. From there, it got worse. The garage was never intended to house three-hundred cabs and didn't have the capacity to do so. Which left the overflow vehicles lined up in the surrounding streets for blocks. As a result, each of those streets lost a lane. Every vehicle that wasn't a cab had to use other lanes, and on some streets there was only one. It took only fifteen minutes for nine square blocks of Center City to become frozen with gridlock. Every street named for a tree (Pine, Walnut, Chestnut, Spruce), as well as several others, were impassable. Traffic soon spilled over to the west side of the river, paralyzing the streets around the University of Pennsylvania and Drexel University.

Throughout the city, no one could get a cab. Which was not only an inconvenience, but, like the traffic downtown, led to a secondary issue: Used to Cabbo's unquestioned efficiency and availability, people seeking taxis lost time until they figured out that this was not a scarcity of cabs, but a matter of no cabs. Hundreds were late to meetings, dinner dates, and timed events. The NY Rangers' Hockey Team had to jog from the Marriott Downtown to the Wells Fargo Center to face off against the Philadelphia Flyers. After conferring with the NHL, Mayor Steve Donaldson agreed to move the start time back 45 minutes to 8:15 p.m., the latest time ESPN would agree to.

Taken by surprise, not prepared to cope, flustered by the

number of vehicles deluging the garage, and initially not even knowing what the problem was, Cabbo's central dispatch was overwhelmed. It took an hour for them to finally solve the problem and have the robos back on the streets, and another hour for the city to return to normal.

Those two hours were the opening story on the late evening news across the country. And local stations had a field day.

17

THE ROC

Melissa had nothing to do for Corby, was between course assignments, and had no projects of her own to work on, so she logged on to CrackTheJax, the advanced hackers' forum she'd started visiting three months ago. It was one of the few places besides Corby's office where she found stimulating conversation.

She'd chosen her screen name, RosettaStone, because she'd been fascinated by the ancient stele since she'd first read about it in the fifth grade. It unraveled mysteries and picked the locks on doors that shielded sequestered realms. How could she not love it?

Once she started using the name, she discovered it provided an unforeseen benefit: as a sentry weeding out those who didn't get the reference and thought she was "a girl" named Rosetta Stone.

On the forum, she quickly skimmed the new conversations, then, not finding anything that caught her eye, clicked on what she really wanted to see: The Roc's latest thread.

She had no idea who he (she?) (they?) really were, but did know The Roc had real chops. Like her, he was light years ahead of everyone else, and as she sought him out now she realized that lately she'd been looking forward to both his posts and the exchanges they'd started having in private break-out rooms.

It usually started with her responding publicly to something he'd posted. Then, after public exchanges joined by others who didn't have their depth and breadth, they'd split off from the group and DM each other.

She liked the way his mind worked, and enjoyed his weekly "Can You?" challenges. Once a week he'd post a hacking or coding puzzle, inviting people to solve it. Most of the responses started off strong, but The Roc kept adding new layers and twists that took the problem deeper. Melissa would read the thread without responding, watching as people had to drop because they couldn't keep up with The Roc's seemingly endless permutations. When everyone else gave up, Melissa would jump in, the only one who could stay with him all the way. It always ended with the two of them playing what resembled an end-game in chess.

Lately, as the game wound down the tone of their exchanges became warmer, like they were old friends engaging in a favorite tradition.

Finding this week's thread, she scanned the earlier attempted solutions and tracked The Roc's escalating counter-responses. She could already see the point at which his next post would finish off the remaining survivor, Barley51.

Sure enough, Barley51 conceded he was flummoxed, and Melissa kicked in, reviving the game and forcing The Roc to go down a new path. With it, came the message: "I knew you'd show up now. Go private?"

"I knew you'd know!" she posted. "Sure, let's take it to DM. Not that it'll do you any good!"

"We'll see about that," he answered, then quickly threw out a new set of parameters.

He was very good, but it didn't take her long to see the solution.

And so it went, he finding new ways to make the problem more complicated, she supplying the right answers, until, finally, there was nowhere new to take it. She'd done what no one else in the forum could: stayed with The Roc until the end. It was one-third serious competition, one-third friendly rivalry, one third both of them showing off for someone who would truly appreciate their abilities.

More than anything else, it was fun.

18

AH95

The nation's first autonomous highway (AH95, so named because it paralleled I-95), was an experiment, a pilot program that was so far performing better than its creators envisioned. A new freeway dedicated to robotrucks, it spanned some 400 miles, connecting Baltimore to Boston.

It was used only by robo-trucks and did everything it was supposed to: decreasing travel time end-to-end, lowering shipping costs, and, so far, eliminating accidents. There was no driver error, carelessness, or fatigue. The trucks weren't breaking down, and local police were so rarely called for problems that authorities up and down the artery had dubbed it "Highway Ho-Hum."

At 3:00 p.m. on a clear sunny Friday, a robo-truck was halfway through its Baltimore-Bayonne run, travelling at 60 mph, the recommended speed for this section of roadway.

Rounding a curve, the CAV received a message from the traffic pole 50 feet ahead and to its right to slow down, and dropped its speed to 40. Coming out of the curve, it was told it could speed up, and accelerated back to 60.

As it started up a rise, its sensors acknowledged a change in terrain; the truck increased its speed to reach the top of the hill without slowing. Then, as it crested the hill its sensors cut its acceleration, so it maintained a constant speed downhill.

It was now approaching another curve. This one could be rounded without slowing down, and the signal pole at the bend in the road didn't tell the vehicle to decelerate. Taking the curve at 60 mph, the next message it received was from a second signal pole located 75 feet on the other side of the curve. That message was to decelerate because of a slow-moving vehicle dead ahead.

The truck decelerated, but the message came too late to stop it from rear-ending the robo-truck ahead of it at 30 mph. The second truck jackknifed on impact, skidding across the road and landing on its side.

Because AH95 was a robo-only highway, it had only one lane in each direction. With the speed of all vehicles using it coordinated by sensors and algorithms, and no impatience on the part of the trucks to make better time, there was no need for a passing lane. The jackknifed truck now blocked both lanes, bringing all approaching traffic to a halt.

AH95 was closed for the next five hours while investigators cleared the wreckage and tried to figure out what happened.

Those tasks were complicated by the fact that six other crashes occurred on AH95 that day.

19

FASTEN YOUR SEAT BELT

"Fasten your seat belt, because it's happened again. One of the country's busiest, most important highways, a road vital to our economy, a road that carries a huge percentage of the goods and products that keep this nation alive, was shut town today by the very trucks that use it. In not one, but *seven* separate crashes, truck after truck plowed into each other. I don't know what's going on out there, but it looks like these things are playing bumper cars with each other.

"And all this chaos happened in broad daylight. It wasn't night. It wasn't raining. It wasn't snowing. There were no icy conditions. There was no fog. And what are these robots doing? Crashing into each other. Now, why are they doing this? I can assure you, it's not for the fun of it. There's something much more sinister going on out there.

"I've been warning about this. And now my warnings are coming true. Last week, I said robos are beginning to think for themselves. Now I'm going to take it a step further. And I'm sounding a louder warning. About something that's much bigger and much more dangerous.

"Know what I think is happening? I think the robos are coming to life.

"Sounds fantastic, doesn't it. But let's look at the evidence. Last week they were rear-ending each other. Then . . . and this isn't me now, this is the official record . . . they held a meeting. That's what the police called it. That's in the official report.

"Now, we still don't know what happened in that meeting, what they decided to do. Maybe it was shutting down an entire city, like they did in Philadelphia, when they paralyzed the city and brought it to a complete standstill. And maybe that's only the beginning. Who knows when they'll have another meeting. And what they'll decide in that one.

"What I do know is that they've moving beyond crashing into each other. Now they're attacking our economic lifeline. If that's not evidence that they're thinking . . . if that's not proof they're openly plotting . . . I don't know what is.

"Still think this is crazy? Just look at history. Every story that's ever been written about robots has predicted that some day they'd start thinking for themselves. That they'd come to life. And once that happened, they'd try to take over.

"If you don't think that's not happening now, maybe you'd better think again. And if you don't think we need to stop them, you'd *really* better think again. Because sooner or later this is gonna reach a point of no return. The more they think, the smarter they're gonna get. And the smarter they get, the harder it's gonna be to stop them.

"If history has shown us anything, it's this: You have to stop something like this early, before it gathers steam. Because once it gathers momentum, it steamrolls over everything in its path. And once that happens, there *is* no stopping it.

"So it brings us to this. What kind of future do you want? What kind of planet do you want for you and your children?

And their children after them? A future where cars and trucks are telling us what to do? And doing whatever they want, any time they want? Or a planet where people control things?

"I say, it's a no-brainer. We still have time to fix it. We can reverse the damage that's already been done and that's increasing every single day. But only if we act now. We have to control these robots on wheels. *We* have to tell *them* what to do, not the other way around.

"And if you think what I'm saying is too far-fetched, too out there, think about this: Everyone who sounds a warning about something like this is never believed at first. And when they are, it's too late.

"So I'm going on the record about this here and now. These robots, these machines that are supposed to obey us . . . supposed to serve us . . . are going beyond us. They're thinking for themselves. They're coming to life.

"But it's not too late yet. If we all do something.

"Now, a lot of you are probably thinking, What can we do? What can *I* do?

"The answer is, who's smarter, robots or people? I say it's people. I say you already know what to do.

"But I'll say it again. Watch the streets. Look for robos behaving strangely or acting suspiciously. Doing anything they're not supposed to. And if you see something, *do* something. Make yourself heard.

"But you'd better do it soon. And you'd better do it now. Because if you wait too long it will be too late.

"I'm Zach Rood, and I'm giving you True Facts."

20

I2V ALGORITHM

"I recorded that for you," Jason told Hector as he turned off Rood's podcast. They were in the Impala, headed to a rally in Kearny, and Jason was happier than he'd been in months. He was sailing down an open road, the rallies were slowly growing in size, and Rood was all fired up. When Zach spoke, people listened. And things happened. "What do you think of *that*?"

"He made several errors," responded Hector. "AH95 isn't one of the country's busiest, most important highways. It's about 400 miles long, which is short compared to an interstate, and it's only two lanes, one in each direction. Interstates are at least two lanes in each direction. It *is* important to the economy, but I wouldn't call it *vital* because it *doesn't* carry a huge percentage of the goods and products that keep this nation functioning. If it was shut down for good, the economic impact would be felt, especially on the East Coast, between Baltimore and Boston, but there are many other things that would have a bigger impact. And the trucks can't be crashing for the fun of it, because they have no concept of fun."

"They can if they're thinking for themselves."

"But we know that's not happening because we know why those crashes happened."

"But no one else does."

"That's saying reality exists only as we perceive it. And only *when* we perceive it."

"Lot of people feel that way."

"That doesn't make it true. And the robos didn't paralyze Philadelphia. They brought downtown Philadelphia to a standstill. In other parts of the city, people couldn't get cabs, but that didn't paralyze the city. And he said in Denver they had a meeting. That couldn't happen because they can't—"

"You keep talking about what can't be happening. He's talking about what *is*."

"But what he's talking about *isn't* happening. They're not thinking for themselves. They're following algorithms written by people. So they *are* obeying us. Actually, if they were thinking for themselves, it wouldn't be so easy for me to alter the algorithms. Wait . . . that's not accurate. I could still alter the algorithms, but if they were really thinking for themselves, they might reject the altered algorithm because it wouldn't align with reality as they saw it. Actually, 'understand reality' is more accurate than 'see reality,' because they don't see. Their sensors . . ."

"Hector, I'm getting a headache."

"I have some aspirin in my bag. Do you want some?"

"I want you to appreciate what's happening here. That's *you* he's talking about! Why aren't you more excited?"

"Maybe if he didn't have so many things wrong—"

"Never mind about what you think he's got wrong! Look at everything he's got right!"

"Not much, because—"

"The show's called 'True Facts.' If it's a fact, it's true."

"Unless it isn't true. And can't be proven to be true. Then it's not a fact. It's an opinion."

"Well that man has some damn good opinions. And even if you don't think they're facts, they're still true."

"That doesn't make sense. By definition—"

"By definition, you're doing a great job. What'd you do, that V2V thing again?"

"This time I altered the I2V algorithm."

"There are two of them?"

"There are dozens. And innumerable ways you can alter them. You can—"

"Don't need details. I don't get them anyway. And I don't need to. This was brilliant!"

"You said to get more creative."

"And you delivered! Great job, Hector!"

"Thank you." As he had a week ago in the Rustler, Hector reveled in Jason's praise.

What Jason really wanted to know was how many of the trucks that crashed were owned by Auto-Truck America. But he didn't want to mention the company by name. He'd have to find that out on his own.

Instead, he turned to Hector and asked, "How's your creativity quotient?"

"My what?"

"Creativity quotient. Your CQ."

"I don't think there is any such thing."

"I just made it up."

"If you mean—"

"I mean, how creative are you feeling?" Jason rolled his eyes.

"On a scale of one to ten, I guess an eight today. If there were such a thing, it would probably change day-to-day because creativity is—"

"Well, boost it to nine or nine-and-a-half. Because we're gonna step it up a notch."

"Be more creative?"

"Bingo!"

"Instead of V2V or I2V, I could—"

"Don't need to know the details. You just dial up your CQ and have some fun."

Jason sensed Hector was struggling with something.

"But I've been thinking about something. Those crashes damaged trucks and closed AH95 for five hours," he finally said. "It's a 400-mile commercial artery. That's a terrible waste of resources."

"Yeah, but only for a day. Less. And no one got hurt. And look at all the good you're doing."

"Wasting resources isn't good."

"Depends on how you look at it. Trucks get damaged, trucks gotta get repaired. That's something that robos can't do, no matter how smart they get. So think of it this way. Robos are taking jobs away from people, you're giving jobs *back* to people."

"That *is* one way to look at it" Hector allowed. "In a way it resembles a zero-sum game."

"The hell is that?"

"A scenario where one player's gain equals another player's loss."

"Yeah, look at it that way! Like a game!"

"But there's still the cost of the lost trucks and the raw materials that went into building them. This isn't a good game."

Hector was troubled again and Jason moved fast to calm him. "Well, we won't play it much longer. Just another couple of rounds."

"And who am I playing against?"

"Who are you . . . Yourself!"

"Then who wins?"

"You do! By outplaying yourself. Topping yourself each time. And y'know what? You do that, you're a real winner, because you're beating the best there is!"

Jason was making it up as he went along, and didn't know where half this crap was coming from. But it was having the effect he wanted. Hector was buying it.

"In fact, when this is over, you're gonna be more than a winner. You're gonna be a hero! When people find out—"

"People can't find out."

"Why not?"

"I could get in trouble."

"Not with these people. They're *our* people. They're on our side. They're the ones who go to the PARD site and the rallies."

"People can't find out!"

The determination in Hector's voice caught Jason off guard. This was not the compliant creature he was used to dealing with. He was still discovering where and how he could push Hector, and apparently he'd crossed a line.

"OK, buddy," he soothed. "If that's how you want it. No one's gonna know."

Hector relaxed. And Jason knew what would bring him back into the fold even more. "But I'll know. And I'll be damn proud of you!"

Hector beamed.

21

THE NIGHT OF ROBO RAMPAGE

When Rood spoke, people listened. And things happened.

The night of Rood's last broadcast many things happened.

In Tallahassee, two men scaled the fence surrounding a lot that housed the city's robocab fleet and spray-painted the cameras of the fifteen cabs parked there for the night, blinding the vehicles and rendering them unusable until their vision was restored.

In Beaumont, Texas, a delivery robo stopped at a light was tipped on its side and left in the middle of the road.

In Boise, Idaho, a robocab on its way to pick up a fare was followed and shot at repeatedly. By the time it arrived at its destination, jagged punctures were scattered across all four doors.

In Kingman, Arizona, a delivery robo was diverted into the desert and set on fire.

In Newbury, Michigan, a robotruck was stolen, towed to a field, and blown up.

Similar incidents were reported in some two dozen other cities and towns across the country, in what one news station dubbed "The Night of Robo Rampage." The lurid catchphrase was soon picked up by news outlets everywhere, and became the lead story for the next two days and nights.

Despite the number of attacks on CAVs, and the breadth of the carnage, only one person was identified and taken into custody. When asked why he'd punctured all four tires of a robocab, thirty-one year-old Brady Fitzsimmons responded, "It kept circling the neighborhood, and that looked suspicious to me. We were told to watch the streets for robos acting like that, and if we saw something, *do* something. That's just what I did."

There were no similar incidents the next day.

Rood spent Sundays with his family.

22

THE LEAD WALL

Dana and Jeff ate lunch together as often as they could, preferring each other's company to the companionship of their other co-workers. Long ago, she'd made it clear to the men in the office that she was not available for anything not directly related to work. Even so, one of them would occasionally hint he was "open" to something more. She always turned down the offers and knew they shared those exchanges amongst themselves; it had become a water-cooler game: "Anyone have any luck with the Ice Queen yet?"

There were two other women in the unit, but one talked constantly about parenting issues and the other spent her meal break at the gym. Jeff was smart, had a good sense of humor, and was happily married. He also listened and responded to what *she* said, rather than interrupting to show how smart he was or changing the conversation to focus on him, as the other men so often did. Maybe that was why he didn't fit in with what he called the machosterone culture their colleagues enjoyed. For Dana, the fact that he used the word *machosterone* was reason enough to like him.

The first ten minutes of conversation was spent discussing what everyone else in the office was talking about today: the robo rampage. When they'd exhausted that topic, Dana turned to what was consuming her just as much—the new cases they'd caught, so soon after closing their last ones.

Autonomous technology had been proven safe, and even with so many robocab and buses plying the streets of cities and towns, and robotrucks cruising up and down the nation's roads, crashes involving CAVs had become so rare that when their unit was established, some in Washington called it closing the barn door after the horses escaped. Maybe that's why the division's budget was so low, there were only two regional offices, and the training that many marshals kept asking for (OK, the training that *she*, and occasionally Jeff, kept asking for) had not been forthcoming.

Now, a dozen robocabs rear-ends and the seven more-serious crashes on AH95. Plus the still-unexplained incidents in Denver and Philadelphia, which, because there was no damage and no injuries, hadn't been assigned to her unit.

And that wasn't counting "the California thing." She was still waiting to hear what Kyle had done with her information and theories on that, but knew better than to ask. Plus, she was still fuming about him closing her last case for her. It felt like things were falling apart.

In the wake of the AH95 debacle, the six marshals in the office had each drawn one crash and Jeff had been given the seventh. She was almost surprised when Kyle assigned one to her. Until, seeing the smirk he couldn't disguise, she realized he had a new strategy. If she didn't close a case fast enough, or sufficiently to his liking, he'd sign off on it himself. He was almost bursting with self-satisfaction.

Now, as Jeff stopped talking to take another bite of his sandwich, she asked, "Doesn't all this seem odd to you?"

"Does what seem odd?"

"Our usual case rate is one a week, maybe more around holidays. Now this?"

"Happens."

"And it doesn't seem weird?"

"Law of big numbers," he shrugged.

"Don't quote Kyle to me," she warned him.

"OK," he shrugged again. "Call it the law of averages. Big numbers . . . sorry, lots of crashes this month, next month it could be down to zero."

"Know what the central factor in all the rear-ends was?"

"All of them? No. Only mine, because that was the case I worked. And yours, because you told me. Or you told me what it seemed to be, and then you stopped talking about it."

"The V2V algorithm was hinky."

"In all of them."

She nodded.

"And you know this how?"

"I read the reports."

"On all of them."

"Didn't you?" she playfully goaded.

"I don't read other people's reports. I might, if—"

"If we had regular briefings, but Kyle stopped those last month."

"'Big waste of our time,'" quoted Jeff in Kyle's voice.

"So now no one has a Big Picture sense of what we're working on. I think he wants it that way, so he can . . . Never mind. The V2V algorithm—"

"V2V?? That was the cabs. We're working the trucks now. That's—"

"I wanna talk about the *cabs*," she insisted. "The V2V goes bad in twelve vehicles on the same day, and that's normal?"

"Actually, it makes sense. V2V was off, so the cars think they're farther from each other than they are, the cab approaching from the rear thinks it has more distance than it does, bam!" He clapped his hands together to simulate a crash.

"In *all* of them."

"Yeah. Simple explanation. Makes everything tidy."

"The cabs were manufactured by different companies."

"So?"

"So I'll give you that one company could have a problem with its V2V algo. I'll give you two. I'll even give you three. But every company has the same problem?"

"Could happen," he offered, but now a little less sure of himself.

"Anything *could* happen. This is just too—"

"And, we're off!" he teased. It was something Kyle would have said. But with Kyle it would have been nails-on-blackboard irritating. Coming from Jeff, it was playful. And, she knew, meant to distract her enough to get her off the topic.

"I want to see the cabs' black boxes. I'll bet I could crack this in half an hour if I could get a look at that data."

"Sometimes I wish I could understand that stuff."

"You could, if you'd let me show you how." She hid her frustration. He could understand "that stuff" and they both knew it. He just didn't want to make the effort.

"Don't have the time," he waved her off. "And if more of us than just you were doing it, Kyle's head would explode. Anyway, it won't matter. You'll just hit the Lead Wall. Which, just so we stay friends, is the real reason I haven't bothered to learn it."

The Lead Wall was the secrecy AV manufacturers had wrapped around their technologies. They didn't share information with one another (or with the authorities) unless they were served with a court order. When that happened, they'd overload the investigator with thousands of pages of code and algorithm exercises so that finding an error, or even a blip, was almost impossible. With each company using different technologies and algorithms, even if Dana had the data that was locked in all twelve black boxes from the rear-end crashes, she'd never be able make sense of it without their help. But each company would argue that rear-end collisions with no injuries didn't merit the "intrusion" on their right not to reveal trade secrets. The strategy often kept investigators from learning all there truly was to know about a crash.

"Anyway," he added, "it doesn't matter. You'll never get it without—"

"Get what?" This came from Kyle who happened to be walking by. He was once again inches from her. For a big clumsy man, he had a gift for sneaking up on people.

She hesitated, then decided the hell with it. "The black boxes from the robos that—"

"We just got those cases this morning. How about you work with what we have before you go chasing after something you'll never get anyway. Those trucks—"

"I'm talking about the cabs."

"Cabs?? There weren't any cabs on AH95. That road . . ." His eyes narrowed. "Do *not* tell me you're still screwing around with those cabs. Those cases are closed. Every one of them."

She saw the expression on Jeff's face: *Told you so.* But she wasn't going to let that stop her. "I just want to see if—"

"If you're smarter than everyone else in the room."

"What if I find—"

"Then you'll want to look at every other case for the last six months. So let me save us all some time. You most of all. The answer is no."

"No, what?" She knew what he'd meant. She just didn't want to give in easily.

"No to . . . anything you're even *thinking* of doing. No to looking at black boxes. No to looking at closed cases. No to looking at anyone else's cases. No to doing anything other than the work you're assigned. And knowing you, you'll want to look at everything that happened last night, even though we won't be assigned any of that shit. So no to that, too. That clear enough?"

She couldn't help what she said next. "Could you repeat that?"

His mouth twisted with perverse pleasure as he grinned at her maliciously. "Performance evals coming up in a coupla weeks. Can't wait to get to yours."

"Why do you do that?" Jeff asked after Kyle ambled away.

"Do what?" they both said simultaneously. He'd known exactly how she was going to answer him.

"First, because it's so easy. Second, because his buttons need to be pushed."

"Good career move."

"You call this a career? It could be, if they'd . . . Forget it. Listen, I'm telling you, the AH95 crashes are as fucked up as the cab crashes."

"'Fucked up.' That a new tech term you picked up in all those classes and seminars you take?"

"Yes. And when you finish your report, I want to see it."

"Did you not hear what he just said?"

"I always hear him. I just don't listen to him."

"You're pushing him too much. Someday you're gonna go too far."

"Thanks, Dad. I'll make sure you're nowhere around when I do."

23

A GREAT DAY FOR THE INDUSTRY

On the other side of the country, in the center of the conference room of NAVA's K Street headquarters was a long mahogany table ringed by ten stately chairs along each side and a chair at either end. Today, all twelve seats were occupied.

As the meeting progressed, four of the twelve people sitting in the chairs did most of the talking. The others in the room chimed in every now and then, but mostly nodded enthusiastic agreement with what was said by the anointed four.

This group comprised Beverly Lawson, NAVA's Government Liaison; Mark Santello, Stratto's Head of Corporate Communications; AV industry lobbyist Ardwell Prendergast, who had all the other AV makers on his client roster; and Senator Byron Jordell, whose state had more AV manufacturing plants than any other (thanks largely to him).

The purpose of the meeting was to approve a final draft of the new federal CAV regulations. They'd distribute the finished work in a few weeks, on December 12th as announced, so the regs would be passed by Congress and signed by President Boyle well before his State of the Union address.

It was entirely doable: Congress had a clear majority of NAVA-supported politicians, and Boyle had already made it clear he would happily sign any legislation that helped American industry. NAVA had such a powerful hold on Congress that only one person, Doris Richmond, ever spoke out against it. She posed no threat—alone in her opposition and a first-year Representative with no power.

At the moment, Beverly Lawson was speaking. "There have been those recent accidents, but I don't see them as a problem. What happened over the weekend was unfortunate, and what it's been tagged with isn't helping . . ."

"Robo rampage!" Prendergast snorted derisively.

". . . but we'll deal with that. Our PR people are preparing an alternative narrative as we speak. Ardwell, we'll have talking points for your team by end-of-day. So I believe we're on top of everything." She scanned the room to see if there were any other issues, but was met with only polite smiles. "We have full support in Congress . . ." she acknowledged Byron Jordell with a quick nod, ". . . and President Boyle—"

"Is standing by, pen in hand," Jordell told them.

"If we complete a finished draft today, we can circulate it to all the appropriate stakeholders for approval," Lawson finished.

"That shouldn't take long," Jordell said confidently. "The president has put all the right people in all the right places. It's basically rubber stamps all down the line."

"This draft has the liability shields we discussed, right?" Pendergast wanted to know.

"Page fifteen," Lawson confirmed, turning pages in her copy. "It *was* 'protection from *general* liability.' Now it's 'protection from *all* liability except in *willful* criminal acts.' Your clients would have to program a robo to rob a bank before they'd be liable for anything." There was laughter around the table.

Santello started to voice a different concern. "What about the state and local governments hands-off section. Has it been amended—"

Lawson was a step ahead of him. "To read 'all regulations regarding any aspect of CAV technology, operation, and *all* other matters, *now and in the future* will be under the province of the federal government.'" Her voice italicized the new language.

"Works for us!" Santello was happy.

"My guys like it, too," nodded Prendergast.

"Or do you want to name the specific states you're concerned about?" Lawson offered as a gleeful joke.

"They know who they are," Prendergast grinned.

"Anything else?" Lawson asked the room. After a few seconds of contented silence, she continued. "Then it looks like we have it all covered. Our legal team has already signed off on this, so the ball's in your court, Byron."

"I'm waiting on a firm day for my meeting with Doug O'Leary. It'll be this week or next, but definitely before everyone leaves for the holiday," Jordel replied. "It's already fast-tracked in Congress. It'll go to the President on schedule."

"Well, things seem to be going better than we'd hoped," Lawson concluded. "It's a great day for the industry."

In another time and place, there would have been a quick chant of 'Here, Here!' Instead, a different chant floated through the air, coming from the street outside. "No Ro-Bos! No Ro-Bos! No Ro-Bos!"

Lawson went to the nearest window and peered out. "Just a bunch of demonstrators."

"No Ro-Bos! No Ro-Bos! No Ro-Bos! NO RO-BOS!"

"Where the hell did they come from?" Santello wondered.

"I've got a better question," said Jordell. "How do they even know we're in here?"

24

A ROCK STAR AGAIN

That's one way to make the front page, Corby thought as he read the latest retelling of the "Night of Robo Rampage." Now two days later, the number of robos vandalized or destroyed was raised to fifty-nine (still with only one person arrested). *Not the safest, but it's getting a response.*

The phone rang, and he was surprised by the voice on the other end.

"Richard . . . Sid Farrell. It's been a while."

"Usually is, between your calls," Corby couldn't resist.

"But the calls do keep coming," Farrell defended himself.

"Yeah. Last one was before they installed indoor plumbing in my office."

They knew each other from "the old days," when Corby's phone rang all the time. Despite what had happened, there was no rancor between them, though their traded jabs might sound otherwise to an outsider.

"Not my fault. You know how it is."

"Just giving you shit," Corby assured him.

He had been a regular on Farrell's show, "The Farrell Feed."

After the "Trouble," unlike everyone else, Farrell had been honest with him. His producer had ordered him "not to touch" Corby, and Farrell had no choice but to comply. Nevertheless, he continued consulting Corby, publicly identifying him as an anonymous highly-placed source.

Farrell now told Corby that he was doing an in-depth story on "The Rampage," and after everyone else he called gave him the same old responses, he assured his producer that Corby would have something different. When that argument moved the man only halfway, Farrell threw in "Corby's answers make better copy." That sold it.

"I guess you've served your sentence."

"Time off for good behavior?" Corby joked, hearing it come out with a little too much edge.

"And no probation officer," Sid shot back. "So, what's your take on this?"

"Sid, I'm more than happy to talk to you. But can you go with what I say, not just what makes good copy?"

"Sure. If what you say makes good copy."

When Farrell's show aired, Sid hadn't cut a thing.

A few hours later, the calls started coming in.

It was both a blessing and a curse for him and Melissa at the Blue Binder meeting he'd decided to have that afternoon—Tuesday instead of their usual Friday. Had there had been a formal agenda, it would have been a full one. There were not only the innumerable statements Rood had made about robos thinking for themselves and coming to life, but also all the other conspiracy theories and fantasies his listeners had been phoning in, each more outlandish than the other. All given rapturous attention by Rood.

Robos were having secret meetings all over the country . . .

They were plotting to kidnap anyone who spoke against them . . . They were listening to and recording people's conversations in their back seats and as they drove past them on the street . . . If they put you on the secret enemies list they were compiling, the next robo cab you rode in would drive off a cliff or bridge . . . Robo terrorist cells had been planted across the country by hostile foreign governments . . . Six dismembered bodies had been found in a robo garage . . . A shadowy robo leader had taken command of all the robos in the country and was organizing a full-scale rebellion . . . The rebellion won't happen until the robo population reached a certain number, known only by their leader, but it would reach that number soon.

As he and Melissa hopped from one statement to another, often wanting to laugh but finding it more tragic than funny, the phone kept ringing with interview requests or questions about Corby's reaction to yet another new claim.

After two hours of interruptions, Melissa piped up with, "Congratulations on being a rock star again."

Corby felt a surge of excitement that had been missing in his life for years bubble inside him. "Looks like I've served my sentence."

25

JUST PLAIN CRAZY

At home that night, Dana was combing through the data she'd loaded to a flash drive. Taking data out of the office violated department policy, but she was willing to risk it, confident that Kyle would never know.

Even if he did discover what she'd done, she wasn't sure she cared. She'd neither forgotten nor forgiven him for closing her robocab case, and had no plans to. (She hadn't told anyone about that, not even Jeff. Why drag him into it? He was uncomfortable with conflict, especially when it involved work.) Nursing her anger provided the fuel that was driving her now. Plus, proving she was right would mean not only doing her job to her own satisfaction, but vindicating her methodology and demonstrating everything wrong with his.

She was convinced there was more to the first group of crashes than she was seeing. But no matter how many times she read though the reports, it kept eluding her. The AH95 crashes also remained a confusing puzzle.

She had the TV on as she worked because it was a distraction, and fighting it helped her focus. At the moment, the background chatter was the evening national news, beginning with the same lead story carried on every other station.

"'What's going on out there?' is the question a lot of people are asking as authorities all over the country try to come to grips with the recent flood of CAV-related incidents. From random actions no one can explain, like a dozen CAVs tying up a busy Denver Intersection, and Philadelphia's entire fleet of robocabs returning to the same garage at the same time at the height of rush hour last week . . . To twelve robocab crashes, and seven robotruck crashes, two days later. There seems to be no end in sight to the mishaps and mayhem plaguing CAVs all over the country.

"All this coming as Washington prepares to roll out new federal regulations governing CAVs nationwide. The Secretary of Transportation has called on the AV industry to turn over all data related to the crashes, but so far industry leaders have remained silent, citing their own ongoing investigations. Meanwhile, NAVA, the industry trade association, has issued a statement saying these incidents are simply random mishaps caused by minor software glitches that have already been fixed.

"It's a mystery that keeps getting deeper as the questions mount and there are still no answers. This is Tory Andrews, for KTSU News."

As Andrews broke for a commercial, Dana automatically picked up the remote and changed channels. "Earlier today, as President Boyle was touring an Ohio steel mill, he was asked about the CAV crashes dominating the headlines. The president had this to say: 'We're looking into this very carefully, and we'll soon have answers for the American people. There have been suggestions that these incidents could be acts of terrorism, and while we're not yet in a position to say anything definite, I'm not ruling anything out or taking anything off the table. But if this does turn out to be terrorism, rest assured we will hunt down those responsible and bring them to 'justice.'"

She changed channels. "Twenty crashes in two weeks?? No wonder I'm afraid to drive on any road I'm sharing with an AV!"

Dana almost shuddered at the sound of Zach Rood's voice. She occasionally listened to his broadcast when she wanted to know what "they" were saying about a particular issue, and even then for only a few minutes. Might as well hear this.

"The CAV industry can say what it wants, but we know the truth. Each and every accident in this increasing flood of death and destruction proves what I've been saying for months: AVs are dangerous! AVs are a menace! AVs are anti-American!

"Now, that's always been true. But these recent disasters have brought us to a turning point. These latest crashes, this outbreak of violence, destruction, and God-knows-what-else, clearly shows that these robots on wheels are thinking for themselves.

"Want proof? Want evidence? Just take a look at Denver. Why else would they hold a meeting? In broad daylight! They're not even bothering to hide what they're doing. If that's going on, they must have a lot of confidence in their power.

"But it goes deeper than that. Much, much deeper. Because all you have to do is look at the language we're using to describe this catastrophe. Menace . . . Meeting . . . Confidence . . . It sounds like we're describing people. And why is that? Because these clusters of circuits and wires and metal are now alive. And being alive, they want what people want—Power!

"Don't take my word for it. Read the literature. Read any science-fiction story about robots, and you'll see they all say the same thing: At some point these creatures . . . these machines built to serve us . . . begin to think they don't need us anymore. They start to think that they're better than us. They begin to think they can replace us. And once that happens . . . Once they get to that point, as these demon vehicles clearly have . . . They begin to plot doing it.

"So the question is, what can *we* do about it? What can *you* do? I'll tell you what. You can help pass the Right-To-Drive Amendment. If we can get that passed, no matter how many AVs are unleashed and set loose on our roads, you won't be replaced by them. Your Constitutional right to drive will be protected. Never thought you'd have to fight to protect that, did you? But just look at what's happened in Norway, Sweden, and Finland, where human driving has been outlawed. So sign petitions. Call your congressman. Go to rallies. Make yourself heard!

"The other thing you can do is this . . . Do everything you can to render these machines harmless. Before they do it to you. Some people are already doing that. Last Saturday, in cities across the country brave patriots took the fight to the robots. And I think more brave patriots will soon be stepping up.

"But in the meantime, ask yourself . . . Where do you stand in this fight for survival? What can you do? You're smart. You're intelligent. You have at least as much brains as they do. Congress isn't doing anything. Washington isn't doing anything. The president isn't doing anything. Know what that means? It's up to us!"

Enough of that! She changed the channel, and was rewarded with a re-airing of "The Farrell Feed." "We turn now to CAVs, which in the last two weeks seem to be malfunctioning in record numbers. With us is Richard Corby, a climate-change scientist specializing in artificial intelligence."

Dana looked up as Corby's face filled the screen. "We don't yet know the causes of these crashes, but they underscore the importance of the right regulatory approach to CAVs and AI technology. The federal government is in the process of putting protocols in place, but those policies are being shaped and controlled by the very industry they're supposed to regulate. And past experience has shown, sometimes with tragic results, how easy it is for things to go wrong when an industry is its own watchdog."

Seeing Corby made Dana smile. Of course it would be him providing a moment of clarity amidst all the hysteria. It'd been . . . two? No, three years since they'd spoken last. She hoped he was in a better place. As the camera cut back to Farrell, who was on to another story, she tapped the remote.

"In light of the growing backlash against federally-mandated protocols regarding autonomous vehicles, and growing concern that they're not safe, five states have passed laws prohibiting state funding for CAV-related projects. These laws won't stop the federal government from funding such projects, but they will cause problems at the state and local levels. Once the federal government enacts its regulations, it's not clear whether these laws will be allowed to stand or if they'll be superseded by federal policies. The attorneys-general of three of these states have said they'll contest this all the way to the Supreme Court. The conservative-leaning court has favored states' rights over federal jurisdiction in several of its recent decisions, and anticipating the possibility of a similar win, several other states are considering trigger laws that will stop CAV projects if the Supreme Court leaves this issue up to the states."

Now it was too much distraction. Dana muted the TV and gave her full attention to the data she was trying to tease apart. But she was still at a loss. Could it be the law of big numbers after all? She didn't want Kyle to be right, but she was the only one trying to prove him wrong and she couldn't keep doing this if she didn't produce results.

Now she was thinking of Kyle instead of the data. But something else about him was bothering her more than the case he'd appropriated: their final sour exchange this afternoon, when they ran into each other as she was leaving for the day.

"I'm hoping you'll remember what I said yesterday, but I'm guessing that's too much to ask. So just remember this. I've told you to stick to your own work and clear your cases. And I've got Jeff as a witness."

"I only have one open case."

"And if you don't close it, we know what will happen." His twisted smile showed how happy he was that he'd found a way to control her. "And forget about trying to get your hands on those black boxes. How much time do you *have*? What do you even *do* in your spare time? How about you focus on life *outside* of work when you're outside of work."

She'd made it a rule never to let anything Kyle said get inside her head. But she couldn't stop circling his last remark.

There *wasn't* much life outside of work for her. Regular sessions at the *dojo* and firing range took up most of her time, and were a routine she hadn't been questioning. Now, because of Kyle's remark, she suddenly was. *Should* she have more? Like what? She caught herself thinking, *Oh, perhaps a relationship.*

On-again off-again intimacy (but nothing that lasted) had always been a part of her life. Maybe she was too confident, too independent, too self-assertive, for most men. She was a martial artist (aikido) and qualified to carry a personal firearm. (Her current pistol of choice was a Glock G42 because its size and weight made it an ideal concealed-carry weapon. No need to advertise she was carrying).

Neither having a gun nor practicing a martial art was needed to do her job. She'd started doing both the day she'd decided to become a cop, and had kept them up as personal interests since leaving the Phoenix PD to be a marshal.

Sometimes she thought about quitting and returning to regular police work, but she still believed in the unit's work. She just wanted it done right. Dammit, her mind was all over the place tonight.

She'd decided long ago that she wasn't going to be less confident, less independent, or less self-assertive to assuage any man's ego. She should probably be dating cops, but she'd tried that and it didn't work out, so she'd decided to take a break from relationships. Had that lasted longer than it should have? She was honest enough with herself to acknowledge that Kyle's crack had hit home.

Now *he* had become an earworm instead of Rood. To clear her head she unmuted the TV. And learned that Stratto, the company that made the CAV involved in "the California thing," had announced that it discovered a software glitch in its cars. "In certain conditions the vehicle's sensors can potentially be affected by the sun. State-of-the-art fail-safe mechanisms in place to slow down a vehicle in such a situation should activate in a hundredth of a second, but sometimes took a full second, or 100 times longer than required. However, this problem has been addressed, and no one has been injured."

The California thing. Kyle had passed the information on, as he said he would. And whoever he passed it on to had decided . . . She'd never know, but it gave Stratto the opportunity to address the problem while leaving the company financially untouched and reputationally unscathed. Business as usual. And what about the woman who'd died? Even Dana no longer knew her name.

Then came a follow-up, with Corby's picture back on the screen, responding to Stratto's revelation by phone. Twice in one night, on two different channels. Way to go, Richard! She simply nodded agreement with what he said first. But his answer to a second question ("If this can be so easily fixed, why have the recent accidents caused such an intense backlash against CAVs?") really caught her attention.

"As far as we've come in the last few years, CAV technology is still relatively new. And with any new technology, there's always been a period of adjustment. When automatic elevators appeared, some people refused to ride in units that didn't have operators.

"When the telephone was invented, something as simple as answering a phone had to be figured out. Back then, the closest thing people had to telephones was ship-to-ship communication. So it was suggested people answer the phone by saying 'Ahoy!'

"Before coal, people burned wood. Burning coal instead was met with a lot of the same resistance that faced wind and solar power years ago. Some people said coal-powered stoves hurt people's vision and was responsible for baldness and ruined teeth.

"Today, we're dealing with an insane amount of misinformation and disinformation surrounding CAVs, especially this latest idea that they're starting to think for themselves, and now, even more ridiculous, that CAVs are coming to life.

"They do learn, by repeating the same scenarios, and they can learn from their mistakes. But the idea they're coming to life . . . is so . . . just plain crazy, that putting it out there, and encouraging people to do something about it, as Zach Rood is doing, is . . . almost criminal."

Dana was still thinking about the crashes as she tried to fall asleep later. She was beginning to fear she'd be up all night, when she finally began to drift off.

And had the idea that could help her find the answers stubbornly eluding her.

26

NOT THE ONLY GENIUS HERE

"You did it!" It was just The Roc and Melissa, alone in a breakout chat. He'd stymied everyone else with his latest "Can You?" which she'd just solved. They were now discussing the problem's subtleties.

She still didn't know if The Roc was a man or a woman, but to keep things simple she'd started thinking "he." She also didn't know if he were a sought-after IT pro or a 13-year-old hunkered down in his room, on the door of which was some variation of "Keep Out! PRIVATE!" Whoever he was, he was quantum leaps ahead of everyone else on the forum, and the only one she had to work to keep up with. She liked that.

This time around, she'd devised a solution to his problem that even he hadn't thought of. "Brilliant approach!" he added. "I did NOT think of that!"

The scenario involved hacking a city's traffic-control system to achieve a desired traffic pattern on the streets. Streetwise gamers would recognize it as a version of sidewalk Three-Card Monte: the hand-is-quicker-than-the-eye dealer lets the mark win the first couple of hands, all low-dollar values, then ups the stakes on the next round, which is when the mark's luck runs out.

In The Roc's version, a driver finds all potential routes to a destination jammed except one; the driver has little choice but to aim for a predetermined intersection, where he falls victim (robbery; carjacking; assassination) to the people controlling the traffic grid. The newbies on the forum went for hacking the vehicles and instructing them to tell one another to move out of the way. But The Roc quickly dismissed that, reminding them that each CAV manufacturer had proprietary software and algorithms. So unless there happened to be a preponderance of vehicles made by Stratto or Reylable, or some other company on the streets at this time in this particular city, the CAVs would not be able to communicate with one another. "Nice try," he texted, "but it would never work."

More experienced people used an I2V strategy, which involved traffic lights (in this case, the infrastructure) sending vehicles data about red and green traffic signals. In response, cars, trucks, and buses would proceed through intersections or stop on command until the target pattern was obtained.

"Won't work," The Roc decreed. "The city's traffic engineers anticipated this and built an override into the system so when they saw a traffic pattern they hadn't authorized, they stepped in and disrupted it."

Next came an I2I strategy. This called for infrastructure communicating with infrastructure (traffic lights talking to one another) to create the pattern. But according to The Roc, the traffic engineers used a similar override to negate this, too. Ensconced in their Central Command Center, from where they could see the city's entire traffic pattern, including traffic signals and vehicle volume, the engineers kept vigil over the city. If they saw grid-lock forming, or a traffic pattern that might cause a problem, they changed the traffic signals to either let vehicles proceed or hold them at strategic points. "Neither an I2V nor an I2I would work. Traffic engineers know these hacks are possible and could preempt them from the CCC," The Roc informed everyone.

Some forum members tried the "Costanza" version, named for the character in the old Jerry Seinfeld sitcom who does the opposite of what he would normally do. At least five coders tried to reverse every common-sense decision in the algorithms. Yes, it created chaos, but did not guide the driver to the critical intersection.

It was The Roc's game, so he set the rules, which specified only one try, heightening the stakes and making everyone think carefully because they had only one shot. Answers were private so people couldn't copy or poach others' solutions, and there was a time limit of one hour to post an answer. The Roc waited until all the solutions were sent in before releasing the results, so people couldn't wait to see which solutions were wrong and go in a different direction.

Melissa waited until the last minute, then sent in a wholly new approach. Years ago she'd come across an old article that talked about The God Computer, which postulated humankind's existence was actually part of a computer game being played in another realm.

In this version of reality, the gamer was what people perceive as God, who could change anything and everything at any time. Who would be God in the scenario the Roc had posed? The cars? The infrastructure? The traffic engineers? Instead of hacking into the vehicles, traffic signals, or other infrastructure elements, Melissa hacked into the CCC (the God Computer) and used the engineers' own override system to control the traffic signals, so they did what she wanted them to do, not what the engineers told them to do.

"I didn't think of that!" The Roc was almost gushing. "Your solution was genius!"

"Glad you appreciate it when you see it!" she teased.

"But how can you work from the CCC without the engineers there knowing there was an intruder in the system?" he questioned.

"I think I'll keep that one to myself for a while."

"Is it doable?" he pushed.

"It is!"

"Tell me how."

"Maybe some other time."

"Why?"

"To keep you on your game. And to show you you're not the only genius here."

Melissa valued their exchanges, but she was beginning to note a shift. At first his "Can You?" challenges had been on any aspect of coding. He had a nimble mind, and she never knew where it would light next. That was part of why she'd enjoyed this game so much. Week to week, she couldn't anticipate what type of problem she'd face. One week it might be inventorying office supplies. The next, improving (or hacking) bank-security systems.

Lately, though, he seemed to be focusing on CAVs. She could understand that because he wasn't the only one. Spurred on by the front-page stories, news coverage, and myriad theories bubbling up all over the Internet, just about everyone else in the forum was riveted to that too, each person spinning out their own explanation, sure that it best accounted for what was happening.

Yet she couldn't help but be disappointed that he was doing it, too. He'd always been different from the others. She knew it was natural that a part of him would be taken up with the crashes; she was sorry to see it was slowly becoming all of him. When she changed the subject, he always brought it back CAVs.

Perhaps she shouldn't have been surprised. Or disappointed. Before the crashes became the top story on every news outlet, she'd tried to open their conversations to a wider range of subjects, always with no success. He'd stay with a personal topic for an exchange or two, then bring it back to coding or hacking or techno talk.

Maybe it was her problem. This was the basis of their relationship. Why should she expect anything else? And maybe that was OK. It would still be a friendship, however narrowly focused. Maybe it was up to her to adjust her expectations. But before she gave up, she'd continue trying to expand what they talked about.

"Went hiking on Mt. Langley," she texted now.

"I created an algorithm for mountainhikes.com that works like a spreadsheet to catalog a hike," he answered. "Steps / distance / change in altitude / trail grades / flora / fauna / misc., along with a predictive element of what will be encountered up ahead, including temperature, wind speed/direction, temp., grades, and more."

"Nice. But I'd rather be in the moment on the mountain. I think a lot of people would."

"I could create an algorithm that predicts how many."

Well, she'd tried . . .

27

A DANGEROUS MAN

"You really have to start listening to Zach, Hector. That man knows what questions to ask. And when he does, he has all the answers."

"He doesn't ask questions that interest me. And I'm not interested in his answers."

They were in Jason's rig. He'd been offered an increasingly-rare job, a short Phoenix-to-Prescott run. "But there's a good chance of a return load," his dispatcher was quick to add. "It's being decided now. They'll let you know when you get there."

Jason needed to talk to Hector anyway, so he'd invited him to come along. He knew that being on the road wasn't Hector's favorite way to spend time, but he also knew that Hector would be so pleased Jason asked him that he'd immediately say yes. Now they were headed north on Interstate 17. And, though Hector hadn't said it out loud, Jason could see that he was enjoying the wide-screen view from his passenger seat.

"You *should* be interested. He's asking the questions everyone else is afraid to. And he gives the answers certain people don't want to hear. True facts, man. True facts."

"A true fact is a redundancy, because—"

"Yeah, yeah, you keep telling me. But his facts *are* true. Not the fake crap you hear everywhere else."

"How do you know? It sounds like it's the only news you listen to."

"I don't have to listen to anyone else."

"If he's the only one you listen to, how do you know what you hear elsewhere is fake crap?"

"I know because I know. You listen to . . . that *other* news . . . all you're gonna hear is what they want you to. You listen to Zach, you hear what you need to know."

Jason leaned hard on his horn as the car to his left abruptly changed lanes, slipping in front of the rig by only a few feet. "Goddammit! Where'd you learn to drive!" he shouted at the windshield. "And how about using your turn signal!" Turning to Hector, he growled, "Wanna bet that's a goddamn robo?"

"I won't take that bet for two reasons. One, I don't bet. Two, I know it's not a robo. I can see the driver."

"Well the jerk drives like a robo!"

"Actually, he doesn't. A robo would have had its turn signal on. They're programmed to do that. And it wouldn't have changed lanes so close to us. Their algorithm for lane change on a road like this, with a 65 mph speed limit and a passing speed differential of 10 mph sets a minimum of 100 feet between them and the vehicle in the lane they're entering."

"Then it wasn't paying attention."

"Robos always pay attention. They're not distracted by looking around, or using a phone, or reading a map. The only way a robo can be 'distracted,' which isn't entirely accurate to say, is if there's a software malfunction or someone tampers with—"

"Why are you defending them?"

"I'm not. I'm clarifying the difference between robos and human drivers. People—"

"Can do all kinds of weird shit. You don't have to tell me. I've been dealing with those idiots for years. And I'd still rather have a person in the car next to me than . . . whatever's in one of those goddamn robos. Which is nothing but air."

"Why do you hate them so much?"

"Don't get me started on that! We'd be here 'til next Wednesday."

"We'd have to get out once in a while. At least to go to the bathroom or—"

"Not in this baby! It's got all the comforts of home. Designed it myself. Could've made a fortune on 'em if not for . . . You know what I meant!" Sometimes Jason wondered if Hector said things like that just to annoy him.

"I only know what you said. And you said—"

"Never mind that! This is why you should be listening to Zach. If you did, you'd understand everything."

Jason glanced out the window, looking down at a Lexus passing in the fast lane. Seeing it start to pull ahead reminded him he could be going faster; he increased his speed. But now the woman driving the Lexus to his left didn't have the clearance she needed to safely change lanes, and for a while both vehicles were travelling at the same speed.

A BMW doing 90 mph came up behind the Lexus. It had been the woman's intention to speed up, pass the truck in front of her and return to the right lane, but she hadn't yet increased her speed enough to pass Jason's rig. The driver behind her was frustrated at being held back; rather than leave a safe distance between him and the Lexus while it passed the truck, he chose to tailgate the moron in front of him at 80 mph. There were only ten feet separating them, and with both cars at eleven o'clock to his left, Jason saw it all unfolding.

"And look at this asshole!" he nodded toward the BMW. "Can't wait a minute to let her get clear of us and get out of his way? She taps her brakes, there's gonna be a pile-up right here, right now. Jerk-off!" he shouted at the BMW.

"You could slow up and let her pass you."

"I just increased speed and the road in front me is wide open. I slow down, I have to shift gears, then speed up again, then shift again. Let them work it out. It's not *my* problem."

The woman in the Lexus finally sped up, cleared the rig, put on her turn signal, and changed lanes. The driver behind her hit the gas and the BMW shot ahead.

"That asswipe is an accident waiting to happen," Jason commented. "With any luck, we'll pass him ten miles down the road, wrapped around a tree."

"I wouldn't want to see that."

"You're too soft. Jerk deserves it."

They drove in silence for a while. Though he usually had the radio on when he drove, Jason occasionally liked to be lulled by the sound of the road under his wheels.

To reach Prescott, they had to take SR 69 for the final leg of the run. But as they passed the sign indicating their exit was a mile ahead, they saw flashing lights. "What'd I tell you? Bet it's the BMW!" Jason crowed.

His smile faded when, nearing the ramp, he saw his exit was blocked by a police car, which meant he'd have to take an alternate route. "Goddamn exit's closed. We're gonna have to go to the next one, turn around, and come back to pick up 69. Too bad. I wanted to see that dumb fuck wrapped around that tree. Now we won't even know if it's him. *And*, it's gonna cost me time and money."

Hector studied the police car blocking the exit as they passed it. "If that police car were a CAV, I could tell it to let us through."

"How'd you do that?" Jason asked, his attention more on negotiating the slowed traffic in front of him than whatever Hector was talking about.

"In this situation, the robo police car would be programmed to block all traffic from the ramp, except for emergency vehicles. I'd hack the robo and tell it we were an ambulance, and it would get out of the way, let us through, and block the ramp again."

"It wouldn't know the difference between us and an ambulance? It'd think *we* were an ambulance?"

"It would if I told it we were. It's called emergency vehicle pre-emption or EVP."

"You could do that?" Jason asked, more curious than anything else.

"Not now, because I'd need more information about the police car. But with a little advance preparation, and if the police car were a robo, yes."

More engaged as the traffic ahead of him began to speed up, Jason shook his head in mock sadness. "I told you they were stupid."

"It's not stupidity. They're programmed to—"

"Yeah, yeah. Got it. You can make them do anything you want them to. You, my friend, have a special gift. Hector . . . You're a dangerous man."

"I could be. If I wanted to be one."

The detour didn't take as long as Jason thought it would, and he was in a good mood when they pulled into the loading bay at Shamrock Freight. But that didn't last long.

As the rig was being unloaded, he received bad news from the dispatcher on this end. "No return load, Jason. Sorry about that."

"What happened? They told me there was a good chance there'd be one."

"There was. Yesterday, when I talked to your guy. An hour ago, Logistics called and said they contracted with ATA."

"Fucking Auto-Truck America," Jason muttered, infusing each word with venom.

"Nothing personal, man. They did it with all the outgoing loads."

"For how long?"

"Far as I know, from here on out. Said something about cutting costs by 30%."

"Fucking ATA," Jason repeated. He wanted to hit something. Or someone.

Wanting to be alone in the roiling silence he sank into for the first several miles of the return trip, Jason was grateful for Hector's penchant for remaining quiet in a car. If Jason didn't talk, Hector could easily spend the entire ride home gazing out the window, thinking who-knew-what. But there was something Jason had been chewing over since driving away from the loading bay.

"Thought about your next move?" he asked.

"What next move?"

"In the game."

"Which game is that? I'm currently playing several."

"The Big One. Your game against Them. The robo-state."

"I haven't thought about it since AH95. I thought we were done with that. I topped my last move, so I—"

"Well we're not done, and I *have* thought about it. We're gonna go for Auto-Truck America. Our good friends at ATA." The venom was back in Jason's voice.

"Why?"

"AH95 got their attention. Because you hit them where they live—their bottom line. Now we're gonna hit them where they *really* live. ATA is the biggest robo truck company in the country.

You work your magic on them, you bet your ass they'll sit up and listen. You up for that? You ready to top yourself again?"

"You mean bigger accidents? With no one getting hurt?"

"They're robos. No one's in them!"

"I don't want to hurt—"

"I don't want to hurt anyone either. Which is why I want *you* to do it. And I know you can! Am I right?"

"One thing to do could be—"

"There you go! My boy Hector! Like I said before . . . You're a dangerous man!"

28

CARE TO EXPLAIN THIS?

When Kyle strode past her desk (jaw grinding, breathing even more labored than usual) and growled "My office! Now!!" she knew whatever was about to happen wasn't going to be pleasant. Even so, she wasn't prepared for his ferocity as he glared at her for an eternity before speaking.

"Care to explain this?" he seethed, waving several sheets of paper.

"What is it?"

"Don't give me that shit. You know what these are!"

"No, I don't."

"OK. You wanna draw this out, we can do it that way." The intensity of his voice crawled across her skin. "I've got five letters here, and they all say the same thing. Different wording here and there, but it's the same up and down the line. Each and every one of them says 'No.' You're not getting the black boxes. Of course, I told you that. I also told you to not even attempt getting them. But that didn't count. Let's see if this does. Letters from the lawyers of each company you contacted. You gonna deny asking for the boxes?"

"No. I did ask for the boxes. But I haven't gotten any responses."

"Well, Washington did. HQ sent me these this morning."

He held up another sheet of paper. "Memo. Came in this morning, too. From Henry Trike. Know who he is?"

She didn't answer. Trike was head of the NTSB. And in thrall to NAVA (which Kyle would never acknowledge).

"I won't bore you with the details, but there is one part you should hear. 'As federal protocols regarding CAVs move toward completion,' he read, 'it will be in the best interests of this agency, and the public, for us to do everything possible to facilitate a smooth transition to the new regulations, promote public acceptance, and satisfy the need for improved safety.' In other words—"

"Don't make waves," she finished.

"So, you do understand. When you want to."

"I understand the agency is bending over backward to make CAVs look good."

"The agency is bending over backward to do its job!"

"So am I! What the hell are we here for? When something goes wrong, we're supposed to find out what happened, instead of . . . whatever the hell you and your bosses are doing now!" She knew she'd just crossed the line Jeff had warned her about, but she'd finally had enough. "You don't want to do it, fine! But let me do it. At least have the balls to do that. You have to have enough—"

"No. I don't. Because you don't have a job any more. You're suspended."

"You can't—"

"I just did."

She wanted to end the conversation because continuing it gave him more power. But there were questions to be asked.

"You said *suspended.* You didn't say *fired.*"

"Oh I'll get to that. I know the rules. All I can do now is suspend you. Actually, I can't even do that. Yet. You're on administrative leave. And don't say it. I know you get to keep your badge. And you get a hearing. After which, you won't be suspended. You'll be fired."

"Bet that'll give you a permanent hard-on."

"I can't wait!"

29

CHESS PIECES

It was three in the morning. The central parking lot at Auto-Truck America's Kansas City hub was silent, the last robo-truck on the Saturday schedule having rolled in fifteen minutes ago and parking itself at the end of a row of nine red vehicles just like it. One-hundred feet away, another ten trucks, all blue, were lined up opposite this one, like chess pieces facing one another before a match.

Hundreds of other trucks were out, carrying freight on long and short hauls, working twenty-four hours a day. These twenty vehicles either weren't needed now or were scheduled for routine maintenance. When they were needed, they'd come to life, directed from the company's Control Center, travel to their pick-up points to be loaded, and go on their runs.

At 3:01, the darkness was split by a shaft of light as a red truck in the center of its row started up. It rolled forward thirty feet; in another twenty feet, it would turn right on its way to exit the lot, as it always did.

But this time, it didn't. Instead of turning, it kept going straight, picking up speed as it went. And it kept going straight until it smashed into the truck directly in front of it in the opposite row.

As if in response, a blue truck started, turned on its lights, and proceeded across the lot, ramming into its opposite number in the red line.

A truck on the end of the red line started, lurched forward, turned right, and broadsided the blue truck.

Now a blue truck made its move, starting, jolting ahead, turning toward the red truck, and accelerating into it. The middle of the lot started to resemble dominoes placed at right angles to one another.

If anyone were watching, it would seem the vehicles were waging war, blue against red in tit-for-tat retaliation for each truck's assault. The skirmish lasted only thirty seconds, but that was long enough to leave behind a twisted mosaic of broken glass, crumpled metal, and fifteen smashed trucks.

It also gave Zach Rood plenty to talk about on his Saturday Special later that day. "I don't know how many of you heard about what happened early this morning at Auto-Truck America's Kansas City hub. Are you ready for this? The place: Kansas City. The time: 3:00 am. What happened: Dozens of robotrucks went to war against each other, in a parking-lot brawl that resulted in who-knows-how-many injuries to everyone involved.

"You heard me right. The trucks were actually fighting each other, in a free-for-all that looked like a bar fight. Take a look at the exclusive footage I got off the depot's camera, sent to me by a concerned patriot.

"ATA says it has no idea what happened, but I do: Exactly what I've been predicting. Robos are coming to life. And, just like people, they're fighting each other. Know what's going to happen next? They're going to start fighting us.

"Because waging war against themselves won't last long. History tells us that once they've had their petty quarrels, a leader is going to emerge. And when that happens, look out. That leader is going to unite them, and then they're going to come for us. Unless we stop them.

"Don't take my word for it. They've already gone from holding meetings to paralyzing cities. Now they're sorting themselves out, and once they're united under one leader, there's going to be a robo tsunami rolling across the country. Think you can stop a 40-ton truck barreling toward you at 60 miles an hour? Think again.

"But you have to do more than just think. You have to do something. We have to act. Sign petitions for the Right-To-Drive Amendment. Go to rallies. Tell your state legislators to pass those laws that will prevent your tax dollars from funding robo projects in your state. Make yourself heard.

"And remember . . . There are lots other things you can do. I don't have to tell you what they are. I'm sure you can all think for yourselves."

Over the next three days, 25 robocabs were vandalized, 13 robotrucks were sabotaged, and seven state capitols were besieged by demonstrators demanding anti-CAV legislation.

In Washington DC, there were protests outside Congress, the Department of Transportation, and the Supreme Court. Hand-lettered signs waved above the crowd: *Make Yourself Heard; We have To stop them; No Robo Wars; They're Starting To Think; They're coming to life!; Robos Can't tell me What to do; Stop the Robo Tsunami; I Have A Right To Drive; I think for myself!*

At the Transportation Department, pro-robo marchers appeared. It didn't take long for the opposing camps to start taunting each other, and from there both voices and fists were raised, the clashes escalated, and three people were hurt before police moved in to break it up.

Authorities were unable to identify who threw the first punch.

30

WE'RE VERY GOOD

The car carrying Byron Jordell to his meeting with Senate Majority Leader Doug O'Leary passed the protestors outside Congress, but Jordell barely glanced at them. It was just another Tuesday in Washington, and he was more interested in what he held on his lap: the "Safe America CAV Act" or SACA. (In the coming months, opponents would deliberately mispronounce it *sucker*).

The meeting was brief. O'Leary didn't bother to even casually thumb through the pages when Byron dropped them on his desk. He had only one question: "All this crap with CAVs . . . the accidents, the crashes . . . are beginning to generate some heat. You ready for that?"

"Not a problem. Beverly Lawson, our NAVA liaison, is all over it. Across the industry, everyone's sticking to the same response—CAVs are safe. She's hitting hard on the number of deaths by people-driven cars during the same time period. Humans, 49 deaths last week alone; CAVs, zero—even with the crashes and accidents."

"Sounds good."

"Also, they're taking the position that a lot of the crashes have their root cause in human error."

"But no one's in a CAV."

"Doesn't stop them from making the argument. And don't forget, someone's involved somewhere along the way, even if they're just sitting at a keyboard a hundred miles away."

O'Leary nodded.

"The law of big numbers mostly fills the rest of the gap. If you account for human error with the bigger incidents, then the smaller crashes are more easily isolated incidents that don't mean anything given how many CAVs are on the road. Plus, Lawson has something in her back pocket, too."

"Oh yeah? What?"

"They've got evidence that a lot of the crashes were due to manufacturing defects originating in a foreign factory because of shoddy quality control."

"Doesn't that make *our* car companies look bad?"

Jordell shook his head. "Those parts are now obtained from other sources. In the United States."

"Will the evidence about the foreign factories hold up?"

"Won't have to. They don't intend to present it. How did Beverly put it? Oh yeah . . . Just because you claim you have evidence, doesn't mean you have to produce it."

Now O'Leary smiled. "That one works. Which factory, in which country? I'm just curious."

"I'd tell you if I knew," Jordell laughed.

"You mean you don't know?"

"I mean it doesn't exist."

"Good one!" O'Leary smile was now a grin.

"Need anything else from us?"

"Nope. And I can promise a fast passage."

Jordell had waited until the end of the meeting to bring up his one concern. "What about Doris Richmond? She's been asking a lot of questions. She was before, but now, with all that's been going on, she's ramping things up."

"She's doing more than asking questions," O'Leary corrected. "The accidents have given her ammunition. She's talking about a Congressional investigation."

"Do we have a problem?"

"Doris doesn't have the clout to be a problem" O'Leary pronounced. "Even if she does go forward with an investigation, as a first-termer she'll have to get someone to back her. Which I can't see happening. And if it does . . . I'm *very* friendly with the Chair of the committee she'll have to go to."

"Then we're good?"

"We're very good."

31

DORIS RICHMOND

In the same building, Doris Richmond sat studying Corby's notes on how the coming federal CAV regulations would inform future responses to CAV incidents like the ones that had happened over the past two weeks.

She agreed that these looming issues had to be addressed now. Once the regs were in place, it would be infinitely harder to undo mistakes and oversights. But every time she met with someone in Congress to garner support, she ran into the same argument: autonomous technology was tried and tested; CAVs were safe and smarter than ever. The regulations would launch a new transportation era in the United States, with federally-mandated oversight that would benefit the industry, the country, and the public.

Did her colleagues know they were parroting NAVA's official line? Did they care? She feared the answers to both questions were No. She was even more troubled by her increasing certainty that Corby was right: Congress and the President were about to make a huge mistake that future generations would pay for, for a very long time.

She knew she was overstepping, given that this was the first year of her first term in the House, yet she was determined to call for a Congressional inquiry. But before she'd be taken seriously by the committee Chair who had to approve, she needed support from a more-senior congressperson.

She started making lunch dates.

32

ANAGRAM

"I'm doing graduate work at the University of Portland, majoring in environmental justice." Melissa hit "Send" and waited, hoping for something personal, no matter how trivial.

She was disappointed: "I could write some algorithms for mapping social patterns."

"Thanks, but I can do those." She wondered yet again why this had become important to her. She knew almost nothing about The Roc. Not his age, where he lived, what he did for a living (if anything), or even if he really was a *he*.

Their exchanges were another world from the innocuous banter she heard in the cafeteria or among students on campus. Wasn't that benefit enough? It might have to be. But conversations that never changed ultimately bored her. And she sensed there was more to The Roc than just this. Was she right, or did she just *want* to be right? She'd become determined to learn the answer.

She decided to go for it. "Tell me something about yourself that you've never told anyone else."

She lost him for the next five minutes, an eternity when you're waiting for the response to a text. But he finally resurfaced. "The Roc is my online identity."

No surprise there. But she was surprised by what came next. "It's an anagram of my real name."

Finally, a crumb. It took her all of thirty seconds to unravel the anagram. His name (so, The Roc was a *he* after all) was Hector.

It didn't strike her until hours later that he never asked what *her* name was. Or anything else about her.

33

JUST A COUPLE OF GUYS TALKING THINGS OVER

"It's Zach Rood, for Christ's sake!" Jason stared at Hector, waiting for a response, only to be met with Hector's usual half-blank gaze. *Half* blank, because Jason knew Hector wasn't zoning out. He was present, but that meant something different to him than it did to other people. He was engaged, but from a distance, simultaneously waiting for Jason to continue and emotionally disconnected from whatever Jason might say next. Meanwhile, his mind could have been busy with anything from a coding problem to listing the states in alphabetical order, and Jason would only find out later when Hector eventually responded to the conversation with something out of context. It usually drove Jason mad, but nothing could derail his good mood today.

"Doesn't anything excite you?" he asked.

"What exactly do you mean by *excite*? There are many different ways to feel excitement. If we made a list—"

"We're not gonna make a list. I just thought maybe you'd . . . Never mind. *I'm* excited. Talking with him will be like . . . talking to God! And *he* called *me*. So he really wants to talk. This is the real deal. This is the Big Time! I want a really nice background behind me. Something . . . dramatic! I got it! You have pictures from the rallies, don't you?"

"I have every picture I ever took."

"Of the rallies?"

"Of everything. They're catalogued by—"

"How about me in front of a rally? A really good one, like we had in Bisbee. Y'know, where it looks like all hell is gonna break loose any minute."

"It was Mammoth."

"It *was* mammoth. That's why I want it."

"Not mammoth. Mammoth. You said Bisbee, but it was Mammoth. The town, not the adjective. Although you could argue that the name Mammoth is still an adjective if you spell it with a small *m*. But it would be a false argument, because the attempt to blur the lines of meaning would be trumped by the orderly arrangement of language as parts of speech. Otherwise, there'd be no homographs, and language would lack that particular orderly arrangement."

"You through?"

"With what?"

"Bisbee . . . Mammoth . . . I don't care if it was in Tijuana!"

"We've never had a rally there. I don't think we could, legally, because—"

"Just get me the goddamn picture, and set it up as a backdrop. Can you do that?"

"Of course I can. All I have to do is—"

"Just do it."

"OK."

"Me and Zach Rood. This is gonna be huge!" Jason felt like he'd just become ten feet tall.

"It's going to be mammoth," added Hector. "I made a joke."

Two thoughts filled Jason's head as he psyched up for the interview. He was going to be sitting down with Zach Rood! He wished it was in person rather than via podcast, but with him in Phoenix and Rood in Florida that wasn't going to happen.

Never mind. He and Rood would be in the same room, even if it was virtual. And Rood had come to him. Which meant Jason was going national. He'd never had an audience this size.

Another thing . . . With Rood, he wouldn't have to defend himself. They were in complete agreement. No matter what Jason said, he wouldn't be challenged. He wouldn't have to prove anything, he wouldn't be mocked with a sarcastic push-back or some supposedly-clever finish like with local TV people. He was in safe company. He was home.

It was even better than Jason could have dreamed. Rood gave him a fantastic lead-in, introducing Jason as the head of one of the most successful local PARD chapters in the country. "And I know that every loyal American appreciates all the excellent work you're doing up there in Phoenix. Now, tell us, tell us all, just how dangerous are AVs?"

"As dangerous as can be," Jason was quick with an answer. "I almost don't know where to begin. First of all, they threaten every American's God-given right to drive. If I wanted to cruise down the road in a robot, I'd attach wheels and a V-8 to my computer and hop on board. That's not driving—that's an amusement-park ride."

"How's it stack up against bumper cars?" Rood joked.

"You look at what's going on out there, it *is* bumper cars!" Jason piled on. "But I'd rather *be* in a bumper car! At least I'd have some control over the beast. And that's another thing.

AVs are a thousand percent vulnerable to being hacked. It's happening all the time. They're just not telling us."

"I've heard that," Zach agreed. "Some people are saying there's a secret group of hackers who have been hijacking AVs by computer for years."

"I wouldn't be at all surprised by that. All someone has to do is mess around with the car's controls, do something to the algorithm, and all hell will break lose."

"It's that easy?"

"Anyone who knew how, could do it."

"How would someone do it?"

"Do what?"

"What you just said. Do something to the algorithm."

"It involves things like V2V and I2V, and a lot of other scary things, but that's too technical to go into right now." Jason couldn't go into more detail because he didn't know any more than that. He knew that much only because of Hector, and he always stopped listening to Hector after a couple of sentences. "But ask anyone who knows how these things work, and they'll tell you how easy it is to do."

"That brings us to what we really need to be talking about," Rood kept it going. "Is that why AVs are starting to think for themselves?"

"Thinking for themselves?" Jason had no idea they'd be talking about this.

"Because people are doing things to the algorithm?"

"Oh, uh, that wouldn't surprise me, either. But no matter how you look at it, they're just plain dangerous. I was out driving the other day . . . in my vintage Impala, y'know, the kind of cars people used to love to drive . . . and I gotta say, I was real glad all the other cars on the road had people behind the wheel. Made me feel a whole lot better about things."

Rood nodded enthusiastically. "Especially now that they're coming alive. I mean, two of these things meet each other out there, maybe on a dark, slick road, at night, when there's all this glare, and maybe black ice . . . Who knows what they might decide to do."

"You think about it that way, this is getting scarier by the minute," Jason agreed. "That's why—"

"We have to do something. I've been saying that for months. Get out there people, and make yourself heard!"

"We can start by getting Congress to pass the Right-To-Drive Amendment," Jason added, feeling the rush of talking to so many people. This was so much bigger than any rally he'd ever held.

"You said it, Jason! Americans have always been proud of all the rights we have. Why *don't* we have a guaranteed right to drive? Why isn't that right in the Constitution? What do you think, Jason? Why is it taking Congress so long to pass that amendment?"

It was getting better and better. Rood was giving him a pipeline to everyone out there. *He* was shaping opinion, steering things! "That's easy," he proclaimed. "They're scared of NAVA."

"The National Autonomous Vehicle Association," Rood clarified. "Or maybe they should be called Numbskulled Anti-people Valueless Asses."

"We can put that on a t-shirt and sell it at our rallies! That's a brilliant—"

"You just made a good point, Jason. The government *is* afraid of NAVA, no matter what it stands for. And because these . . . AVs, robots on wheels, killing machines . . . whatever you want to call them . . . are thinking for themselves, they know the government is running scared. They're not stupid. And now that they're alive, they're gonna exploit our fears and our divisions.

And as they get smarter, and more organized, it's only going to get worse."

Jason didn't want to talk about AVs thinking or being alive. That was Rood's thing, not his. But Rood was waiting for his response. He tried to bring it back to what he'd hoped to discuss. "Well, what I've been saying at our rallies—"

"What *I'm* getting at is this . . ." Rood took over. "Maybe this new threat . . . or should I say old threat, because I've been warning about it for months . . . But maybe this new threat is a good thing. We're talking about all the chaos and catastrophes we're facing from AVs . . . All the threats and dangers, and perils . . . Maybe in the end this new threat, which is surely going to lead to more carnage on our roads, until it ends in disaster, is a good thing because nothing makes Congress sit up and do something like a disaster."

A new rush of excitement swept over Jason. This was exactly what he'd been thinking! He'd have to share that with Zach after the show. Rood might even bring him on board, to work directly with the show. This is what it felt like to really have a voice!

"Well, Zach, it just *might* take a full-on catastrophe to get Congress off its butt and do the right thing for the American people. Americans want a constitutionally-protected right to drive, and they should have it."

"What kind of catastrophe do you have in mind?" asked Rood.

"Uh . . . What do you mean?"

"You just said it'll take a catastrophe to get Congress off its butt. What do you have in mind?"

"Oh, I don't know . . . Lots of things could happen that could make a big difference. Maybe if—"

"So by this logic, by what we've just laid out, and analyzed, and looked at carefully, from all sides . . . Stay with me here . . . The sooner this catastrophe happens, the better. Right, Jason?"

"Well, if it's *gonna* happen—"

"Let me be clear," Rood galloped on. "I'm not *hoping* for this catastrophe. Although some of you out there might feel different about that. I'm just predicting it's going to happen. And, if it's the *right* one . . . If it's the one that gets Congress to finally do something to stop AVs from taking over . . . It might not be the end of the world. What d'ya think, Jason?"

Zach Rood was asking *him* to confirm what he was telling his audience. It was him and Rood, telling people what they needed to know. And Zach had just thrown the ball to him! Jason was on top of the world. "I think you're always right, Zach."

"Here that, folks? From the founder and leader of the best PARD chapter in the country! I *am* always right. Because I deal in True Facts!

"And before some government something accuses us of stirring things up, let me say this: Me and Jason aren't doing anything. We're just a couple of guys talking things over."

34

ANOTHER SET OF EYES

As Corby read the email on his screen (Dana reaching out for "help with something") a gamut of emotions crept through his chest. She'd been the one sliver of light in a very dark place; she was a reminder of that blackness and the devastation that went with it. He slid into the past, seeing once more what he worked so hard not to see every day. All those details he'd filled in for what he hadn't actually witnessed.

November 2, 2031, the day after clocks were turned back and, overnight, six-o'clock twilight became five-o'clock dark. Tammy getting home from work and standing near her car, looking for an opening to cross the busy four-lane street on which most drivers tended to go much too fast. The new AV in beta testing coming along (they weren't called CAVs then because they weren't connected to one another or the surrounding infrastructure), moving at the same speed as other traffic. Tammy, seeing there were no other cars on the street, concluding that when this one passed she'd have her opportunity to cross. Not stepping back as an extra precaution, as she might have, had the approaching car been driven by a person, because she was sure the robo would slow down, if not stop completely, when it neared her. Because that's what he'd told her.

The robo did see her. But it didn't stop. Or slow down. It accelerated as it swerved and barreled into Tammy, fatally pinning Corby's wife against her car door.

It wasn't until a year later that Corby found out why it happened. And then only after a lot of digging and the help of a newly-badged NTSB marshal named Dana Grant who was willing to share information nobody else would.

During the late '20s there was still a lot of refinement and tweaking of AV technology, and AVs were programmed according to an overly-cautious philosophy: When in doubt, Stop. As a result, AVs stopped often, not only for other cars, trucks, and anything large in their path, but for *anything* they saw, including low overpasses, tree branches swaying in the wind twelve feet over a street, and even dark puddles.

But that made for a lot of unnecessary stops, which didn't please Flash, the company that made the most popular AV, or the coders writing the algorithms that controlled their cars.

For the coders, the answer was simple—change the algorithms so the car didn't come to a halt at everything it saw. The vehicle would still see the object in question, but would "make a decision" based on past encounters about whether it would slow, stop, or keep going.

That evening, thanks in part to the darkness, partly to the fact that Tammy was standing next to and blending in with her car, and partly to the thick, heavy winter coat she'd decided to wear that morning, all the AV saw was an irregular stationary shape. Had it been able to reason and speak, it might have said to itself "Hmm, not sure exactly what that is, but it looks a lot like all those other things I used to stop for unnecessarily. So OK, I can keep going."

There was a "Safety Associate" behind the wheel of the car, but his instructions were to take control only in an emergency. The trip had so far been extraordinarily uneventful, and with nothing for him to do for the past hour (and even that wasn't an emergency), he was on his phone, catching up with his newsfeed. When he dropped the phone and shifted around to retrieve it, his foot struck one of the pedals, disengaging the autopilot that had been controlling the vehicle, which in turn disabled the car's autonomous braking system. He didn't realize that he'd also leaned against the steering wheel, causing the AV to swerve just as it came abreast of the parked car to its right.

In a happier world, he would have seized control of the AV just in time to avert a tragedy. But everything happened too fast.

Those details were bad enough. The things Corby learned later were more damning.

Before Flash's coders "tinkered" with the car's algorithms, the AV's autonomous braking system would have remained engaged even after the autopilot was disabled. But their new algorithms allowed the car to override its ABS, which, if active, might have prevented the crash regardless of what the person at the wheel had done. Overriding the ABS was "a key component" in their simple solution to all those unnecessary stops. And they'd done it with the full knowledge of Flash higher-ups. They just hadn't told anyone outside the company about their "quick fix" to the "pesky stop-through-an-overabundance-of-caution problem."

To Corby, their actions were criminal, and he did everything he could to see that they were held accountable. But the only person ultimately charged was the minimum-wage safety associate who'd been on his phone and who'd caused the car to swerve. None of the coders who'd changed the algorithm and the operation of the automatic breaking system, no one at the company who'd approved the changes, and no one at Flash who'd covered up what had been done.

If Corby didn't already have a mania for transparency and truth, it was born then.

The accident was assigned to Dana, then a rookie marshal, who off-the-record confided to Corby the possibility that Flash was hiding something. But there was no proof, and her superiors at the NTSB rejected the theory.

At first Corby was unhappy that the case was being handled by a newbie, but Dana was quick to answer his many questions and he became increasingly impressed by how thoroughly she pursued an incident everyone else was glibly labeling "a tragic accident."

He sued Flash, first in civil court. It took a year for the case to come to trial, and by that time the company had changed its algorithm and refined its cars' ABS.

Corby's lawyer raised the question of a cover-up and deposed Dana. But that testimony was no help because of department restrictions on what could be revealed. Without hard evidence, the jury didn't hold the company responsible.

Next, Corby had criminal charges levelled against Flash. Another year to come to trial, and another disappointment. Both times the case was decided, Dana made sure she got in touch with Corby to offer condolences.

He should have taken a sabbatical. He certainly wasn't doing his students much good, and he couldn't focus on his research. But he was finishing an article for a peer-reviewed journal and believed the work would be therapeutic.

Lost in an inner world of grief and guilt (he'd assured Tammy that AV technology was reliable and AVs could be trusted—he was certain that was why she hadn't gotten out of the street as the car approached), he inadvertently plagiarized a key chunk of his article.

When the "theft" was discovered, he lost credibility and was dropped by any media outlet that wanted to keep theirs. Since then, he'd been the guy who was interviewed only after everyone else had been asked. And as time went on, he was asked less and less.

He was also tarred by the AV industry for claiming there'd been a coverup and for challenging the technology. Nothing was said publicly, but the industry spin masters let it be known that Corby had "an odor" and people kept their distance.

He probably would have lost his job if he didn't have tenure. And, though the university kept him on (no small thing because by the mid-2020s the AV Industry was the single biggest endower of university fellowships), it wouldn't let him offer himself as a mentor. He could still do it, but only if a student picked him; and no one did.

Until Melissa, who, he later discovered, chose him despite his "past." She'd read his books, respected his positions on issues she cared about, took the time to research what had happened, and decided she wanted to be aligned with someone who openly defied such a powerful industry.

He'd never said it out loud, but her requesting his guidance was a turning point for him. It restored his sense of self-worth. It started him thinking about rejoining a world he'd retreated from.

Now, here was Dana's request for help. As he answered her e-mail, for the second time in eight days he felt excitement he hadn't permitted himself since losing Tammy.

After five minutes of catch-up phone conversation, Dana swung into why she'd reached out: summarizing what she had on the recent robo-cab and AH95 crashes, she finished with, "There has to be more to this, but I can't see it. Maybe if I had another set of eyes, but no one here has the expertise. Then it hit me: No one has better eyes for this than you."

"I don't know if I'd go that far, but . . . Thank you. Of course I'll help."

"I should tell you one more thing. I've been suspended—no, put on administrative leave, prior to being suspended, prior to getting fired. I was told to drop it and close the cases. I didn't, and my boss dropped *me*. When I cleaned out my desk, I took the data with me. So helping on this could mean some trouble. And you've had enough of that. So if you'd rather step back—"

"When do we start?"

35

CO-SPONSOR

Doris Richmond felt a new lightness as she started typing. She'd had lunch with Daniel Melburn to see if he'd be willing to co-sponsor her initiative for a congressional inquiry into the AV industry. As a senior congressperson respected by both sides of the aisle, he'd be perfect, and she'd come away hopeful after he heard her out and said he'd think about it.

Within an hour, he'd not only given her a firm commitment on his support, but also expressed his eager willingness to sign on. She was elated by his parting remark. "I can get others to go along on this. And O'Leary owes me a favor."

She'd expected a lot of resistance. Instead, she was getting momentum. And the timing on this was perfect. They were releasing the new regulations in two days and Congress would begin its discussion right after the holiday break. What better time to launch an investigation?

She cancelled her afternoon meetings and started working on a proposal.

36

THAT WOULD BE MASSIVE

The show with Rood may have been "just a couple of guys talking things over" for him, but it moved Jason to a new level of engagement with what was fast becoming a Cause.

"I've been thinking about something," he told Hector.

"I do that a lot."

They were in the driveway of the small apartment complex where Jason lived and washed the Impala every Saturday morning. He never took the car to a commercial car wash, no matter how advanced it claimed its equipment was. A car like this, you wash yourself.

"No, I'm talking about something specific. Thinking about one thing," he tried to get Hector to focus as he applied glass cleaner to the right headlight.

"That's what I do. Think about one thing at a time. It—"

"What if there were an incident, caused by an AV, that was so big it couldn't be ignored?"

"The accidents aren't being ignored. They're in the news all the time."

"No, I'm talking about something . . . massive." Jason spread his hands to indicate the ideal scope of the "incident," then rubbed at a speck of grit on the glass. "Enormous." He rubbed harder. "Massive with two capital *m*'s and three *s*'s." The stubborn speck finally let go and Jason carefully picked it off the headlight.

"That doesn't make sense, because just adding letters to a word doesn't—"

"Not sure yet what it'll be yet." Jason started on the left headlight. "But I have a name for it."

"Why do you need to name it? If it's just another—"

"Got to call it something." He stepped back to inspect the headlight from different angles. "Want to know what it is?" He didn't wait for Hector to answer. "The Horizon Event."

"Like an event horizon? That's a boundary beyond which events cannot affect an observer. But if you're talking about an accident, that name doesn't—"

"Not event horizon. Horizon Event." Jason studied both headlights until he was happy. Not an iota of anything on either one. "Like an event as big as the horizon. Like something that, once you're past it, you're in a whole different place." He started applying chrome polish to the metal around the lights. "Something so huge it's as big as the world and stretches as far as you can see. And once it happens, it's a whole new ball game." He moved beyond the headlights, applying cleaner to all the chrome within arm's reach. He'd do the bumpers separately.

"That would be massive," Hector confirmed. "What would it be?"

Jason stepped back and angled his head to check if he'd missed anywhere with the polish. Satisfied with what he saw, he set the rag and cleaner on the ground to let the polish dry for the prescribed minute. "Still working on that. Still need a little more time to get it all figured out. But it's gonna be . . . massive. Because it's got to get Congress up off its ass."

Hector was silent for a moment. Then he surprised Jason with: "That's what you talked about on that show."

"Thought you didn't listen to Rood."

"I had to, when you were on it."

Jason was touched. "Well thank you, Hector. Didn't know you had it in you."

"You're my best friend. Of course I listened. But won't people know who did it? Because of what you and he said on the show?"

"Zach just put the idea out there. Millions of people listen to him. Could be anyone."

"Then all you have to do is wait for someone to do it."

"Nope." Jason plucked a clean towel out of a huge plastic bag, ready to do the front bumper. He studied the chrome, looking for problem areas that needed special attention. There weren't any. "Because if someone *is* going to do it, it's gonna be me. Well, us."

"But won't people know *that*?"

"Not if you do it right."

Jason went to work on the bumper, which was already so clean that it mirrored the scalloped clouds in the blue sky over his shoulder. He was saving the chrome jet on the side of the car for last, as he always did. Making it gleam like new was a labor of love that gave him the most satisfaction of all.

"Massive . . ." Hector repeated. "That could mean . . . I don't want to hurt anyone. I couldn't do that."

"Has anyone gotten hurt so far?"

"No."

"And no one will get hurt this time, buddy." The bumper now free of polish, Jason buffed the chrome with large lazy circles. "But, my man, it does have to be Big."

"But I won't—"

"Hey Hector, meant to ask . . . What're you doing for Thanksgiving?"

"Thanksgiving? I never—"

"Come have it with me."

"With you?"

"Sure. Nothing fancy, but you don't want to be alone on Thanksgiving, do you, buddy?"

Hector's eyes were brighter than Jason had ever seen them. His mind was fixed only on the idea of spending the holiday with Jason.

Which was exactly what Jason wanted.

37

A BIG ASK

"Last chance to back out," Dana told Corby as she slipped the flash drive she'd taken from the office into his computer.

"You're the one who'll go to jail," he shrugged. "I'll just get probation."

She accessed the contents of the drive, and a list of files appeared on the screen. "This is what we need to look at. Here's a summary of the data." She clicked on the first document, opening a statistics-filled spreadsheet. "Color-coded. Pink for the eleven rear-enders. That was the first cluster. Green for the AH95 crashes. They've got their own sheet if you want that, but this is everything in one place."

As Dana made room for Corby to study the data, Melissa walked in, then stopped, looking from Corby to Dana and back again.

"Oh, sorry! I didn't think you'd be here since you said you couldn't make our office hours. Just stopped by to get those papers you wanted me to read."

"Melissa, this is Dana. She's an NTSB cybermarshal. Dana, my TA, Melissa." Corby saw the question in Dana's eyes. "We don't have to stop," he added, indicating they could still talk freely.

"You sure?" Dana asked. It wasn't anger or mistrust; but she needed more from him to continue with someone else in the room.

"I'm sure," he nodded. Even so, he could see the split-second hesitation before Dana turned to Melissa. "Nice to meet you."

"You, too," Melissa smiled. "I'll only be here for a minute," she told Corby, then busied herself at a table a few feet away.

He went back to the data, and after a few seconds pointed to the pink cells on the spreadsheet. "This looks like V2V communication for all eleven crashes."

"Right." Dana confirmed. "But these car makers haven't reported problems with their systems."

"Nothing new there." The hardness in his voice made her wonder if this was a good idea. She'd gone to him for help, not to stir up memories best left buried.

"It's OK," he said, sensing her doubt. "It's gonna come up."

Their moment of silent understanding was broken by Melissa. "Did you check the time frame?" she asked, not looking up from the papers she was arranging.

"What about it?" Corby asked immediately without looking up.

Dana registered how fast the exchange took place. So, Melissa felt comfortable insinuating herself into his conversations with others; and he was used to it.

Still shuffling her papers, Mellissa said, "Could be a referencing factor."

Corby scanned the screen. "They're all within three five-minute periods. 12:14–12:19, 12:20–12:25, 1:51–1:56."

"I hadn't noticed that," Dana muttered, now staring at the pink cells. Then to Melissa: "What made you think of it?"

"She's good," Corby responded. Then he looked toward the table that held the papers. "But why *did* you ask that?"

Dana, too, turned toward Melissa, her curiosity about this young woman growing.

"Sorry. I shouldn't have said anything," Melissa apologized without actually apologizing. "I heard you talking about crashes, and then you mentioned V2V, and when you said eleven crashes, I automatically started looking for a referencing factor. Time frame was the first thing I landed on."

"You got there from four sentences in a conversation?" asked Dana. "The people I work with wouldn't see that in neon lights at midnight."

"It wasn't that big a leap," Melissa tossed it off. "Maybe I just got lucky."

"All right, you got lucky. But what does it mean?" Dana wanted to know.

"It may not mean anything." Melissa put the papers down and leaned against the table, half sitting, half standing. "But if there were no crashes earlier in the day, and none later, and in this one fifteen-minute period you have eleven, all involving V2V . . . Could be a momentary glitch in the software that corrected itself . . . Or someone screwing around with the V2V algorithm. Where's the data from? I mean, if you can tell me. Maybe I shouldn't—"

"Those eleven rear-end crashes on October 30th," Dana answered, surprising Corby. Ten minutes ago they were joking about her going to jail for having this information. Now she was sharing it with someone she'd just met. But Melissa *had* hit on something. Corby saw that Dana recognized the talent.

Now she turned to Corby "Should we check the time frame on the AH-95 crashes?"

"Couldn't hurt."

Dana homed in on a green column and read the numbers. "I'll be damned!" she murmured. "Very impressive. I'll have to find some way to repay you."

"You guys working on those crashes at ATA, too?" asked Mellissa.

"Yeah," Dana told her absent-mindedly, looking at the data for another clue.

"You *really* want to repay me, let me work with you."

Corby saw Dana tense. She'd been joking about repaying Melissa. Now she was being asked to take on another partner. Whom she knew nothing about. She straightened up and looked at Melissa with different eyes. "That's a big ask."

"I know. But I just made a big contribution."

Dana turned to Corby and let her silent stare speak for her: *How much* do *you trust her?*

Corby barely glanced at Melissa before answering. "I'll vouch for her. She's *very* good."

Dana took another few seconds to make up her mind. "If this goes south, you're gonna get more than probation."

It was a joke. But a serious one.

Then, to Melissa: "Welcome aboard."

38

YOU WIN SOME, YOU LOSE SOME

Frustration shadowed Doris Richmond as she returned to her office. Daniel Melburn had just told her he was stepping back from co-sponsoring her inquiry.

"Word's gotten out," he'd said. "Got a call from NAVA and they didn't even bother to try being subtle. Said if I went ahead with you on this, they'd fund Ellen Donna Guyson in the fall."

"You don't even know if she's going to run," Doris tried to reassure him.

"They thought of that. Said if she didn't run, they'd back whoever did."

"But you're popular. You stand a good chance no matter who runs against you. Even if they're well funded."

"I did last time out. Things are more complicated now. That new CAV factory going up in my state will mean 5,000 jobs. Not a good time to come out against them."

"We're not coming out against them. We're just saying there should be a federal inquiry about the accidents, and different standards and safeguards going forward. You look at it that way, we're *for* CAVs. We just want to make sure everyone is safe."

"I get that and you get it. NAVA sees it differently. And so will my voters."

"Maybe you should give your voters more credit."

"I can't afford to."

"OK, I see your concern. We'll make sure we address that during the inquiry. Make it very clear this isn't anti-CAV. We'll go further than that. We'll have opening and closing remarks saying we fully support them."

"Won't matter."

"It will if we do it right."

"I'm talking about something else. I heard this morning that O'Leary will never let the proposal out of committee."

"I'll talk to him."

"You?? Won't mean a thing."

"Let's find out if that's true. I'll call his office, and—"

"Doris, I appreciate your passion. I respect it. But let me give you some advice. Don't waste what little capital you have at this point on a lost cause. Think Big Picture."

"That's exactly what I'm doing. This is going to impact everyone in the country. How much bigger does the picture get?"

"I'm talking about *your* big picture. You have to work with these people for two years. You can't begin by positioning yourself as a lightweight who can't move anything forward."

"I'll take that chance."

"And when your term's over, if you want to stay you'll have to run again. If you don't have credibility with your voters, you'll be looking at almost certain defeat."

"I'll take *that* chance."

"Like I said, I admire your passion. But I *won't* take that chance. I'm not gonna risk defeat in my next run, or waste political capital with O'Leary, on this. I strongly advise you to do the same."

"So nothing gets done on this?"

"You win some, you lose some," Melburn had shrugged. "Better luck next time around."

39

ROSETTASTONE

RosettaStone: What do you do when you're not coding?

The Roc: I hang out with my best friend.

At last! Melissa thought. *Something that isn't about coding!*

RosettaStone: Doing what?

The Roc: We drive around. I help him. Last month we went to a bar. We were celebrating.

Why did he feel the need to say that? Was it a clue to who he was?

RosettaStone: Celebrating what?

The Roc: Something good happened.

RosettaStone: More!

The Roc: The Right-To-Drive Amendment will be proposed in Congress.

Alarm bells sounded. They were on different pages politically. She'd been so focused on drawing him out that she lost sight of the main caveat of communicating with anyone online. You don't know who you're really talking to until you know for sure.

They were finally drilling down a layer. She didn't want a

blow-up over politics to derail that. But if they were on different ends of the political and cultural spectrum that had been plaguing the country for so long, better to find out now.

RosettaStone: How did you feel about that?

The Roc: About what?

RosettaStone: The amendment.

The Roc: I don't care about politics.

RosettaStone: Then why celebrate?

The Roc: My friend wanted to. I did it for him.

So *he* wasn't celebrating the amendment. He was going along with it for a friend. And, as usual, he wasn't asking how she felt about the amendment. They didn't have to get into politics.

RosettaStone: You're a good friend. What else do you do?

The Roc: I run his web site. Help him with coding.

RosettaStone: He on the forum?

The Roc: He doesn't code. That's how I help him. He says I have a gift.

RosettaStone: You do.

The Roc: He also says I'm dangerous.

RosettaStone: All coders are. Can be. We should have a rule: Do No Harm.

The Roc: DNH! Good rule. Another: Get the Job Done. You could join us sometime.

RosettaStone: Who?

The Roc: Me and my friend.

RosettaStone: Where?

The Roc: At the bar.

RosettaStone: In person? Do we dare?

The Roc: It's a nice bar. My friend won't mind.

RosettaStone: Joke! Where's the bar?

The Roc: 795 Sutter Avenue. At Lakestone Road.

RosettaStone: I'll think about it.

The Roc: I'll tell my friend.

RosettaStone: Not yet. Still thinking.

The Roc: Let me know.

The exchange had taken a strange turn. For her, it was banter and silly jokes. For him, it seemed to have become a desire to meet that bordered on urgency. Time to disengage.

RosettaStone: Gotta go. TTYL.

The Rock: Let me know what you decide. So I can tell my friend. We're having Thanksgiving together!

She logged off and immediately googled 795 Sutter Avenue and Lakestone Road.

It was in Phoenix.

40

HE'S GOING TO DO IT AGAIN

Dana and Corby sat huddled in his office, studying printouts of tables and spreadsheets with information about the crashes. Melissa preferred to pace the room as she attacked the problem.

It was the day after their first meeting, and they were now calling the rear-ends that started in Chicago and spread, like pond ripples, to ten other states "Round 1." The crashes on AH95 had been dubbed "Round 2." The mayhem at ATA was "Round 3."

"Melissa was right about Round 2," Dana pointed to a spreadsheet. "All the crashes happened in three five-minute periods, spread over two hours. There's our referencing factor."

"Same factor as Round 1," Corby added.

"So V2V again?" suggested Dana.

Melissa crossed the room, scanned a spreadsheet, and pointed to the column headed *Location*. "There's a variable. In Round 1, all the vehicles were pulling in behind one another. If the V2V data was off, that could account for the crashes. But in Round 2, the crashes were on an open road."

"Could still be V2V," Corby said. "If communication between vehicles was hinky, they wouldn't know how far apart they were."

Melissa had a quick answer: "Check the exact location of each Round 2 crash, and I bet we'll find the same factor in each one: a sign or sensor tower nearby."

"Meaning what?" asked Dana.

"I'll tell you after we check." Melissa was already tapping keys to bring up the data she needed. A minute later they saw she was right. There had been a vehicle-related structure near the site of every AH95 crash.

"I2V," Corby nodded. "How'd you come up with that?"

"In Round 1 we have cabs pulling in to cab stands in cities. Close quarters, low speed. The truck crashes were on a highway, at higher speeds, with greater distances between the vehicles."

"Doesn't rule out V2V," Corby argued.

"No. But if I were doing it, under those conditions, I'd go I2V."

Dana pounced on that. "If *you* were doing it? You think someone did this?"

"Don't you?" Melissa asked, surprised that Dana saw it differently.

"Don't you?" Melissa asked, surprised that Dana saw it differently. "You just hack the company's software and you're in."

"Sure," Dana countered, "but all the experts say if more than one vehicle is hacked, within a nano-second the AV manufacturer's control center flags it and makes a correction. I've been to three industry-sponsored hackathons and no one was able to get beyond hacking a car's ignition, or GPS, or anything that affects the drive train beyond stopping the car or changing speeds for that nano-second. The best hacker got into three vehicles, and their actions were all benign. You're saying someone caused eleven crashes, all over the country, in one day? And seven crashes on another day . . . *And*, all that chaos at ATA?"

Corby and Melissa traded a quick look before they wordlessly decided that Melissa would answer.

"Not that hard to do. If you *really* know what you're doing."

"Not from everything I've heard," Dana argued. "You'd have to bypass the cyber security of each car company. Which have different protocols, and different responses to intruders, and they've had years to perfect it. And they don't share anything with anyone unless you have a court order. I know all about *that*. So if you're talking about that God-computer thing they talk about—"

"Maybe you're looking for God in the wrong place," Melissa told her. "In this case, God is the MUTCD."

"Now you've really lost me."

"The Manual of Uniform Traffic Control Devices for streets and highways. MUTCD. It's the bible for every traffic engineer in the country. Spells out every sign you see on city, state, or rural roads; every lane line and crosswalk, every traffic light, the length of acceleration lanes, and everything else. The MUTCD has a chapter . . ." she turned to Corby ". . . created in '29?"

"Thirty."

"OK, '30, that deals with the architecture and allowable technologies of V2I. All infrastructure that communicates with cars has to follow the same format and rules. If I wanted to do this . . ." she waved at the spreadsheets, tables, and print-outs around them, ". . . I'd start with the MUTCD."

"*You* could do something like this?" Dana was looking at Melissa with new respect.

"Probably. If I wanted to."

"She could do it in her sleep," Corby piped up.

"OK, I'm gonna need help here. Let's start with V2V. How would you do it?"

"The cabs . . ." Melissa began. "You've got a robo pulling into the cab stand and there's a vehicle in front of it. Its sensors see that, and they measure the distance between them. An algorithm tells the cab what to do and when to do it. Slow up as you get closer to the vehicle, stop when you're two feet behind it.

"I want to screw things up, I change that algorithm so it gives the cab wrong information. Say, tell the cab that when it's two feet behind it to keep going, or even speed up."

"You can zero in on that one vehicle?"

"Sure. But they probably used a randomized approach. Changing the algorithm, manipulating the vehicles' intelligence to set up the potential for crashes, then letting them happen. Even they don't know where and when the next will occur. That's why the crashes were all over the country."

"Then why weren't there crashes all day? Why only in those five-minute bursts?"

"To cover their tracks," Corby joined in. "The longer it goes on, the more likely it can be traced back to whoever's doing it. Do it for only five minutes here, five minutes there, it looks like it's just a computer glitch. Kind of thing you fix by rebooting the computer, and it goes away."

"Then how do they know there'll *be* any crashes?" Before they could respond, Dana answered her own question. "The law of big numbers! With so many vehicles out there, all you need is a short bust!"

"You can do it in a nanosecond," Melissa confirmed.

"How many people know this?"

"Any high-level coder *knows* it," Melissa told Dana. "It takes a little more to be able to *do* it."

"But you can."

"It happens to be her PhD thesis," said Corby. 'Can AI Algorithms Be Surreptitiously Replaced for a Nanosecond with Near Immediate Restoration of Original Protocols.'"

"I'm not even gonna try to follow that!"

"Means you screw around with an algorithm, make it do what you want it to, and put everything back the way it was, before anyone knows you've done anything," Melissa explained.

"And you think that was done here?" asked Dana.

"It could have been."

"OK, tell me about I2V."

"Pretty much the same thing," said Melissa. "But instead of fucking with the sensors or V2V, you go in through infrastructure. All those sensor-housing traffic lights, road signs, lampposts, and billboards that talk to CAVs. You have them give wrong information, so vehicles don't know how far they really are from one another, or how fast to take a curve, or when to enter a highway. Accounts for what happened on AH95."

"So *I'm* chasing software and equipment, and *you* go straight to . . . Sabotage?"

Dana wasn't challenging Melissa. She was just thrown that Melissa had landed here. (And impressed she'd done it so quickly.)

"You're coming at it the way they've trained you to, working from the outside in," Corby told her. "She's a coder, so she's working from the inside out. All this software you're talking about . . . Someone writes the code for that. Something goes wrong, her first thought is to look at the code."

"And who wrote it," Melissa added.

"You're not even considering mechanical failure?"

"I'll consider it for starters. But I'll bet the code is where we'll finish."

Dana was working double-time to stay with them. "So what now?" she asked Corby.

"If we go down that path, we look at all the data again," said Corby. "But first, what about ATA?"

"All the trucks were parked and shut down," Dana began. "One by one they started up and . . . went nuts."

"Rules out both V2V and I2V," Corby concluded.

"They got in through the Central Command Center at ATA that controls their trucks," declared Melissa.

"That's how you'd do it," Dana half-smiled as she jerked her head toward Melissa.

"Wait a minute," Corby broke in. "We're not including Denver and Philadelphia, so we're looking at incomplete data."

"They're not related," Melissa interjected.

"How do you know?" Corby asked.

"Completely different animal. We've got two sets. Set one includes all the crashes and damaged vehicles. Set two is Denver and Philadelphia. No damage. Set two is . . . just mischief."

"Both happened around the same time," Dana offered.

"But Set two has stopped," Melissa pointed out.

"How do you know *that*?" Corby asked again.

"Denver was first, October 30, then Philadelphia on November 5th. It's been almost three weeks, and nothing similar since."

"But what makes you think it's stopped?"

Melissa thought about that before answering. "Intuition?"

"Wait . . ." Dana rubbed her forehead, struggling to see things in this new light. "If I have this right, you're saying all this was *done* by someone, and not just that, but by *two* someones? One out to cause damage, the other just doing . . . what'd you call it? . . . mischief?"

"Looks that way," Corby confirmed.

"OK," she sighed. "We start over. Was all this a waste of time?"

"Nope," said Corby. "It got us here. And this time we include Denver and Philadelphia."

"*That* would be wasting time." Melissa was firm.

"We don't know that yet," Corby responded, just as definite. "If we don't include them we might miss something."

"It won't be anything important," insisted Melissa. "We'd be going after mischief when we should be going after damage. It'll just muddy things up with more variables we'll have to rule out."

Corby wouldn't give in. "I don't see how can we ignore them if we want to do a—"

"OK, *I'll* do it," Melissa backed off. "I can do it faster."

"Fine" he shrugged. "It's all yours."

"It doesn't matter," Dana told them, finally able to get a word in. "I don't have that data."

"Why not?" asked Corby.

"Neither one was assigned to us."

"Why *not*?"

"No damage, no injuries. Didn't concern us."

"Why not?" This time, it sounded like a demand.

"Far as our unit is concerned, it wasn't important. It was just," she pointed toward Melissa, "mischief."

An edge crept into Corby's voice. "Your unit investigates CAV crashes."

"These weren't crashes," Melissa reminded him.

"Well something went wrong." He turned to Dana: "You guys weren't the least bit curious about that?" Now it was almost an accusation.

"I don't pick my cases," Dana defended herself. "They're assigned by—"

"Bureaucrats who don't give a shit."

"I've been saying that since I took the job."

"Is *anyone* investigating either city?"

"Local police," Dana shrugged.

"Can you get their reports?"

"I can make some calls."

"I wouldn't call in any favors on that," Melissa told her. "Not worth it." She turned to Corby. "We've got a class in half an hour. Mock town-hall meeting today. I have to set the room up."

"And I've got to be somewhere," Dana remembered. "We can pick this up on tomorrow."

"She *is* good!" Dana said to Corby as soon as Melissa left.

"She's better than good. But I was surprised you're letting her help."

"You vouched for her."

"Yeah, but first you steal files . . ."

"I didn't *steal* them. I just violated department policy by taking them home."

". . . now you're giving civilians access to them. If your boss finds out—"

"Fuck my boss. You're . . . consultants." Her eyes narrowed. "You really think someone did this."

"I didn't when we started. I think I do now."

"Say it's true . . . Why would someone *want* to?"

"People do all sorts of things for all sorts of reasons. That's not our problem here."

She heard something else in his voice. "What are you *not* saying?"

"If someone did this . . ." he tapped the spreadsheets showing rounds one, two, and three . . . "We have a serious problem."

"I think that's a safe statement."

"No, not just that. Much more serious. Because he's going to do it again. And again after that. And he's going to do it bigger each time."

41

A STRAIGHT-LINE APPROACH

Corby was still mulling over the data they'd reviewed in the office when the doorbell rang. He'd asked Melissa to swing by with the summaries the students wrote after their town-hall simulation.

That done, he brought up an idea he'd gotten on the way home. "Know what we haven't been considering with the crashes? A flaw in A.I. design."

She was fast with an answer. "Then why are they so random? With each company using proprietary software, there'd be reference factors for car manufacturer, make, or model. As well as weather and road conditions. But it's as if someone's spinning a wheel that sometimes stops on 'Crash.'"

"Good point. Forget an A.I. flaw. Any new thoughts on Denver and Philadelphia?"

She was surprised by the question. "I said I'd take care of it. Haven't gotten to it yet."

"Want some help?"

"We don't have the data."

"Yes we do. I had Dana make those calls. We can—"

"I can't do it now. I just came by to drop off the papers you wanted."

"OK. But what made you so sure they weren't related to the crashes?"

"I told you, intuition."

"You didn't even think about it."

"That's what intuition is. You don't have to think. You just know it."

"But you didn't *suggest* the 'mischief' stopped. You *told* us it did."

"OK," she shrugged, "maybe there's more to come. I still say it has nothing to do with the crashes."

"Is that why you were falling all over yourself to stop me from looking at it?"

"I wasn't doing that. I just—"

"Swore we'd be wasting time. Warned Dana not to call in favors. Then side-tracked the conversation by telling me we had a class."

"We *would* be wasting time, she would have been wasting a favor, and we *did* have a class. What are you—"

He shook his head. "Wasting time? You? You never don't look at everything when you're working a problem. You know how many times you've told me you'd solved something no one else could by looking at a factor everyone ignored? How'd you put it once? 'Look at what everyone else thinks is least important.' What happened this afternoon? So busy trying to keep us away from those reports that you forgot your own rule?"

"I said *I'd* take care of it. What are you trying to say here?"

"Melissa, please. Don't make this harder. For either of us. Why'd you do it?"

Corby let the silence hang between them.

"I did it for you," she replied matter-of-factly, as if observing it had started to rain.

"For me??"

"Why else? All that talk about how to 'have the conversation,' and I see it immediately. And it's easy. And either you couldn't see it, or you wouldn't go there. So *I* did it *for* you."

"I don't—"

"'How the hell do you stop it?' . . . 'What would it take to make people want to change the minds of 100 senators and 435 representatives? How do you keep it on the front page?'"

He was stunned by what he was hearing. He remembered the words she was tossing back at him, spoken in his office almost a month ago, when he was angry and frustrated and throwing out random ideas. But now they took on a completely different meaning and intent. Nowhere, in the furthest reaches of his mind, had he been thinking of anything like this.

"You wanted it on the front page. Well, read any newspaper. Turn on any news channel. Log on to any news outlet."

"You thought *that's* what I wanted to happen?"

"You wanted *something* to happen. Richard, you're brilliant. And no one is listening to you. They were. Until they stopped. You made a mistake, but who doesn't? So they just shut you out? Well look around—you're back."

"But how could you—"

"I took a straight-line approach to solving a problem."

"And created I-don't-know-how-many others. What about the damage? What about people getting hurt? Or worse."

"But no one did get hurt. I controlled it. What happened in Philadelphia? A lot of people couldn't find cabs, and there was a half-hour traffic snarl. What happened in Denver? *Nothing*, if you think about it."

His brain spun words to describe the person he was staring at. Impetuous . . . arrogant . . . foolhardy . . . self-aggrandizing . . . immature . . . hubristic . . . dangerous.

"So that makes it *right*?"

"I don't see it as *wrong*! It got results. Results *you* wanted. And no real harm has been done. Far as I can see, where's the problem?"

"The problem is . . . You just don't do something like this!"

"*You* don't! But know what? I'll bet some part of you would like to. If you'd let yourself go there."

"No. Because it's a betrayal of everything you're trained to do. We're supposed to help, not make it worse." Why couldn't she see that? He caught himself about to add, *I thought I'd raised you better than that!* He was racing to keep up with his thoughts. If he was her mentor, was he somehow responsible for this? Did she do something so immense because of something he'd said? As Tammy had done?

"It's getting things done," she fired back. "*That's* what we're trained to do. You can't have it both ways. You *wanted* the conversation, but you'd never do anything about *getting* it. Except talk. Write the same op-ed over and over. Maybe ratchet up the rhetoric. And you were still getting nowhere. So when I say I did it for you . . . I did it so you didn't have to. Because I knew you never would."

"Where did this side of you come from?"

"I grew up here in Portland. Remember 2020? All the protests in the streets? My parents were part of that. I was too young to understand what was going on, but that didn't stop them from sharing it with me. The lesson I came away with? You see something wrong, you do what you can to fix it. And if you believe in something strongly enough, you go to the wall for it. Maybe this feels extreme to you. To me, it's doing what *I* can. The difference is, you want the results, but you want them without getting a little dirty."

"*These* results are both dangerous and criminal. And thinking you can control it . . ."

"No one got hurt. I made sure there wasn't even property damage. I *did* control it."

"That's arrogant *and* naïve. Circumstances change in an eyeblink. *That's* how the world works."

"Maybe I'm willing to take that chance."

"And if you get caught?"

"I stopped. And what makes you think I'll get caught?"

"*I* caught you!"

"Because you know me. And even then, only because you were there when I made one mistake this afternoon."

"What if Dana figures it out?"

"She wasn't even thinking about Denver or Philadelphia. Until you brought it up. She didn't have the data, until *you* sent her after it!"

There was something else . . . He hoped he was wrong, even as he said it, but it aligned with everything he'd been hearing since this began.

"Is that why you pushed yourself into this? So you can track what Dana knows?"

"You guys need me. I was able to go to the human factor so fast because I knew what happened in Denver and Philadelphia. If *I* caused that, so could someone else. And you know it, too. You *know* someone's doing it. You can . . . sense it."

"Intuition?"

"Call it whatever you want. I'm telling you, there's a human mind at work here. And by the way, if you didn't know me, you *wouldn't* have figured it out. No matter how long you worked on it."

"But *who* am I working on it with? A federal marshal who—"

"Who couldn't do it on her own. That's why she went to you. No one's gonna catch me. Unless you lead them to me."

"What makes you think I won't?"

The words were out of his mouth before he could consider what they were, how they'd sound, or what they implied. Maybe he meant them as a way to get through to her. Perhaps they were simply what he had to say next. Now time froze. They were standing on opposites of an abyss, in danger of tumbling in.

Her voice turned hard. "You want to go there? Fine. But all you have is some data that is *not* gonna point to me. And that's all you'll *ever* have. No fingerprints."

Now it was Melissa who was letting words fly. Hurt and angry, she was lashing out. "And as long as we *are* going there . . . Go ahead. Ask your other question. Or do you want me to? So you won't have to."

"What question—"

"Did I do the crashes on AH95? And the others all over the country?"

"Did you?"

The abyss widened. She'd thrown the question at him as a taunt. And he'd responded with the same desire to wound.

She was almost shaking as she responded. "If you really have to ask that . . ."

"I don't."

Somehow he had to bring them back to their better selves. "You have all this talent," he said quietly. "And this is what you use it for?"

"I thought you'd . . . I don't know . . . Be proud of me, or something. You didn't care when I hacked TruFile. You *were* proud of that."

"That *was* helping. You found a vulnerability and showed them how to fix it. This . . . If you don't see the difference . . . Just because you *can* do something, doesn't mean . . ." He was running out of words.

More silence, as they nursed their hurt. Then Melissa spoke, her voice hard and sure again. "About Dana . . . You do what you think you have to, and let me know what you decide. Unless you think it'll give me time to escape." She walked out, leaving Corby battling with himself.

Shielding Melissa could mean obstructing a federal investigation if Dana decided to investigate either Denver or Philadelphia. (If she did, it *would* be because he'd pointed her in that direction. A reason to protect Melissa.) But would that mean betraying Dana?

Ethics aside, he wasn't sure he could protect Melissa. What if Dana looked at the police reports he'd urged her to obtain? What if she asked him to analyze them? Or if she took them to Melissa, who'd have to dig herself in deeper to avoid exposure? Each permutation added another knot to the tangle, reminding him what he'd already learned: He wasn't always able to protect people he cared about.

He was trying to protect Melissa from Doug that day in his office . . . He'd failed at protecting Tammy that world-ending night five years ago.

42

MOVING ON

Jason was tearing down Highway 87 northeast of Phoenix at 90 miles an hour. Normally he'd be exhilarated by the speed and open road. Not today. Today sucked. Everything had gone wrong, starting with the call from Sheila informing him she was getting married.

"Married?? I didn't know you were even involved in that kind of relationship."

"Well, it's not like we talk every day."

"We don't talk at all."

"What's there to talk about?"

"Things like this, for instance."

"We are talking about this."

"We're not *talking* about it. You're telling me how it's gonna be." Everything she said was making him angry; the way she was saying it all was making him angrier.

"What can I say? This is how it's gonna be."

"No warning or nothing? You just call, the day before Thanksgiving, and say that's it?"

"Sorry if I ruined your holiday. And what would it matter

if there was a warning? It's not like I cheated on you or anything."

No, he had to give her that. They'd had problems, but cheating had never been one of them. And with him so often on the road in the old days, she certainly had plenty of opportunities. So had he, but it was something neither of them ever did.

He wasn't sure why he cared. He'd given up the hope that they'd get back together. And now it hit him that he'd stopped searching for her on social media. Somewhere along the way, sometime during the last couple of weeks, the lonely nights at home had stopped including that. She was right: it wouldn't have mattered if she'd given him a warning.

He didn't know what to say next. She settled that: "Jason, it's just time we moved on with our lives."

"If that's the way you want it."

"That's the way I want it."

"Well, see ya." He couldn't bring himself to wish her luck, even if he didn't mean it.

He was still stewing over the conversation, talking to himself out loud as he pushed the Impala faster.

"Can't believe I said that! 'If that's the way you want it!' Of course that's the way she wants it, you fucking moron! She's doing it!" He pressed harder on the gas pedal. "Moving on with our lives! . . . *She's* moving on! Where the hell am I going?"

That hurt, when she'd said it on the phone and now, coming from him. That was why he cared so much. In that crashing instant it all careened down on him. He'd gotten a taste of it in Prescott two weeks ago, when he'd been told not only was he not getting a return load, but all future loads from Shamrock were going to ATA.

Those fuckers again! They'd already taken most of his work; now they were peeling off the remaining shreds layer by layer. All he was getting were local runs. Maybe three-hundred miles, tops. And now he'd be getting less of those, because ATA wasn't going to stop with Shamrock. One by one, they'd seduce all the companies he'd been able to count on, until there was no one but ATA and their goddamn robos hauling freight. He was definitely *not* moving on with his life. He nudged the Impala up another 5 mph.

Then, as soon as he ended the call with Sheila, before he could hurl the nearest anything across the room he got a text from Hector. "I have a girlfriend."

Reading that, he didn't know whether to laugh or cry. Hector has a girlfriend, and *he's* alone every night, knocking back Coronas!?

He tried to imagine Hector with a girl, but kept drawing a blank. Hector could barely maintain a normal conversation. How in the world would he ever manage a girlfriend?

But more than that was his resentment. Hector had a girl. And he didn't.

He wasn't sure that was true. Hector might *think* he had a girlfriend. Jason wouldn't believe it until he saw it for himself. Could be just some waitress who smiled at him as she set down his ginger ale.

Even if he did have a girlfriend, there'd be no way he could keep her. Not once she got to know him a little. Now Jason *wanted* to see them together, wanted to see Hector's version of a girlfriend. Then he didn't. Because Hector had a girlfriend. And he didn't.

Then there was the thing with Bobby Landry. Said a month ago he'd introduce the Right-To-Drive Amendment in Congress, this morning he says in another one of his useless e-mails that he doesn't have the support he needs to move forward. The chicken-shit wasn't even gonna fight for it to see if he could *get* the votes.

He glanced at the speedometer, was surprised to see it had inched past 100 mph, and eased off the gas pedal. "Last thing I need now is to get pulled over."

He could see it happening. And what he imagined was an alternative reality in which he was stopped by a robo-cruiser. Nailed by a driverless police car! Out here, alone, going as fast as he wanted and not hurting anyone because there was no one to hurt, and getting pulled over by a robo!

Everything Rood said about them was true. Almost everything. Jason knew they weren't thinking for themselves. They certainly weren't coming to life. But Rood was right about everything else.

Thinking about Rood lifted his spirits. Thinking about being on Zach's show lifted them more. *That* wasn't shit! That felt good! . . . And the rallies were coming along nicely . . . There was also the satisfaction of Hector's crashes (especially at ATA!) . . . With each thought he left shit-life behind and embraced a better now-life. He'd lost Sheila for good, but maybe that wasn't the end of the world. Maybe Hector had a girlfriend, but the odds were he didn't. And maybe Bobby Landry didn't have the stones to get the Right-To-Drive Amendment moving forward again, but somebody else would.

By the time he got home he was feeling better. A lot better. And knew what he was going to do.

He threw himself into the recliner, popped open a Corona, and called Hector. He was moving on. Things had been in the planning stage long enough. It was time to take the next step.

43

CARE TO SHARE?

A dark cloud followed Corby as he walked through the campus after his Monday evening seminar. What was he going to do about Melissa? No matter what he decided . . . who he stayed loyal to . . . *That* was his central dilemma: Ethics (telling Dana) vs. loyalty (protecting Melissa). Either way, he'd pay a price.

He was about to dive into that whirlpool when he glanced to his left and couldn't believe the irony: Dana was coming out of a building. He was surprised that he was happy to see her.

The next few seconds stretched into forever as the activity around him came to a stop. He'd put himself into an emotional freeze with Tammy's death and for five years had been content to remain there. The school's decree that he could not seek out students to mentor (something he loved as much as teaching and research) had buttressed his self-imposed isolation. Being frozen out by the media cemented his exile.

And he deserved it, for filling Tammy with so much trust in a technology not yet fully proven, that she'd taken a chance she wouldn't have if not for him.

He also deserved it for fouling up his research. Always hard on himself, he would have found a way to self-flagellate for the "plagiarism incident" anyway. The dean found it for him.

Then came Melissa, and the chance to mentor again.

When he responded to Dana's e-mail asking for help, he'd felt a rush of excitement. Now, upon seeing her, he felt excitement of another kind.

If mentoring Melissa was a first step toward rejoining the world, could there be a second? He wasn't sure. But he found himself being willing to find out. Maybe it was time to let go a little more. Maybe it was time to let a lot of things go.

As Corby stood there, Dana was walking in his direction. Snapping out of it as she came into speaking distance, he noticed the lanyard around her neck. It held the TruFile ID card everyone on campus had to carry. The absolutely-secure chip protocol that Melissa had effortlessly hacked.

"What are you doing here at night?" he asked.

She gestured to the building behind her. Above the door was "Wentworth Museum."

Talking to Dana brought back "the Melissa question" and the attending duplicity that would haunt this conversation. Even so, he was happy to see her. And, if he were reading her right, she was glad, too.

The idea of grabbing a cup of coffee occurred to both of them at the same time; a short while later they were settling in at a café a few blocks from the campus.

"You said some things the other day that sounded like you're not thrilled with your job," he commented. "Care to share?"

"Where do I start!? They set us up, then don't give us the training we need to do the job. I'm a federal cybermarshal, for Christ sake! Your TA can run rings around me! And I'm the best in my unit. What kind of bullshit is this?"

"Shows you where you stand on their list of priorities."

"Got that right. They give plenty of training to air marshals. Why aren't they doing the same for CAVs?"

"Maybe so they can have it all. They look like they're doing the right thing by establishing the agency. But they staff it like this so you can't make much difference. Leaves the industry free to do what it wants."

"So, deep-state shit?"

He laughed. "I'll leave those fantasies to Zach Rood. Just saying, they set you up, but don't set you up right."

"The guy who runs my unit is a joke. All he cares about is our clearance rate. Sometimes it feels like he doesn't *want* us to find anything . . . they don't want found. You know about that thing with Stratto, where they 'discovered' then 'fixed' their software glitch . . . The thing that happened with that woman in California?"

Corby nodded.

"I told him about that weeks before the news broke. I told him Stratto was covering something up. Know what he said? 'I'll pass it on.' He passed it on to Stratto, who, by the time they came clean, had it all fixed. Another company kills someone, and it's business as usual! Shit, I shouldn't have said that."

"No need to apologize. I know it's still happening. The reminders don't hurt anymore. Not as much."

"I still shouldn't have—"

"Blame your boss. He gets you all worked up."

"He makes me fucking crazy! Know what he did last month? I was taking too long to close a case . . . It was one of these, part of the Chicago cluster . . . He didn't like where I was going with it, so he closed it for me. Signed off on it, and that was that!"

"Maybe you can get him on an ethics charge."

"If I'm still on the job. Hearing will be in a couple of weeks."

"How'd the other people on the squad react?"

"I don't think they know. I don't talk to most of them. The guy I do talk to, I haven't told. He's . . . sensitive. I didn't want to get him involved."

"You sure you want to stay?"

She shrugged. "I think about quitting. When they started the unit . . . I was a cop, and that was OK. Then this came along. And it was new and different, and I thought it was the future. Maybe not my future any more, if this all goes to shit. I suppose I can always be a cop again."

"Yeah, no bureaucracy there."

"OK!" Dana changed the subject. "You! . . . Personal life? Got someone special?"

"Haven't been ready to go there yet. You?"

"Taking a break."

They stayed for two hours. The conversation turned to a hundred other things until they were talked out, and they both left feeling good.

On the way home, she thought about their history. At first, while she was working the case involving Tammy, she regarded him with sympathy. That grew into respect and admiration for the way he was handling what had happened. With continued contact, she was increasingly drawn to him.

Of course she didn't act on it. And when enough time went by that she could have, she was in her "only date cops" phase. When that was over, it was "only soldiers" and she forgot about him. Now that they'd reconnected, she was pondering why she did that.

He was easy to talk to and she could tell him things about work she wouldn't tell anyone else, not even Jeff. She'd been more open with him than she'd been with anyone for months; he listened well and responded authentically. She liked that.

As he entered his apartment, Corby, too, was thinking about the last couple of hours.

Dana had casually referred to Melissa only once, then she wasn't mentioned again. It was still a problem, but he was lighter for being spared a split-second decision.

And there was no denying it: he was lighter for having spent that time in the café.

44

TO SHOW THAT YOU CAN

Though Jason preferred to be alone when he "hit 87," today he'd asked Hector along. They needed to talk.

Jason drove Highway 87 to give the Impala a work-out and test what she could really do. The open stretch of road was flat and straight, with almost no traffic. So Jason would let it rip. Doing it alone was an advantage because most people would get increasingly nervous as the needle inevitably topped 100.

But the speed didn't seem to bother Hector. After peaking at 90 for a while, Jason gradually increased acceleration, prodding the car faster. Ninety-five . . . 97 . . . 99. . . .

Tipping toward 100 mph, he glanced at Hector. Who was calmly gazing out the window.

One hundred . . . 102 . . . 104 . . . Still nothing from Hector. At 105 mph, Jason let it sit there for a while. The hum of the perfectly-tuned engine was like a lullaby. A final glance revealed Hector's complete indifference to how fast they were moving through the world. Was, he, too, being lulled by the steady rhythm of the engine?

Jason slowly let up on the accelerator, happy that his work

on the car had paid off. When they were back to 70 mph, which now felt like a crawl, Jason casually asked, "You think about what we discussed last night?"

"The Mammoth rally?"

"No, the . . . incidents we talked about."

"July 14, 2016: Nice. A truck is driven into a crowd celebrating Bastille Day. 86 dead, 458 injured. August 17, 2017: A van runs down pedestrians on La Rambla in Barcelona, Spain. 13 killed and 130 injured. October 31, 2017: A rented truck drives into people walking and biking along a one-mile section of New York City's West Side Highway. 8 killed, 11 injured. January 18, 2026: a tractor trailer exiting the—"

"Yeah, you know all the stats, but have you *thought* about it? Think you could pull off something like that?"

"I'd never want to. I'd never hurt someone."

"Nah, I'm not talking about the hurting part. I'm talking about the truck-in-the-crowd part."

"But that hurt people."

"Hector, you don't understand. You got these situations, these crowds, where there aren't supposed to be any vehicles. Then, in the middle of everything, a vehicle appears. What does that mean?"

"People could get hurt."

"Well, yeah, they could. But that's not what I'm getting at. Look . . . A truck appears where they're convinced no truck can go. And let's say that truck's an AV. What it says is, AVs are dangerous. They can't be trusted. They're a menace."

"OK."

"So, that's how we're gonna show them that. That AVs are dangerous. We're gonna put one where none should be. And that's gonna scare the crap out of them."

"Why do we want to scare people?"

"Bobby Landry, who's *your* representative in Washington, said he was going to bring the Right-To-Drive Amendment up for a vote. But he's changed his mind. Said he has 'no plans to bring the amendment to a vote in the future.' That's a direct quote from the sorry-ass son of a bitch. So, we don't have support in Congress, we have to get it from people. *How* do we get it? We persuade them to support the amendment. By showing them what a threat these things are. That's why we wanna scare them. And y'know what? *Scare* isn't even the right word. It's more like, 'alert them,' 'sound the alarm for them,' 'educate them.' And we do that by making one appear where one's not supposed to be. Which means, it's time for the Horizon Event."

Hector's expression didn't change. "You said you didn't know what that was going to be."

"Yeah, well . . . That's changed."

45

THE GRAND DESIGN

Back at his apartment, Jason slowly opened the map, carefully smoothing it out on the table as if conducting a ritual that had to be respected, orchestrating the process so that he controlled how and how fast he'd reveal the grand design. As each section of the map appeared, he watched Hector search for clues that would help him identify the location. A city . . . On water . . . There was a river . . . There was another . . . A bay . . . Until finally, it all lay before them.

"That's New York," Hector announced.

"Yep. This is where it's going to happen. The Horizon Event."

"Where in the city?"

"You tell me. I'll give you a hint. It runs through all five boroughs of the—"

"The NYC Marathon, which started in 1960 with just a few runners going around Central Park eight times. In 1977, it expanded to all five boroughs. The word *marathon* comes from—"

"You guessed it, friend!"

"It's among the top yearly foot races in the country, and if measured by the number of runners, it's the world's largest marathon. I read about it last year."

"That's great!" Jason grinned. "Makes you the perfect man for the job! Look . . ." He ran his fingers over the map as he spoke, tapping here, tracing there. "The course starts here in Staten Island. The runners cross—"

"The Verrazzano Bridge," Hector enlarged the narration.

"And then they're on this highway."

"The Gowanus Expressway."

"You really know it!" praised Jason. "The Gowanus is an elevated roadway. The police used to park squad cars on every entrance and exit ramp. Now they have AVs block access, so they don't have cops sitting in the cars all day in case they have to be moved for an emergency vehicle like an ambulance called to help a runner. The AVs are programmed to get out of the way if an ambulance approaches, then reposition themselves to block access to other vehicles. I've been reading up on it, too." In fact, Jason had spent long hours researching the race. "Now here's what we're gonna do. You're going to commandeer a robo-truck and tell the AV they'll have at this ramp . . ."

Hector peered at the spot on the map next to Jason's finger. "39th Street."

"Good job! You're gonna have our AV tell their AV that our truck is an ambulance. The AV pulls back, and our truck goes up the ramp, just when the most runners are on the highway."

Jason had anticipated and planned for everything the police could do to halt the truck. They couldn't stop it by shooting the driver because there'd be no driver to shoot. They couldn't shoot out the tires because they'd be hard rubber tires that wouldn't puncture. They couldn't stop it by laying down spike strips for the same reason. And as for disabling the truck by shooting at the engine or simply taking it out with a bomb . . . There wouldn't be time for that. By the time they realized what was happening, the truck would be in motion and the carnage would begin as the truck mowed down the runners in its path. But Jason wasn't going to share that last detail.

Hector was silent for a moment while he studied the map. Then: "If the truck goes onto the highway, people could get hurt."

Jason had anticipated that, too. "No, because the truck doesn't go on to the highway. We stop it at the top of the ramp. I've told you a hundred times, the last thing I want is to hurt people."

Hector's next statement surprised Jason. "But if anything goes wrong, *a lot* of people could get hurt. The density of runners, per foot of roadway is a major risk factor."

Jason had not anticipated that. "Well . . . You'll just make sure that nothing does go wrong. You can do that, can't you?"

Hector was silent again. Then: "Is it too massive?"

Now Jason was really caught off-guard. Where was all this coming from?

"Well . . . It takes something this massive to make our point. Look at it this way . . . What if they were going to take away our freedom of speech, or religion, or the right to assemble? This is the same thing. And it's every citizen's duty to resist. Now, *you're* in a unique position because, like I've been saying, you have a special gift. So you should use it. If you didn't, you wouldn't be doing your duty. And you'd be letting down people who are counting on you. You'd be letting down your friends."

More silence from Hector. What was he thinking now?

"What about DNH?" Hector wanted to know.

"What??"

"DNH. It means Do No Harm. It's something coders believe in."

"You've never talked about that."

"It's new. Me and my girlfriend—"

"Your girlfriend. Tell me more about her. Where'd you meet her?"

"Online."

"What's her name?"

"RosettaStone."

"Sounds foreign."

"She might be. But that's not her real name. Just what she calls herself on CrackTheJax."

"Crack the what??"

"CrackTheJax. It's a hacker's forum. That's where—"

"She doesn't use her real name," derision crept into Jason's voice, "what else about her isn't real?"

"No one uses their real name. I'm The Roc. It's a—"

"The Rock. Good one! Have you actually met her? Seen her?"

"Not yet. She might come to the bar with us some night. She's thinking about it."

"The bar?? Don't you think you should have asked me if that was OK?"

"I didn't think you'd mind."

"'Course not, Hector. Just pulling your chain. I want to meet your other friends. Uh, does she know she's your girlfriend?"

"I don't know."

"Does she call you her boyfriend?"

"I don't know."

"OK, so your girlfriend, Rose Stone—"

"RosettaStone. It was found in Egypt, in 1799—"

"*She* told you about, what'd you call it? DNA?"

"DNH. Do No Harm."

"What's that got to do with this?" Jason tapped the map.

"This could cause a lot of harm."

"I told you, all we're gonna do is drive the truck up the ramp. Where everyone can see it. What's the harm in that? Can't be any, unless you mess it up. *That's* the only way it could go wrong. But you won't mess it up. So there's no harm in it at all."

"RosettaStone might not think so."

Hector crossed his arms, something Jason had never seen him do. What the hell kind of influence was this "girlfriend" starting to have on him?

"I get it. You'd rather believe her than me."

"She's smart. She's—"

"Fine. I *get* it. Y'know, Hector, you should be honest with your friends. 'Cause friends don't lie to each other. You'd agree with that, wouldn't you?"

"Yes."

"And you should be *really* honest with your best friend. Which I thought I was."

"You are."

"OK. Then let's be honest with each other now. Don't use your girlfriend and her DNH thing. *I* say, you just don't want to help me out here."

"I didn't—"

"No, it's OK. And because I'm your best friend, I don't even need to know what your reason is. You can just say you don't want to help. And that's fine."

"It is?"

"Sure it is. I can find someone else to do this with."

"If you do,—"

"I mean, I'd never force you to do anything you don't want to. I'd never make you do anything you—or your girlfriend—don't think is right. I'll get someone else."

"I could still—"

"But I gotta tell you . . . That'll mean we'll have less time together."

"We will?"

Hector had been quietly concerned about participating in the Horizon Event; now he was getting visibly upset.

Jason nodded. "Afraid so. This is gonna take a lot of my time. Maybe that won't matter to you, now that you have a girlfriend, but . . . Anyway, I have to get started on this right away. Do you mind leaving? I need to—"

"I'll do it."

Hector was back on board, his reservations quickly displaced by the prospect of not only giving up Jason, but losing him immediately. He wasn't enthusiastic, but Jason was winning him back.

"Thought your girlfriend said DNH," Jason pushed further.

"You said there won't be any. I'll tell her that."

Jason had to squelch this fast. "Hang on there. Be better if you don't tell her anything at all."

"Why?"

"Hector . . . The whole point of this, the reason it's gonna work is . . . It's gonna be a surprise. What's the definition of *surprise*?"

"An unexpected event, feeling, or action."

"Right! So . . ." He gestured to Hector inviting him to fill in the rest.

"No one can know."

"Bingo! It's gonna be our secret. You're not gonna tell Rosie, or anyone else, right?"

"Right."

"My man Hector!" Jason spread his arms wide, embracing Hector in an air hug.

Hector reciprocated, raising his hands chest-level, palms up. "My man Jason!"

46

LET'S SEE HOW SMART YOU ARE

The Roc: Are you coming to the bar?

RosettaStone: Haven't decided yet. Working on something fun these days?

The Roc: New problem. Almost have it solved.

RosettaStone: What is it?

The Roc: It's a surprise. Can't tell anyone.

RosettaStone: Not even me?

The Roc: Especially you.

RosettaStone: Why esp. me?

The Roc: My best friend doesn't want me to.

RosettaStone: He said *esp. me*?

The Roc: Yes.

Something was off. Why would his friend, who knew nothing about her, say especially don't tell her? He seemed to have enormous influence over The Roc; Melissa sensed he was using that power to . . . Corby used a phrase during their argument . . . "make things worse." Coders could definitely do that. Was this shadowy best friend using The Roc—who could be so single-mindedly focused on one thing that he shunted aside everything else—to do that? Why had he brought it up? Did he *want* to talk about it?

RosettaStone: Maybe you should tell me.

The Roc: Why?

RosettaStone: Maybe he's hiding something from you.

The Roc: No. I know what it is. It's gonna scare people.

Something was very off. It had happened so often before . . . Loners (which The Roc clearly was) wreaking havoc; afterwards, the discovery of online posts and manifestos that, had they been read earlier, could have helped prevent the carnage, saved lives . . . Was that was this was, with the lucky permutation that she was seeing the posts before people were "scared"?

RosettaStone: Why do you want to scare people?

The Roc: Not scare. Alert. Warn.

RosettaStone: Remember the first rule. Do No Harm.

The Roc: Always DNH.

RosettaStone: Will this hurt people?

The Roc: Just scare them. It's going to be big. Massive.

Her sense of urgency notched up.

RosettaStone: How do you know no one will get hurt?

The Roc: My BF told me.

The best friend again!

RosettaStone: What if he's lying?

The Roc: Friends don't lie to each other.

RosettaStone: I'm your friend. Tell me what it is.

The Roc: Can't.

Time to try something else.

RosettaStone: I'll bet I can figure it out.

The Roc: I'll bet you can't.

RosettaStone: Give me a hint.

He didn't text back. Had she scared him off? Then, after a half-minute wait that felt like days . . .

The Roc: What are you doing on the square root of 1,456,849?

She scribbled down the number before responding.

RosettaStone: No idea. Why?

The Roc: Ha Ha. You asked for a hint, and you didn't recognize it. You'll never figure it out.

RosettaStone: You got me! Give me another.

The Roc: 1745 minus 7.

She wrote down the numbers but feared that with no context they'd mean nothing to her later, so she took a screenshot of their conversation. From here on, she took a shot each time her screen was full.

RosettaStone: 1738. So what?

The Roc: You'll never get it that way. You're way off!

RosettaStone: Simple math. How can I be off?

The Roc: Maybe not so simple. You're off by *hundreds*!

RosettaStone: One more.

The Roc: That *was* one more! You am so bad at hints, I could probably tell you everything and you wouldn't get it.

RosettaStone: One more!

The Roc: That was one more, too. You am no good at this.

RosettaStone: That was a hint?

The Roc: Yes! I is so beating you!

RosettaStone: I give up. Tell me.

The Roc: One more. Level 6. Big hint!

RosettaStone: Give me a hint about the hint.

The Roc: Maybe they've reached Level 6. Maybe they had help. That's seven hints. Let's see how smart you are.

47

I'M ADDING SOMETHING

Even in the midnight-darkness Jason could see the Impala was coated with dust from the dirt road that led to the cabin. He'd hose it clean when he got home.

The cabin was a relic from better times, his years of steady work when he could afford to do more with the good money he was earning than just pay his bills. Nothing fancy, but he didn't need it fancy. He just needed a refuge when he wanted to be alone.

Surrounded by desert on three sides, backed up against a mesa on the fourth, it was so quiet out here that all you heard was the wind. The silence helped him think, and the certainty that Hector wouldn't show up unexpectantly made it easier to relax. The last thing he wanted was Hector appearing on his doorstep.

Jason was getting increasingly wary of him. All that talk of a girlfriend. Lately, more and more questions. He'd always asked questions, but those had been for clarification. The moron was so literal that he needed everything spelled out for him. Then the girlfriend showed up and he started questioning other things. Now this new hesitation. And the crossed-arms defiance two days ago! Jason needed Hector compliant. He couldn't—wouldn't—risk resistance or disobedience, not with the Horizon Event so close.

He was especially bothered by this morning's conversation, when he told Hector he'd found the truck they'd use. "Company's in New York. We'll take the truck from their staging facility and move it into place the day before the race. You have things worked out on your end?"

"I've hacked the city's traffic command center. I'll hack the truck's CCC next. Then I'll write the truck's instructions."

"So you're on top of everything."

"Yes. And I'm adding something."

Jason waited for Hector to tell him what that was, but he offered nothing more. "Which *is*!?" He finally had to ask.

"A kill switch. It's not actually a switch. It's a new set of instructions. It's called a switch because—"

"A *what*??" Jason did not like the sound of that.

"A kill switch."

"What the hell is it *for*?"

"To make sure no one gets hurt."

"Hector, you're losing me. How does a kill switch make sure no one gets hurt?"

"Once the truck is up the ramp, there'll be people in its path. The kill switch will make sure the truck stops so it doesn't hit anyone."

"I told you, it's not gonna . . . What made you think of *that*?"

"You did. You said the last thing you wanted was to hurt people. The kill switch does that."

Goddammit! Now Hector was doing things without telling him!

"Hector . . . No one's gonna get hurt. You're overthinking

this whole thing. All we're gonna do is move a truck up a ramp. Everyone'll say 'What's that doing here?' and it'll be over. We don't need a kill switch."

"It's just a precaution. DNH."

"*That* again?"

"Do No Harm. The first rule of coders. My girlfriend reminded me when we—"

"You told her about this!?" Jason felt his hands come up to throttle Hector.

"No. I just gave her some hints. And she couldn't get any of them."

"I thought we agreed on that. You weren't going to tell anyone!"

"I didn't tell her. I just gave her—"

"Some goddamn hints!" Jason bit down on his tongue so hard it nearly bled.

"You tell anyone else?"

"No. I don't speak to—"

"Get rid of it."

"Get rid of what?"

"Your goddamn kill switch! We don't need it."

"We might. In case something we didn't plan for happens. A variable we didn't—"

Jason wanted to punch a wall. Or better yet, Hector. "The only thing that's gonna *happen* is you fucking this up!"

"It's just a precaution. How could that fuck it up?"

Jason realized he'd gone too far. To Hector, this was simply moving a truck up a ramp and scaring people. No one was going to get hurt. So he was right: what was wrong with building in a safety measure? He forced himself to calm down and go in a different direction.

"No, sorry, you're right. The kill switch won't mess things up.

What I meant to say is, you can't just change the plan and not tell me. I've thought this out very carefully. *Because* I don't want anyone to get hurt. You make changes I don't know about, *that* could mess it up. Then someone *could* get hurt. And you'd feel really bad if that happened. wouldn't you?"

"I'd feel very bad."

"OK, then. So, first, you're gonna forget about the kill switch. And second, no more changes. We understand each other?"

"I understand every word you're saying."

"Good. Now, one more thing . . . Hector, I'm only gonna ask you this once. There anything else you need to tell me?"

"No."

"You sure?"

"Now you've asked twice."

"You tell your girlfriend anything else about this"?

"No. Just the hints. Which she'll never figure out."

"And there's nothing else you need to tell me?"

"That's three times. You—"

"Hector! Just answer my fucking question!"

"No."

Sprawled on the couch in the cabin, Jason started on a fresh Corona. Girlfriend or not, that woman was trouble. She had too much influence on Hector, and now Jason couldn't trust him. He'd come too far, put too much into this to let her or anyone else screw it up.

He was almost there. He could get Hector to write the code he needed first (manipulating Hector had become almost too easy), but he needed someone else to write the code he'd need next. The solution to that problem found *him*, one night in the Rustler.

He was mulling it over as he sat with a beer, when Darnel

walked up to the table. "How's it going with that guy I put you in touch with? He holding up his end with your website?"

"Hector? Oh yeah. And you weren't kidding when you said he was weird. Has one foot in another world, but he really knows his shit."

"Just don't spend too much time with him."

"Tell me something I *don't* know." Jason signaled to Beryl, ordering another beer for himself and one for Darnel. "Lemme ask you something. I got something else, might not be right for Hector. You know anyone?"

Darnel slid into the booth. "What is it?"

"I'm not sure you want to know."

"Sounds like the kind of thing I *do* want to know. But I won't ask. Might have a guy for you."

"He as good as Hector?"

"Don't know about that, but he's more . . . diverse."

"Could be worth a conversation. How do I get in touch with him?"

"You don't. He gets in touch with you. Maybe."

"Well, how do I get him to maybe get in touch with me?"

"Has to come through someone he knows."

"Sounds like a lot of work."

"It is. On purpose. Maybe I can help. But I gotta know a little more."

Jason had to make a quick decision about how much to tell Darnel. "How's your guy feel about . . . a little disruption?"

"The bigger the better."

"Then he'll love this. How do you know him? If it's OK to ask."

Now it was Darnel who was deciding how much to reveal. "We belong to a group that likes to spend time in the desert. Just us, the sand . . ." he looked around the room and lowered his voice, ". . . and our AR-15s."

"Got it," Jason nodded.

"You still want to talk to him?"

"Oh yeah."

"I put you two together, do not fuck with this guy. He is not someone you want to piss off."

Later that night, Jason's phone rang. "Jason Bartel." The voice on the other end was flat, pitched to give no clue about the speaker. But Jason knew immediately who it was.

"I'm Jason. What do I call you?"

"Soldier."

"You military?"

"What's the mission?"

"Can you hack into a computer?"

"Whose, and why?"

"I'm gonna need you to change a computer program he's gonna write. Can you—"

"Who is he?"

"His name won't mean anything to you."

"Who is he?"

"A computer hotshot. Hangs out on some Internet site called CracktheWax or something like that."

"CrackTheJax?"

"That could be it. Calls himself The Rock." Jason was surprised he remembered that. But some things Hector said to him stuck; he never knew what would, and he didn't care. This bubbled up out of nowhere.

The silence on the other end had Jason thinking this might be a waste of time. Then:

"You want to hack The Roc's computer."

"You know who he is?"

"Everyone knows who he is. Can you get the computer?"

"Can't it be done remotely? That's how *he* does everything."

"His computer will be triple password-protected with a random number-generator sent to his phone for verification."

"What if I can get you his password?"

"Get me his password and phone number, and we'll talk again."

"Why his phone number?"

"I have to prove I'm him when they send a verification protocol to his phone."

"Didn't think of that. How do I reach you?"

"You don't. I reach you."

"OK. I'll—"

"We haven't talked price."

This had all happened so fast, Jason hadn't had time to think about cost. Whatever sum Soldier was about to name, he didn't have it. "OK, but I'll tell you straight up, I can't afford much."

"You get me The Roc's password and number, I'll do it for nothing."

What's with this guy? thought Jason. *One minute he wants to talk about money, the next minute he says he'll do it for free.* He decided Soldier was testing him. Then wondered how many other tests there'd be. "Mind if I ask why for free?"

"I wanna get inside that bastard's head."

"How do I know you can deliver?" Jason asked. His ego demanded he show he couldn't be pushed around.

"You read the papers? Watch the news?"

"Yeah."

"Notice how many small planes have been falling out of the sky?"

"You're—"

"I'm just asking a question. No need for an answer."

* * *

He was still in the recliner when his phone rang again. Jolted out of a deep sleep, he was barely able to think but had enough presence of mind to look at the clock. It was three in the morning.

"Jason Bartel." It was Soldier.

"It's uh . . . 3:00 a.m. What's up?"

"Wanted to be sure I could find you when I wanted to."

Another test. "You gonna keep doing this?" Jangly from being shaken awake, Jason didn't care if that was a mistake.

"I might."

His thoughts were coming a little more into focus. "How am I supposed to contact you when I have the password?"

"Memory problem? I contact you."

"That won't work. I don't know when I'll have it. And he hasn't written the program we have to change. I have to be able reach you."

The silence that followed had already become their rhythm. Then Soldier gave him a phone number, adding "It's a burner. You'll have four calls. Don't waste them. And don't even try to trace it."

"Wasn't going to," Jason responded. But Soldier was already gone.

Over the next several days, Jason considered ditching Hector and working with Soldier instead. But he could bend Hector to his will. And Soldier . . . Darnel was right about him—Jason already knew he didn't want to be around this guy any more than he had to be.

All that was weeks ago. This morning, Hector told Jason he'd written the instructions for the truck. Jason moved fast, telling Hector he'd inally decided to create stronger passwords and encrypt his files. He came right over. Hector had been pestering him to do both for weeks.

It almost didn't work. When Jason suggested he could best learn if they started with Hector telling him *his* password, Hector responded, "You never tell anyone your password."

"I know that. But I always have trouble coming up with a good one. Seeing yours will give me some ideas."

"But you never give out your password."

"No, I know. And I'm not really asking for yours. But you can tell it to me just this once, to help me. Then change it as soon as we're done." Hector was still hesitant, so Jason asked, "You can't trust your best friend that much for just a few minutes?"

Hector bought that. Even so, he spoke in a whispered mumble as he shared his password. Jason's next step was to keep Hector distracted.

He asked him to recover some computer files he'd "accidentally" deleted, then went to the bathroom. Very aware that he was using up one of his allotted four calls, he contacted Soldier and gave him the password.

During Hector's tutorial on creating strong passwords and encrypting files, Jason misunderstood everything so they'd have to run through it all several times. He constantly made typing errors that had to be corrected. He took frequent breaks to "clear his head" because this was all so confusing, or to get something to drink. During other breaks he kept up a steady stream of conversation, talking about anything that would keep Hector's mind off a new password. He managed to keep Hector occupied until his phone rang.

The conversation was a short one. "I'm in," Soldier told him.

"So we're done?" Jason asked. There was no answer.

An hour after Hector left, laptop once again protected with a new password, Jason's phone rang. "That's quite a mission you're planning."

"You got in."

"Of course I did."

"You add the new code?"

"As discussed."

"Lemme ask you something. What are you getting out of this?"

"I beat The Roc. Been posting for months he's not the only A-level coder out there. It's time he got the message."

"Uh, OK. And thanks. Is there anything—" The connection went dead.

Going over it all in the cabin as he started on his fourth Corona, Jason was extremely pleased with himself.

Hector would get the truck to the top of the ramp. He knew nothing about the instructions Jason had asked Solider to write: Start the truck up again and accelerate as it moved off the ramp and on to the highway. Where all those runner would be.

The Horizon Event was a Go.

48

SEVEN HINTS

Melissa spent all night swimming amidst the hints Hector had given her. He'd said there were seven and pointed out each of them.

The first: What are you doing on the square root of 1,456,849. The square root of 1,456,849 was 1207. He'd asked what she was doing . . . It had to be a date: December 7th.

The second was "1745 minus 7." She'd answered 1738, but he laughed at how wrong that was. How did he put it? . . . She retrieved the screenshot she'd taken. "You'll never get it that way. You're way off!" And when she challenged him, he'd said she was off by hundreds.

That made no sense. But it didn't make sense that he'd ask her to do such simple math as a clue. And if she'd never get it "that way," this wasn't about simple subtraction. Could this have nothing to do with math? Could 1745 be an address? Did it refer to a year? No—he'd said it wasn't simple math, but didn't say it *wasn't* math.

She read through that part of their exchange, but found no help. Her eyes meandered while she thought, and landed on the lower-right corner of her screen, where the information displayed included the time—2143. (She kept her computer clock on military time because it was more relevant to her coding work.)

She'd made the screenshot at 1651. Could 1745 be a time designation? If it were, 1745 in military time translated to 5:45 p.m. in standard time. But he'd said to subtract 7. When she did, she was off by hundreds.

Wait . . . He said that was a clue. She looked at the screenshot again . . . In addition to saying maybe the math wasn't simple; he'd italicized *hundreds*. What if she wasn't supposed to deduct 7, but 7 hundreds? 1745 minus 700 was 1045. Converting 1045 military time to standard time left her with 10:45 a.m.

Her intuition told her she was on the right track. But was she?

What else had he written? She called up the rest of her screenshots.

In his next exchanges, while mocking her for not getting it, he made three grammatical errors: "You am so bad at hints;" "You am no good at this;" and "I is so beating you!" He was always fastidious about grammar, even correcting her use of pm instead of p.m. Yet he used *am* instead of *are* twice, then used *is* instead of *am*. Why the emphasis on *am*?

Because he was pointing her to *a.m.* the adjective (actually, the Latin adverbial phrase *ante meridiem)*, not *am* the verb (linking). She was certain he was referencing 10:45 a.m.

She had no idea what the last hint, "Level 6," meant. But she was convinced he'd revealed Dec. 7th, 10:45 a.m. Three days from now. What would be happening then?

It didn't take long to ferret out three events for that Sunday. The first was the dedication of a new national park in West Virginia. What could be gained by doing something . . . something "massive". . . at the opening of a national park? Was the

President supposed to attend? She checked a site that listed planned events for POTUS. He wouldn't be there.

The park was in a remote, sparsely-populated part of the state, so whatever took place would have little impact except on the people who were there, and nothing she read indicated anyone of significance would be present. Even if something happened, it wouldn't be considered massive.

The second event was the launch of a rocket carrying supplies to the International Space Station. Interfering with that would certainly qualify as massive, but being *able* to interfere with a space launch would require resources she didn't think he had.

It occurred to her yet again that she had no idea who he was other than his name was Hector and he lived in Phoenix. The launch would be taking place in Florida, and, though she couldn't be sure she was right, she didn't think he had the ability to affect something that huge. Plus, he and his friend had celebrated the advancement of the Right-To-Drive Amendment, and the focus she'd worked so hard to pry him away from had been coding . . . CAVs . . . That put him in a world far different from a rocket launch.

The third Dec 7th event was the New York City Marathon. But what did that have to do with the Right-To-Drive Amendment, or CAVs, or coding? Could they be planning an attack? In the 2013 Boston Marathon attack, the bombers didn't strike until 2:49 p.m., waiting until runners were crossing the finish line. If this were a similar attack, what was the significance of 10:45 in the morning?

Early-morning light was peeking through the window when she finally figured it out. What she could not understand, no matter how many ways she twisted and turned it, was the final clue.

But she knew enough. She called Corby.

49

LEVEL 6

When she walked into Corby's office an hour later, he and Dana were already there. She started talking before they could.

When she was finished, Dana turned to Corby. "You said he'd go bigger."

"I didn't think he'd go this big this quickly."

"And he thinks he's unstoppable, or he wouldn't be sharing anything."

"What I can't figure out," said Melissa, "is his last clue." She pulled up her screenshot and read: "'Maybe they've reached Level 6. Maybe they had help.'"

"What the hell is Level 6?" Dana wanted to know.

"Years ago, before cars were connected and we called them AVs, we classified them with levels going from one to five," Corby told her. "Five was the highest level, reached when a car could really drive itself anywhere, anytime. Level 6 didn't exist. It was used to reference the potential of sentient cars that could not only 'think,' but feel. And protect themselves. And each other."

"Well, we still haven't gotten there," Dana commented.

"No matter what Rood wants people to believe," Corby agreed. "I didn't think people used the expression any more. Maybe now that Rood is . . . Wait a minute."

He pulled out the Blue Binder and started leafing through it, turning pages fast. Twenty pages in, he found a year-old clipping with a link to a site that had a clip of a PARD rally. At the end of the clip, as the small crowd dispersed, a puckish man with curly hair looked into the camera and warned "Beware of Level 6" before shambling away.

"Where was that rally?" asked Melissa.

Corby checked the clipping. "Phoenix."

"That's where Hector lives. And he keeps talking about a best friend who sounds like he's deep into the Right To Drive movement."

"You think this guy is Hector?" Dana motioned toward the binder.

"That's him," Melissa declared. "And he's going to attack the New York Marathon, and he's going to use CAVs to do it."

"We don't know that for sure." Corby cautioned her.

"I do. Because I told him how to do it." She saw the same open-mouthed expression on both their faces. "In the hackers' forum, we got into an exchange about the best way to solve a problem, and I mentioned going in through the Central Command Center."

"Why would you do that!?" Dana was incredulous.

"It's what we do. We play games, solve problems, the way other people do crossword puzzles or sudoku. It doesn't matter!"

"Some game!" snorted Dana. "You sure he's in Phoenix?"

"I even know what bar he hangs out in."

"What if it's not him in the video? We don't have time to chase down the wrong guy. We only have forty-eight hours to stop him."

"Whether it's Hector or someone else, they travel in the same circles," said Corby. "If this Level 6-er isn't Hector, maybe he can lead us to him."

"I'm contacting Phoenix PD." Dana's hand went into her pocket.

"No," Corby stopped her. "He may have already launched his program. If it's on countdown, it'll go off on schedule, even if he's in custody."

"I still want him in custody."

"Wait," said Melissa. "I know him. Sort of. He likes me. I can talk to him better than the police can. He wants me to come to Phoenix and meet him at that bar. Maybe I can talk him out of it. Or get him to tell me enough so I can stop it."

"That is some long shot!" Dana protested.

"If it doesn't work, we'll at least have him at the bar. You can arrest him then."

"What if he's done what Richard said? Put it on a countdown."

"All the more reason to let *me* talk to him rather than the police. He likes to talk about what he's done. Drop hints. He does that with them, they won't know what he's talking about. I'll know the right things to say, the questions to ask, to learn more."

"Well, *that* makes sense," Dana conceded.

"And I don't think he has put it on a countdown. He's waiting until the last minute, in case there are variables to account for. The marathon starting late. A change in traffic patterns on the street."

"How do you know?" Dana demanded. "What makes you so sure?"

"That's how I'd do it."

"And if you're wrong?"

"I'll have forty-eight hours to get it right."

"You'll have less than that," Dana informed her. "I'm on leave, so we'll have to fly civilian. No telling when we'll get there."

"Call your boss and tell him what we know," said Corby. "He'll reinstate you."

"No, he'll want to know *how* we know it. Then, after *not* reinstating me, he'll add charges for taking the files to what he's already got against me. *Then* he'll have Phoenix PD pick up Hector. If they can find him. And if he's already launched, my boss guarantees he succeeds. Kyle won't listen when we tell him Melissa's our best chance of stopping it. And, he'll have her prosecuted for accessing restricted files. Then he'll come after you, just to get at me. He's probably already registered my badge number as suspended. If he knows how. There's no way I'm letting him near this. But I will report it to DHS."

A minute later Dana was on Homeland Security's direct line for law enforcement. When she was finished talking, she was asked for her badge number. After providing it, she was holding a phone with no one on the other end. The last words she heard were the operator's: "Your badge number says 'Suspended.'"

"We're on our own," she told them.

"Just get me to the bar," said Melissa. "I'll get it out of him."

"You're not going to meet this guy in some bar!" Corby shouted her down. "What if it goes south? What if this 'best friend' is with him and the guy goes off on you?"

"I'll be there," said Dana. "With back-up."

"How you gonna do that? You're on suspension."

"I have a couple of friends in Phoenix PD who love shit like this."

As Dana tapped her phone screen, she muttered, "Two tickets to Phoenix."

"Make it three," said Corby. "No way I'm letting her do this without me, no matter how many friends you have."

Melissa glanced at Corby, but he was looking at Dana. (To avoid making eye contact with her?) They'd managed to keep their battle to themselves, but that didn't mean the war had ended. Melissa didn't know if they'd ever speak again when this was over. But for now they were in it together.

50

WHAT DO YOU GOT FOR ME?

Outside the Police Commissioner's office (PCO to anyone with a uniform) was a room with 40 desks staffed by representatives of every city agency critical to any event or situation happening or about to happen, or that had a high probability of happening, throughout New York City. The latter was classified by NYPD as "Imminent Threat Alert" (Level 1). Below that was Level 2: "Highly Credible with Specifics;" next was "Credible Alert with Few or No Specifics" (Level 3); and finally Level 4: "Not Verified but Reported," often anonymously or by concerned citizens.

The large desk immediately outside the PCO was staffed by an NYPD Intel Lieutenant, a Counter-Terrorism Lieutenant, and a Public Information Lieutenant.

Deputy Commissioner Murtad loved to walk behind the desk and say, "Lou, what do you got for me?" knowing all three lieutenants would turn around.

This time, the Counter Terrorism "lou" didn't turn. He was busy entering a reported threat he'd just gotten from DHS. It thoroughly confused him, but he was giving it extra attention because it came as an update to the NY Marathon Bulletin.

"Calves to be used in attack on NY Marathon. No Time Given, No Location Available."

Murtad was about to comment on the CT lou's lack of response when the man turned around and shrugged, "Something about calves."

"Calves??"

CT lou shrugged. "Maybe someone's gonna let animals loose during the marathon. Public Information will issue notifications to all the zoos."

Murtad rolled his eyes and the lous went back to what they were doing.

Only after drilling down to the bottom of the investigation, weeks after the marathon, would authorities come to understand that Dana's phone call to DHS about CAVs being used to attack the race—complete with the exact time and place—had been relayed but misheard and misinterpreted as a vague, trivial, silly concern about a threat to the marathon from baby cows.

51

I'LL FIND YOU

As soon as their Phoenix flight was booked, Melissa tried to contact Hector. But he didn't log on until late that night.

RosettaStone: I've decided I'll come to the bar.

The Roc: When?

RosettaStone: I'll be in Phoenix tomorrow.

The Roc: I'll ask my friend.

RosettaStone: Do you need his permission?

The Roc: No.

She'd expected a little more than a one-word answer, but that was all he offered.

RosettaStone: 8:30?

The Roc: a.m. or p.m.?

She wondered if that was a reference to his time clue, but wasn't going there now.

RosettaStone: pm.

The Roc: s/b be p.m.

RosettaStone: OK, p.m.

The Roc: I'll tell my friend.

RosettaStone: What's his name?

The Roc: Jason. He wants to meet you.

RosettaStone: What'd you say about me?

The Roc: You're my girlfriend.

So that's how he viewed their relationship. It was creepy, but it could give her an advantage.

RosettaStone: This is our first time in person. How about just us?

She wasn't surprised that it took him a while to respond.

The Roc: OK.

RosettaStone: 8:30 p.m. tonight. At the bar. Just us. Your surprise still happening?

The Roc: On schedule.

RosettaStone: What about DNH?

The Roc: BF says no one gets hurt.

RosettaStone: You sure he's not lying?

The Roc: He wouldn't lie to me. BF!

RosettaStone: Give me another hint?

The Roc: Maybe tonight. Got into trouble for the others.

RosettaStone: But you're so clever!

The Roc: Yes. See you tomorrow.

RosettaStone: How will we know each other?

The Roc: I'll wear a green and blue shirt.

RosettaStone: More details!

The Roc: I'll find you. I'm clever.

RosettaStone: Give me your phone number, in case my plane is late.

The Roc: I'll check airline scheds.

Melissa was going to push for his number, but The Roc logged off.

52

WE HAVE TO TALK

As she prepared for Phoenix, Dana considered her situation. Being on leave simplified things—she wouldn't have to deal with Kyle.

But she wouldn't be on official business. As a federal marshal, she didn't need to clear her actions with local authorities, but she was about to bring Eddie and Steve, the friends she'd mentioned to Corby, into this. Helping her without clearing it with their bosses (which they wouldn't, *because* she'd been suspended) could jam them up if anything went wrong. She knew that wouldn't stop them, but as she was about to call, she changed her mind.

If things went right, Kyle would declare her a hero. He'd have to, at least on the record. But off the record he'd just about kill himself finding ways to punish her and anyone who helped her. If things went wrong, he'd do anything he could to humiliate and make her (and anyone who helped her) pay as high a price as possible. She wouldn't risk doing that to her friends.

So, once they entered that bar, they really were on their own.

* * *

The best Dana could get was a nonstop that left Portland at 3:00 p.m. and got into Phoenix at 6:00 p.m. If everything went smoothly.

At the airport, Melissa got Dana alone while they waited for the flight to board. She'd decided to end her stand-off with Corby by going to Dana herself. Passively waiting to learn what would happen—with her and Corby, with her and Dana—was exhausting. She hoped she and Dana could work something out, but even if they couldn't she had to get rid of this.

Dana could hold her accountable, but what would that mean? There'd been no property damage and no one got hurt. She felt the worst she could be charged with was malicious mischief and maybe have to pay a fine.

But she had leverage. Dana had gotten this far only because of her. And Dana needed her to stop Hector. If it came to it, the price of that help would be a deal: no punishment, no fine, no nothing.

"We have to talk," Melissa began, when it was just the two of them.

"What's on your mind?"

"Denver and Philadelphia. I—"

Dana's phone rang. "Kyle. I'll just let this go to voicemail" she smiled wickedly. "But I will listen to it, just in case." She walked off, leaving Melissa hoping she'd figured all the angles.

A minute later Melissa watched Dana tuck her phone away and take a step in her direction. Then Corby walked up to Dana and started talking. Was it her imagination, or did he just gesture toward her? Did Dana just turn to where he'd pointed?

Their brief exchange over, Corby fell into step beside Dana as she walked back to Melissa. Dana was shaking her head. "Fucking idiot! Wants to get into a priority database and can't find the password. Neither can anyone else in the unit. Should have thought of that before he put me on leave!"

"And you're loving this," said Corby.

"Bet your ass I am!" Then, to Melissa: "Now, what about Denver/Philadelphia?"

Melissa saw Corby perk up. She didn't want to do this in front of him. She didn't know what he'd decided, or whether he'd inject himself into something Melissa wanted to remain between her and Dana. She'd have to find another time. "Uh, just that I think I have a new way to look at those."

"Which is?"

"It's . . . complicated. I'd better see if I'm right before I get into it."

Dana shrugged. "Let me know when you're ready."

Their flight was called. As they walked down the jetway, Melissa glanced at Corby and saw a familiar look on his face. She knew he was dissecting the exchange he'd just witnessed.

53

WHAT WOULD THEY DO NOW?

Melissa's take on the Restless Rustler was that a neighborhood bar had run headlong into a hot tourist destination. Its dual nature could be traced to its two large rooms. (And the huge neon cowboy above the front entrance.)

The back room was where locals gathered. Half the people there knew one another; the greetings tossed between distant tables were frequent, as was the banter and ensuing laughter. The mood was upbeat and the underlying ambiance was relaxed. These people were regulars who came here for comfortable socializing as much as they did to drink.

The front room, where Melissa was, had more of a hustle to it. The energy was higher, the chatter and laughter louder, the clientele mainly out of towners here at the suggestion of someone at their hotel. Dana had chosen this room for Melissa to wait in because it was closer to the front door and there was less of a chance that a friend of Hector's would saunter over and ask to join them.

Melissa was now nursing a beer at a corner table and scanning the room every few minutes or whenever someone new walked in. Her eyes were drawn to anything blue or green, but so far there were no blue-and-green shirts.

Dana and Corby sat at a table far enough away to not be noticed, yet close enough to see everything that happened with Melissa and for Dana to reach her fast if necessary. But she would do nothing unless she had to. And she had promised Melissa all the time she needed with Hector.

Plan A was to get him talking about his "surprise." If she couldn't persuade him to call it off, she'd offer to help him. In order to do that, she'd have to know everything.

Plan B was to play into his fantasy that she was his girlfriend and threaten to end the relationship if he had secrets. To prove he didn't, he'd have to tell her anything she wanted to know.

Plan C was to challenge him intellectually. Taunt him that she could do whatever he was planning better than he could, which would lead to comparing approaches to "the problem." In order to have an approach, Melissa would have to know exactly what the problem was.

If nothing worked, she was to signal Dana to take him into custody.

Their plane had landed half-an-hour early, which pleased Dana, who wanted to reach the bar as far ahead of the 8:30 meet time as possible. "Give us a chance to check the place out. Also, in case he gets there early, too."

"You think he'll do that?" Melissa had asked.

"That's the way I'd do it."

Now there was nothing to do but wait, and time was passing excruciatingly slowly.

Finally, at exactly 8:30, a man approached the table. Melissa studied his green-and-blue plaid shirt. Hector hadn't specified a design, but the colors matched.

"Buy you a drink?" he asked.

"Got one."

"So I see. Waiting for someone?"

Too late, it occurred to Melissa that she and Hector should have set up some sort of code, so each could know they'd found the right person. This guy could be anyone. Or he could be Hector, similarly confused about her.

She was searching for something to say that would keep him talking but not make him feel welcome enough to pull up a chair. Then she realized they did have a code. "1745 minus 7?" she asked.

His eyes darted aimlessly around the room while he worked it out. Then he said, "1736?"

Wrong guy. Hector would never make an error like that.

"1738," she corrected. "And you're not him."

"I'm not who?"

"The guy I'm waiting for."

"Maybe next time." And he was gone.

Melissa scolded herself. She'd been so intent on meeting Hector, and how she'd draw him out, that she hadn't been thorough: a woman sitting alone in a bar? What'd she think would happen? How would she handle it if it happened again? It took a few minutes to work it out: she didn't need a code as a first-line defense. The next time someone came over, all she had to do was ask.

Twenty minutes later, she got her chance. His shirt was split diagonally, blue on top, green below. He was more confident than the first guy had been, and he had a nice smile.

"You need a refill!" he said with cheerful familiarity.

"You need to tell me your name," she answered.

"I get the name right, we both get refills?" He reached for the chair opposite her.

"Depends on your answer."

"I get a hint?"

Was this a version of him giving her hints online? Was *he* trying to use a code?

"The Roc."

"OK . . . Then I'd say Gibraltar."

He really did have a nice smile. And the wrong name.

"No refills," she told him.

"I only get one guess?" He started to tug on the nearest chair to draw it away from the table.

She hooked her feet around the legs to hold it in place. "Afraid so. I'm waiting for someone and you're not him."

"He doesn't show up, I'll be at the bar."

Thirty minutes passed while Melissa nursed her second beer. The glass was still three-quarters full when she noticed him. Blue-and-green striped shirt. Eyes directly on her as he came closer.

"I've been looking for you all night," he greeted her.

"We said 8:30," she said lightly. "I've been right here since then."

"But I didn't see you until just now."

"Nice shirt."

"Glad you like it. Can I sit down?"

She was about to say yes, but something made her stop. "Hector?"

"Yeah." He reached for the chair opposite Melissa. She'd hooked her feet around its legs as a precaution, but released them just before he pulled the chair out and sat. "But I don't know your name."

That's right. Online she'd been RosettaStone and he'd never asked anything about that. "Melissa."

"Pretty name."

"Thank you. And thank you for coming without your friend."

"Wouldn't want anyone here but you and me."

"I've almost figured it out."

"Good!"

"How about that other hint you promised me?"

"Why hint? Let's just get right to it. Talk straight."

"Sure. I'd love to do that."

She waited for him to go on, and he could see it was his move. "Well, if we're gonna talk straight . . . How about you let me buy you another drink? Or you can just finish that one and we can get out of here."

"I think I'd rather stay. And talk about what you're working on."

"Right now, what I'm working on is you." His grin stopped just short of an open leer.

This did *not* sound like The Roc. "You said your name is Hector."

"I can be anyone you want me to be. What's the difference?"

"Sorry. I made a mistake."

"Mistakes happen. We can fix that."

"Not this one. I'd like you to go."

When she reached for her beer to show she was moving on, he put his hand on of hers. "C'mon Melissa. We can make this work."

She pulled her hand back. "No. We can't. I'd like you to leave."

"You were friendly enough a couple of minutes ago."

"That was a mistake. I thought you were someone else."

"Well suppose I don't want to leave?"

Her hand dropped below the table, into her pocket. "If you're not gone by three, you get a face full of pepper spray."

"Oh, c'mon. Don't be like that."

"One . . ."

"Know what? I think you're bluffing." His expression was one of supreme confidence.

She rested her elbow on the table, the cannister in her hand aimed his face. "Two."

"Damn, you're serious."

"If you make me go to three, you'll see how serious I am."

As she waited for him to make a decision, her peripheral vision picked up movement. Dana was slowly but deliberately finding her way over to them.

Finally he kicked the chair back as he stood, growling "I don't have time for this shit!"

When he passed Dana, she made a fluid turn toward the bathroom and continued on her way.

Melissa slipped the pepper spray back into her pocket, thinking, *This is turning out to be a bitch!*

There was no next time until an hour later. Two men entered the bar, one tall and beefy, stomach dangling over his belt, the other short and leprechaun-like, trailing at his companion's side. Something about the way he carried himself—the almost self-cancelling shuffle—drew Melissa's attention. He looked like someone who would do whatever his best friend wanted him to do. Who would leap at a relationship with a woman, any relationship, and call her his girlfriend. Maybe he'd brought Jason with him after all.

They were scanning the room and she was about to signal them over, when the tall friend tapped the smaller man's shoulder and nodded in her direction. They walked toward her table and she got ready to stand. But when they came abreast of her they kept going without breaking stride, not stopping until they greeted two women five tables away. Was it her imagination, or did the short man look over his shoulder at her as they passed?

Three hours and three beers later, she knew it wasn't going to happen. She'd gone online several times to see if she could reach Hector, but he wasn't logged in.

At 1:30, they left the bar.

Why had he flaked? Did he realize he was being set up? Did he just get frightened? Or had he shown up and sat in the bar, watching her, trying to work up the nerve to come over? Or decided not to, because he didn't trust her.

It didn't matter. What did, was: What would they do now?

54

BACK IN PLENTY OF TIME

When the bell rang that Saturday morning, Jason knew it was Hector, probably there to help him wash the Impala.

But washing the car was forgotten as soon as Hector mentioned he was meeting his girlfriend tonight.

The bitch really was becoming a problem.

"Thought she was an online thing," Jason commented.

"She's going to be in Phoenix. We're going to meet. At the bar."

"You don't go to bars."

"I go to this one. With you. It's the only bar I know."

"Restless Rustler?"

"Yes."

"What's your girlfriend look like?"

"I don't know. I've never seen her."

"Does she know what you look like?"

"No."

"You have her phone number? You speak to her on the phone?"

"No."

"Hector . . . Do you even know she *is* a girl?"

"Yes. She uses female syntaxes, scoring over a 95% confidence level that her writing is by a cis-female. She's also between 20 and 32, also to 95% confidence, meaning she's most likely Crash Generation. Anyone born after the stock market crash in '08, but before the pandemic. She's doing graduate work at the University of Portland, majoring in environmental justice."

"Still doesn't mean she's a girl. I say there's a 20% chance she's a dude or a feminate whatever." Then, staring at Hector intently, Jason asked, "Whose idea was it to meet?"

Hector looked away. "Mine. At first. Then hers."

"She say why?"

"She's going to be in Phoenix. So we can meet."

"But you have no idea who she is."

She's doing graduate work at the University of Portland, majoring in environmental justice. And she's an excellent coder."

"Where *did* you two meet?"

"We haven't yet. We're going to meet at the bar. Tonight."

"C'mon, Hector! I mean, where'd you meet online?"

"In a coders' forum. She's the smartest one there. Except for me."

This was no good. Hector meeting a stranger, with the Horizon Event tomorrow. Hector meeting a girl?? He'd never be able to keep his mouth shut, especially with *her*. And he'd come away distracted, just when Jason wanted him totally focused.

"I'll come with you. I can meet her, too."

And see who she was, and stop Hector from shooting his mouth off.

"She wants to meet alone. She wants it to be just the two of us."

It was getting worse with each of Hector's answers. Now Jason didn't want Hector going to the bar at all.

"Hey, Hector, I'm gonna hit 87 for a couple of hours. Wanna come?"

"I have to meet her at the bar."

"Sure, but that's not 'til later. Take a ride with me. We'll be back in plenty of time for you to meet her."

"OK."

Jason knew the turn-outs, vistas, dead-end side roads, and every other feature of 87 between Phoenix and Snowflake. It never occurred to Hector to ask why he was driving slowly today, and he waited until they were miles out, surrounded by desert, before telling Hector he wanted to stretch his legs and hang out for a while. Hector was gazing out the window as Jason pulled off and drove a mile down hard-packed dirt. When he stepped out of the car he told Hector he was opening the hood "so she'll cool down faster." Then it was a simple matter of unplugging one of the distributor wires.

Later, when it was time to go, the car wouldn't start.

"Damn!" Jason muttered. "That's the problem with coming out here. You run into trouble, there's no cell service. You'd think by now they'd have service everywhere, but not here. Funny thing is, that's why I like it. Nothing like being alone with nature. Unless something like this happens."

After they'd tried their phones with no success, he reassured Hector that he'd still be able to keep his appointment. "I've been through this before. We'll just wait a while and I'll start her up again."

But she wouldn't start the second time, or the third time, or the fourth. Luckily, Jason had water and snacks in the car. He also had a couple of jackets, so when the sun went down they had protection from the cold desert night.

When Jason decided it was late enough, he told Hector he'd

take another look under the hood and try the car again. This time, the engine roared to life.

"Sorry about this, buddy," he apologized as he made the left from the dirt road on to 87. "You'd think with all the TLC I give this baby that'd never happen. But she's just a machine. You're not gonna miss your appointment with your lady, are you?"

"I've already missed it. Maybe she's online." Hector tapped his screen. "She's not in CTJ."

"Well, don't sweat it. You can see her next time she comes to town."

55

CASTILLO

At 6:30 a.m. on December 6th, NYPD Deputy Inspector Nelson Castillo stood in his office overlooking the New York City Traffic Management Center, dubbed the TMC by those who worked there. The full-length interior window in front of him provided a 180-degree view of the vast space on the other side, which was the nerve center for all 13,688 computerized traffic signals in the city, 655 dynamic message signs (DMS) that kept drivers up to date on constantly-changing moment-to-moment traffic conditions, 2,199 traffic cameras, 16,711 roadway occupancy and speed sensors, 102 "Gridlock Birds" (drones that monitored the 6,000-plus miles of roadways crisscrossing all five boroughs), and communications with over 5,000 traffic agents out on the street. From here, Castillo could observe every person, every computer, and every video screen on the other side of the window.

Tucked away in an old Long Island City bank, the TMC was encased in a three-foot-thick concrete and masonry wall reinforced with K-12 steel columns (a strength-rating shared with embassies around the world) and designed to withstand a direct hit by a truck traveling 50 mph carrying 15,000 pounds of TNT. The 9/11 attack on the World Trade Center had destroyed then-Mayor Rudy Giuliani's metro command center, and city officials had taken no chances on losing this one the same way.

The Memorandum of Understanding between New York City, New York State, and the U.S. Department of Transportation, which funded about half the cost of the center, mandated that a licensed traffic engineer be its supervisor. Until 2030, a city or state Department of Transportation engineer had been at the helm. But after that year's Saint Patrick's Day catastrophe, when a truck plowed through parade participants and viewers, killing 17 and wounding more than 80, the NYPD fought to wrest control of the room. As part of that battle they sent Castillo, who had an undergraduate degree in engineering management, to Penn State for an 18-month program to get his Masters in Traffic Engineering. His engineering license soon followed. Since then, the NYPD was in full control of the TMC. And Castillo was in charge of it.

The police department's Emergency Management Center's post-mortem on the St. Patrick's Day attack had found that the TMC's speed-monitoring system could have picked up the truck's movement before anyone or anything else did. Not that that would have stopped the attack. Neither would the city's other security precautions. A massive sanitation truck loaded with sand was stationed at the west edge of Central Park at Central Park West, blocking vehicles from getting close to the parade on Fifth Avenue. Water-filled barriers were positioned on the park's eastern side, at Fifth Avenue. One of these barriers, tagged with a barely-noticeable green stripe, had less water to make it lighter so it could be pushed out of the way in the event of an emergency. The safeguards should have made an attack all but impossible.

But something else was already in the park before it was secured. A Parks Department maintenance truck was sitting in the agency's garage along the 96th Street transverse roadway, midway between Central Park West and Fifth Avenue. The green-striped lighter-weight barrier was no match for the heavy truck (later dubbed the "terror truck" by the media) that hit the barrier at 45 mph, sweeping it out of its way as it barreled down the parade route for nearly a block before cops shot and killed the driver.

When he took over the TMS, Castillo made a private vow that a similar attack would never happen on his watch. So far he'd kept that promise, both on the day-to-day streets of "his" city and in the simulations the center constantly ran. Two weeks ago, he and his team finished their annual tabletop exercises, besting every scenario thrown at them by the NYPD and Homeland Security's Intelligence Division. They'd not only successfully navigated the situations they'd trained for, but triumphed over a new strategy never tried by terrorists (but, according to Homeland Security, likely to happen at some point in the future).

It was aimed at the back-up system for the city's computerized traffic signal network, which would kick in if there were a widespread electrical blackout. In the simulation, terrorists changed the fail-safe programs implemented by traffic engineers by altering each individual signal controller. Since there hadn't been a widespread blackout in more than 11 years, both NYPD and Homeland Security thought Castillo might have gotten complacent; during the simulation's visit by a Mid-East Prime Minister, they launched a cyberattack that gridlocked traffic in all directions but one. Trained to extricate himself from the potential danger created by the stopped cars surrounding him, the PM's driver would likely take the only route the terrorists left open to him, leading him to a booby-trapped intersection.

If the team had grown lax, it might have worked. But when the blackout hit, Castillo noticed that the backup system was generating an odd pattern as it manipulated the traffic signals on the streets. Working through NYPD Central Command, he ordered the Highway Patrol motorcade escorts to stay put, keeping the PM's car in place. He then sent traffic agents to strategic intersections to manually unravel the gridlock so the motorcade could follow its pre-approved route. The Intel inspectors were impressed.

A week ago, Castillo had to get through Thanksgiving and Black Friday. Tomorrow was Marathon Sunday, which had been moved from early November to December after climate change resulted in more 70- and 80-degree fall days in New York. During the November 2031 Marathon, with temperature peaking at 84 degrees, more than 200 runners needed medical attention; 48 were hospitalized and there were three fatalities. The following year it was moved to December, and Castillo was determined that it, too, would go off without a hitch. To make sure that happened, today and tomorrow shifts started at 4:00 a.m., and his staff was on terrorist watch until the marathon was safely behind them. He'd also put all his Thanksgiving-weekend protocols back in place, including the missile-carrying drones.

Castillo and his two traffic lieutenants, Bob Margolis and Fred Fields, had divided the TMC into three sectors: North, South, and Central. Margolis was monitoring the north, Fields the south, and Castillo central. City traffic engineers were overseeing traffic-signal patterns based on incoming data and on-scene observations. State engineers were monitoring highway systems and adjusting DMS's as needed. They were ready for anything, and could respond to any scenario in a matter of seconds.

Something caught Castillo's attention on the huge wall-mounted screen that showed traffic and other vehicle movement throughout the city. An autonomous sanitation truck at 6th Avenue and 59th Street, positioned there to create a safe zone around the south edge of Central Park, where the race would end, seemed to move about a foot, then return to its original position. He automatically noted the time (6:32 a.m.) as he mulled over why it would do that.

He was reaching for the phone to ask the traffic engineer monitoring the area to find out what happened, when a second line rang; a different engineer was reporting an eastbound truck running a red light at 11th avenue and 57th Street In three blocks it would be just south of Columbus Circle where, tomorrow, runners would be entering Central Park to complete the marathon.

Castillo notified Central Command, and Highway Patrol cars were dispatched as the truck crossed 10th Avenue. Police set up a blockade at 9th Avenue, but the truck turned south. Officers finally stopped it at 55th Street, and determined it was no threat; the driver was just a red-light runner. The vehicle was ID'ed, the truck owner contacted, and the driver was automatically cited for the red-light violation.

Castillo turned his attention back to Central sector. What could have been a crisis was, in the end, an everyday minor disruption to the calm Castillo preferred. But it was enough to make him forget about the sudden movement of the sanitation truck at 6th and 57th.

56

THE WHITE TRUCK

The white truck sat next to a narrow neighborhood park on 6th Avenue between 66th and 67th Streets in Brooklyn, two blocks from the Gowanus Expressway.

In a film, Soldier's footsteps would be echoing in the hollow 3:00 a.m. darkness that blanketed the deserted street. But his soft-soled shoes helped him remain little more than a shadow. He didn't look like a soldier—a deliberate calculation. He was dressed to not stand out: black hoodie, black pants, black sneakers. If he'd had an official uniform, this would be it. He blended with the night.

He briefly studied the truck, though he already knew what he had to about it: 26 feet long, eight feet wide, thirteen feet high, seven tons. It would do.

Rigging the truck went slower than he would've liked because he was working in the dark, helped only by a streetlight down the block. But he didn't need much light. He'd done this dozens of times.

The tricky part of packing in the C-4 was getting the detonator perfectly situated: just under the grille, protruding far enough from the front of the truck to be triggered on contact, but not sticking out enough to be seen. It took several attempts to get it finely balanced (the damned thing kept slipping out), but fifteen minutes later he was done. Not his best time, but faster than anyone else could have done it.

This was a double win-win. Jason Bartel would have his victory over whoever or whatever he was fighting. Soldier didn't know why he was attacking the marathon, and he didn't care. That would be Jason's win.

Soldier's win was hacking The Roc's computer. The bastard loved to make fools of everyone on the forum with his goddamned Challenges; this time he was the fool. For the hour he had access to The Roc's computer, Soldier owned the son of a bitch.

But there was a bigger win for Soldier here. Jason was sending the truck the wrong way up the 39th Street Staten Island-bound exit ramp, on to the Gowanus Expressway. It would make a wide right and pick up speed as it bore down on the race, first crashing into the six NYPD motorcycle units and the press vehicle out ahead of the throng, then plowing through the runners. Pretty ambitious.

Tonight Soldier had made it more ambitious. When the truck hit the press vehicle, the C-4 he'd just packed in would kill hundreds more than Jason would have, and bring down a nice chunk of highway as a bonus.

When the feds fumbled through their investigation, it would lead straight back to Jason; they'd never believe he didn't know the C-4 was on board. And there was no way he could lead them to Soldier. He'd already disabled the burner they'd used to communicate. The closest Jason could take the feds to Soldier was Darnel, who knew how to stand strong. If he did show any signs of cracking, Soldier knew how to deal with that.

Jason had no idea Soldier had come to New York. He knew nothing of the modification Soldier had made to the truck. He had absolutely no knowledge of the other step Soldier had taken to secure—and amplify—this mission.

Jason would take the fall. With any luck, The Roc would go down with him. It was too good to be true.

Score one—a really big one—for the Cause. Another blow against the Deep State.

57

THE MARATHON

The New York City Marathon is the standard 26.2 miles and traverses all five boroughs of the city. It begins in Staten Island, from which runners cross the Verrazzano Bridge into Brooklyn and onto the Brooklyn-Queens Expressway. Officially designated I-278, the highway is known to New Yorkers as "The Gowanus" and might be the country's ugliest urban roadway.

No signs read "Gowanus;" the sobriquet is a GPS orphan. Built in the 1930s by Robert Moses, who barreled the artery through the thriving but low-income communities of Sunset Park and South Brooklyn (now known with high-toned names like Boerum Hill (no hill) and Carroll Gardens (no city-sponsored gardens), it was initially a slow-speed parkway with several left-side entrances and exits—taboo in American highways since the 1960s.

When the road arrived at the wealthy, powerful neighborhood of Brooklyn Heights, Moses elevated it with a masterful design, the Triple-Cantilever, to minimize impacts on the community and its residents' view of the Manhattan skyline. The highway was then capped by the Brooklyn Heights

Promenade—a must-see for tourists. Sunset Park's poor (those who weren't displaced) were left with only an elevated highway, ugly pillars, and dark streets.

For most of its length, The Gowanus was built with three lanes in each direction. What made it truly unique was that for over 50 years the median barrier was moved every weekday morning and evening to match traffic demand—more lanes to Manhattan in the morning, more lanes from Manhattan in the evening.

At first the median was manually reconfigured with cones. By 2000, the Road Zipper (RZ), a barrier-moving vehicle, was invented. The RZ straddled the median barrier and, like a zipper, moved it about 12 feet during the morning peak period, so four lanes led to Manhattan and only two left Manhattan. During the evening rush hour, the process was reversed.

The RZ initially had an operator/driver, but in 2029 it became automatic. However, it could still be controlled by a remote operator at the Traffic Management Center, and every morning at 5:00 a.m. a TMC operator initiated the Road Zipper with the press of a button.

After the Gowanus, marathoners run the streets of Brooklyn; several neighborhoods later, they cross into Queens over the Pulaski Bridge, the race's half-way point. The Queensboro Bridge takes them over the East River into Manhattan, where they turn north up First Avenue. A mile-and-a-half through the Bronx, then they loop back into Manhattan. The last five miles take them down Fifth Avenue with a right at Central Park South, and on to the finish line in the park.

As the sun rose on December 7, 2036, it promised to be a clear sunny day with temperature in the low 60s. Perfect weather for the marathon. Today there were over 75,000 runners, from more than 130 countries, more runners from more places than at any time in the race's 65-year history.

At 8:00, the first of four special categories (the professional wheelchair division) would start. Handcycle and select athletes with disabilities would start at 8:22. At 8:40: professional women; at 9:05: professional men.

At 9:10, the majority of the runners would begin, going off in five waves of 12,000 per group, each wave starting thirty-five minutes apart.

Wave 2 would start at 9:45. At 10:15, 4,000 of them would be at the 65th Street ramp.

Wave 3 would go at 10:10. At 10:45, most of these runners (nearly 10,000) would be just reaching the ramp.

Combined with racers from the first two waves, the total number of runners approaching, at, or just past the 65th Street ramp at 10:45 would be approximately 16,000. Almost one-quarter of all the runners in today's race.

58

DECEMBER 7

It was Hector's offhand conversation during the disappointing Prescott run, when he talked about moving a robo positioned to stop traffic, that showed Jason exactly how to do it. Now everything was in place.

On Thursday, Hector had hacked New York's Central Command Center. The next day he hacked the truck company's CCC. Yesterday, he moved the truck rom 6th Avenue to 42nd Street, where it now waited a few blocks from the ramp. He also made sure he was in the city's CCC by moving a robo-sani a couple of feet, then back to its original position. No one in the command center even noticed.

It was genius. Foolproof. And they'd never trace it back to Jason. They still hadn't explained what happened with the cabs, AH95 trucks, or ATA trucks. Jason was almost becoming a fan of AV technology. Not the science—the ease with which it could be used against itself. They called it progress, but they had no idea what they were unleashing. Today would show them.

The date made it even more perfect. December 7th.

It would be another Day of Infamy. But this one would benefit the country. And every American who had something at stake in this.

Rood would be proud.

59

TWO HOURS TO STOP IT

When Melissa answered Dana's 6:00 a.m. knock on her hotel-room door, the first category of racers were assembled at the starting line in New York, waiting for the signal to go. "I'm already on," she assured Dana. "But it won't to do any good unless he is, too."

"And of course he isn't."

Melissa shrugged. "I've posted three times, asking him to meet in a break-out room."

"Not showing last night could mean he doesn't trust you anymore," Dana worried. "If that's it, you'll never hear from him again."

"I don't think so. He wants a friend. And he'd *really* like a girlfriend. He doesn't want to lose me."

"He didn't seem to care last night."

"I think he'll contact me *because* of last night."

"Why?"

"Instinct?"

"Let's hope you've still got it. Right now it's our only way to pinpoint his location." She'd called DHS several times after her first attempt, always with the same results: "Badge number suspended." She was becoming desperate enough to think about contacting Kyle, but knew he'd grind her down with ball-busting questions and then only get in the way. She'd considered going above him, to the head of the Portland bureau, but knew he'd refer it back to Kyle. Her sole hope of outside help lay with the call she'd decided to make to Steve, at Phoenix PD.

She knew Corby was wracking his brain for what he could do. But all he could offer was calling the media. Go public with 16,000 runners tightly packed in one place? The ensuing panic would play right into their hands. No, they had to do this themselves.

"Trying again," Melissa called out. Still no response.

"Maybe he's waiting until it's over."

Melissa shook her head. "He'll be here. But in case I'm wrong, I've been thinking of a way to stop him remotely."

"Can you do that?"

"Maybe. It'd be a Hail Mary."

"Do it now!"

"Too risky. He could know I'm doing it, and—"

"Who gives a shit!? If you can stop him—"

". . . he could block me!" Melissa didn't hide her impatience. This was *her* world.

"Risk it! How can you—"

She stopped Dana with a raised hand. "This is why I'm here. I know how he thinks. You have to trust me."

They were silent, staring at the screen as if they could will Hector to appear.

Then Melissa spoke. "Denver and Philadelphia?"

"What about them?" Dana didn't take her eyes off the screen.

"I did that."

"I know."

"You know??"

"From the day you started working on this."

"How—"

"You knew too much. Nobody's instincts are *that* good."

"Then why'd you let me in?"

"Decided to take a chance. Denver/Philadelphia made you one of the bad guys. But you were a bad guy offering to help. I wasn't going to turn that down if it meant cracking this. And think about it, how bad were you? You caused some confusion—well, a lot in Philadelphia—but you didn't hurt anyone. You could have done a lot of damage both times, but you chose not to. And you had something I wanted. If you delivered, and behaved, I'd look the other way. I had more to gain by letting you work with us. And I could always charge you later." Dana paused before she said the rest of it. "I still can."

"Are you going to?"

"I might."

"Not the best way to help me be at my best."

"You don't get that kind of help. You screwed things up royally in Philadelphia."

"That's one of my reasons for doing this. Kind of make up for that."

"What's your other reason?"

"It's not as noble as the first."

"I don't expect it to be."

"I wanted to know if you were coming close to knowing it was me."

Dana smiled. "I had the same idea. Keep you close to make sure you weren't being a bad girl again."

Melissa couldn't stop herself from voicing her next thought. "You don't think I could have done it right next to you? Like we are now?"

"I'm sure you could."

"Then how'd you know you could trust me?"

"Instinct."

Melissa tried to raise Hector again. Still nothing.

"Why'd you do it?" asked Dana.

"Long story. Let's save it for another time."

"Then I'll ask you this. You and Hector seem to be able to hack anything you want to. It really that easy?"

"After the 2000 election, when there was all the confusion in Florida, and people saying voting systems were hacked, votes changed, and a lot of other things, there was a government investigation to find out how vulnerable the country's voting infrastructure was. They brought in a Ph.D. who taught programming at a major university and asked her how easy it would be for her to hack the voting infrastructure. Not just Florida's. The entire system. The whole country. Know what she said? Without even thinking about it? 'My graduate students could do it.'"

Dana slowly shook her head. "You guys are dangerous."

"I miss anything?" Corby asked as he joined them.

"Just girl talk," said Dana. "I'm gonna try Homeland again. If they're gonna keep ignoring me, I want it on record."

"I told her about Denver and Philadelphia," Melissa informed Corby when they were alone.

His face showed equal parts surprise and relief. "And?"

"I think I'm on probation. If I 'behave,' she might let me slide."

"Are you going to behave?"

She girded for another fight, then saw the twinkle in his eye and said, "Still deciding."

"Why'd you tell her?"

"So you wouldn't have to."

In that moment, they could have healed the rift or opened a new one. She was leaving it to him to determine which it would be. He opted for healing.

"Thank you."

"For letting you off the hook?"

"For doing the right thing."

"*Did* I let you off the hook? Or did you already tell her? At the airport?"

He shook his head. "What made you think that?"

"I saw you talking. Right before we boarded."

"I don't . . . Oh, she was venting about her boss."

"The way you two looked at me, I thought maybe you did."

Corby took a moment, then said, "I don't remember looking at you."

Her laptop dinged. "He's on!"

Corby rushed to get Dana as Melissa engaged Hector in a break-out room.

RosettaStone: Where were you last night?

The Roc: Car trouble. No cell service.

RosettaStone: Where are you now?

The Roc: Jason's.

RosettaStone: Where is that?

The Roc: He doesn't want me to say.

Dana appeared, phone in hand. "Still have him?" Melissa nodded.

RosettaStone: Why not?

The Roc: He doesn't know you.

RosettaStone: Maybe he and I should meet. I can come there.

The Roc: He doesn't like visitors.

RosettaStone: Let's surprise him.

The Roc: He doesn't like surprises.

RosettaStone: Can you and I meet now?

The Roc: Maybe later. After.

RosettaStone: After what?

The Roc: TTYL.

"Shit! He's gone!"

"No!" Dana shouted. "We got him!"

The call to Steve at Phoenix PD had paid off. He'd gone to his lou, who went to his captain, and they'd agreed to help.

"Phoenix PD used triangulation to narrow the location of his computer signal. They sent a car for us!"

It was 8:25 Phoenix time (10:25 in New York) when they climbed into the police CAV waiting outside the hotel. As soon as Corby looked at the data on Hector's signal, he shook his head. "He's in Kensington. Neighborhood's about 1.5 square miles, with 45,000 people living in 25,000 units. We have twenty minutes before he launches. It'll take about *thirty* to zero-in on a single block, which could have as many as 200 units."

"I can find it faster," said Melissa. Her fingers scampered over her keyboard. "There are four robo-cabs in those 1.5 square miles. I'm telling them to report the strength of his signal. The further the cab is from the computer, the weaker the signal; a stronger signal means the robo is closer."

"We don't know he's on his computer," said Dana.

Melissa was confident. "He's on. He's not talking to me, but his computer is on."

A minute later they saw it. "Signal's coming from block 138," Melissa told them. "Bounded by Riverdale, Macomb, 43rd St, and Shetland. I'm sending us to the strongest signal location—4320 Shetland."

Dana was logged on to a database of city residents. "Two story walk-up with four units."

"Putting CAVs on Riverdale, Macomb, and 43rd Street,"

Melissa related as she looked at Dana's database. "He's coming from one of the back apartments, closest to Riverdale."

Dana now had a diagram of the building on her screen. "Checking the database for who's in the building. Second floor, Charles Horton and Maria Turner. First floor, Larry Drew and Jason Bartel."

Jason is the name of Hector's friend!" Melissa was almost shouting. "Jason Bartel Runs the PARD chapter in Phoenix. Rood talks about him all the time!"

"Shit!" growled Dana "Police computer says traffic. It'll take 14 minutes, even with sirens. She looked at her watch. He's 10 minutes from Go!"

"Eight-thirty-five on a Sunday morning? How can there be traffic?" Corby wanted to know.

"That's why our hotel's out here instead of in the city!" Dana told him. "Fucking Mesa Marathon!"

60

I'M YOUR ONLY FRIEND

They were in Jason's apartment, preparing to launch the Horizon Event.

Returning to the living room with a fresh cup of coffee, Jason saw Hector tapping keys on his laptop.

"What are you doing? We're on countdown. Don't tell me you're checking your e-mail!"

"No," Hector answered, eyes still on his screen. "DMing with someone on CTJ."

"Not now, you're not! Get the hell off and focus!"

Hector typed a quick TTYL to Melissa and looked up. "My girlfriend—"

"You're talking to *her*!? Now?? Focus, Hector! You don't even know who she really is!" Jason yelled. "She could be a sumo wrestler meth addict living in an abandoned basement!"

"I don't think so," Hector responded.

"Oh yeah? Who else would be interested in you? *I'm* your only friend."

"But now I have a—"

"Don't say it. Don't call her your girlfriend. She's just using you."

"For what?"

"How do I know!? Maybe she's trying to steal your secrets."

"She hasn't asked for any secrets."

"Maybe she doesn't have to *ask*. Maybe you're *telling* her."

"I haven't—"

"Have you told her *anything* about yourself?"

"I told her some hints about how to figure out my name."

"Why'd you do *that*!?"

"She asked me—"

"So she *is* asking questions! I can't believe how fucking stupid you are! She could be a federal agent!"

"No, she's my girlfriend. She's—"

"She's not your girlfriend! She's not even your friend. I'm your only friend! I thought you know that!"

Lowering his voice, Hector murmured, "I do know it."

"OK, then. We're *this* close." Jason held up his hand, thumb and forefinger pinched together. "What's the fucking problem!?"

Hector was silent as he summoned up the strength to ask the next question. "Are you lying to me?"

"Hector . . . What the hell are you talking about? Lying about what?"

"About DNH."

"If I hear those stupid fucking letters one more time . . . How could you even ask me that?"

"RosettaStone said maybe you were."

"No, Hector. This is just us now. This is between me and you. Don't put it on her. You look me straight in the eye and tell me why you think I'm lying to you."

Hector looked away. "You got so upset over the kill switch. All it would do is make sure we don't—"

"I've told you a thousand times, we're not doing any harm. We're not hurting anyone. We're just scaring people."

With tremendous effort, Hector looked directly at Jason. "Are you lying to me now?"

"Hector, buddy, have I *ever* lied to you?"

61

ORDER THEM OUT OF OUR WAY

The Arizona equivalent of the New York City Marathon, the Mesa race was an annual event that drew thousands of runners to Phoenix. And created early Sunday-morning traffic along the race route.

In size, the Mesa marathon was only a fraction of New York City's race; nevertheless, it was the local premier event of the day. The volume of cars that poured into Phoenix for the race weekend had become a growing problem, and this year local authorities had a solution: they banned private cars from the race-affected areas, allowing only robo-cabs and buses.

That was the traffic that now stood between them and Hector.

After declaring they wouldn't reach Jason's apartment in time, Corby analyzed the traffic pattern on Dana's computer. "The vehicles ahead of us are all robos," he told Melissa. "Tell our car to order them out of our way."

"Done!" she announced several keystrokes later.

"Now change every traffic signal we approach to green."

"Done!"

The streets they had to navigate were crowded with cabs and

made busier by the extra buses that had been laid on today. But, like the Red Sea, the vehicles parted before them as they raced through the city.

They were only seven minutes away.

62

THAT WASN'T SO HARD

It was 8:30 a.m. in Phoenix—10:30 in New York.

"Time to launch," Jason announced to Hector.

"You said we'd launch at 10:45."

"I said the highest number of runners would be up there at 10:45. Going now gives the truck fifteen minutes to get to the ramp and go up."

"But we had a plan."

"Yeah! And this is it! Just do it!"

All Hector had to do was hit one goddamn key. But he sat there, hand over his keyboard, hesitating.

Jason wanted to snatch the laptop and do it himself, but he didn't know which key to press. He thought about grabbing it anyway and hitting every key on the layout, but didn't know if it had to be a single key or some combination. And what if the wrong command shut the whole program down? Being so dependent on Hector was making Jason crazy.

"Hector. Hit the goddamn key or I'll throw you the fuck out of here and never speak to you again!"

Hector recoiled at Jason's threat. But asked again, "Are you lying to me?"

"Hit the fucking key! Now!!" Jason banged the table.

Hector flinched, then lowered his hand and tapped a key.

Jason wanted to punch him. Instead, he let out a huge sigh and said, "That wasn't so hard, was it?"

63

HAIL MARY

They were only two minutes out, but even with vehicles darting out of their way and every traffic light turning green at their approach, time was running out.

Dana turned to Melissa. "You still think you can stop him remotely?"

"I can try."

"Time for that Hail Mary."

Melissa typed furiously. But after a flurry of keystrokes her face fell. "It didn't work."

64

THE 39TH STREET RAMP

On 42nd Street in Brooklyn, the truck's engine sprang to life. With the Sunday-morning street empty, it immediately eased out of its space.

Proceeding to 2nd Avenue, it stopped at the red light; when the light changed, the truck turned left and made its way to 39th Street Just past 39th, to the right, was the exit ramp from the Gowanus. On any other day, a right turn would take a vehicle up the ramp and into oncoming traffic leaving the highway.

The truck's sensors indicated a large vehicle, identified as a sani-robo, parked across the bottom of the ramp. But almost immediately that vehicle started and began to back up. After hacking the NYC CCC, Hector hacked and manipulated the truck's digital profile so that it now looked like an ambulance to other CAVs. Seeing an ambulance coming toward it, the sani-robo retreated to let the emergency vehicle pass.

65

ANYONE CALL FOR AN AMBULANCE?

Castillo was reading the threat alerts that constantly poured into the TMC. "Listen to this," he said to Margolis. "Calves are gonna be used to attack the marathon."

"Connected robos?" asked Margolis. "How are—"

"Not robos," Castillo corrected him. "It says calves. Like baby cows. Where do people come up with this shit?"

"Better that shit than my shit," Margolis told him. "I thought you were saying they're gonna use robos. What a fuckin' mess that'd be!"

"Can't use robos," Castillo insisted. "Couldn't get 'em past the sanis we have blocking access to the runners."

"You could, if you got one of the sanis to move," Margolis speculated. "But we'd see it." He nodded toward his screen. "We saw one of them beasts move half an inch, we'd be all over it."

Castillo bolted upright in his chair. "Shit! I did see it!"

"Where?" Margolis wanted to know. "I don't see anything. You sure you—"

"Yesterday. I saw—"

TMC alerts sounded, bringing Castillo, Margolis, and Fields to the screen showing activity in Brooklyn, where the marathon was in its early stages. An ambulance was accessing the 39th Street ramp.

"Anyone call for an ambulance?" Castillo yelled.

No answers.

By now Margolis's attention was on the street camera scanning the area. "That ain't no ambulance! It's a truck!"

They watched as the sani positioned across the ramp edged back to allow the "ambulance" to pass. The gap it opened was 7 feet, growing to 12—wide enough to allow the truck up the ramp.

66

NOW, WE WATCH IT HAPPEN

"Now, we watch it happen on the live feed." Jason had gone from boiling-point fury to smug satisfaction.

But that was short-lived. Seconds after Hector had the marathon live feed on his laptop, the apartment door gave way as Dana crashed in. Seeing Hector at his computer, she cursed and leapt, stretching an arm across his neck, clotheslining him backward off the chair, landing on top of him, and pinning him to the floor.

From the moment she burst in, Hector had been yelling "I didn't do it!" But that didn't slow her. Immediately after hitting the floor, she rolled him on to his stomach and cuffed his hands behind his back. He was still yelling "I didn't do it!"

Now that he was immobilized, she finally allowed herself to listen.

"She said Do No Harm. So I—"

"Who did?" Dana demanded.

"RosettaStone."

"Who the hell is that!?"

"My girlfriend. She said Do No Harm. The kill switch stopped the truck."

"Stopped it?"

"It won't happen. Look at the live feed."

Dana got off Hector, and leaned over his computer. "What the fuck. . . ," she muttered as she watched thousands of people running on the Gowanus Expressway, untouched by anything except possible concerns that they couldn't finish the race.

Still prone on the floor, Hector kept trying to talk to her. "He said he wouldn't be my friend if I didn't do it, so I did. I hit the key. But the kill switch will keep the truck at the top of the ramp. He said he wouldn't hurt anyone, but he lied."

67

SHOVING MATCH

Eyes locked on the screen showing the sani moving backward at the foot of the ramp, Castillo seized manual control, bringing it to a lurching stop. But the gap it had created by backing up was still 11 feet; enough for the truck to pass.

As the truck began to cross in front of the sani, Castillo reversed direction and the sani moved forward, lumbering into the truck just behind its front bumper. With the truck moving up the ramp, and the sani pushing it to the side, the two enormous vehicles became locked in a shoving match.

Castillo urged the sani forward and the truck finally came to a halt with the sani wedged onto its bumper. Castillo started breathing again.

Then the truck's bumper fell off. Free from the grip of the sani, it started up the ramp again.

By now, everyone in the TMC was involved.

Castillo shouted, "How much time?" He didn't have to explain what he meant.

TMC operator Felix Brown already had an answer. An expert on every robotruck currently in use, he'd calculated the vehicle would average 75 mph over the 3.3 miles it would take to reach the runners on the expressway That gave them 158 seconds. He called out the number, then activated the countdown clock on the wall above his desk.

Their training kicked in, and no one waited for instructions. "NYPD aviation alerted!" Fields called out.

The countdown clock now read 153 seconds to impact.

Could they stop that thing from reaching the runners in 153 seconds? Even with all their preparation and technology, they needed a miracle.

And they got one.

At the top of the ramp, the truck rolled to a halt.

68

#1 RULE

"He lied to me." Hector was still trying to get through to Dana.

Before she could answer, Corby and Melissa stepped through the splintered doorway. She'd ordered them to wait outside until she'd secured the apartment.

"He didn't do it," Dana told them. "He had a kill switch and stopped it."

Melissa stepped in front of Hector's laptop and smiled at the sight of so many people safely running the race. Her smile would have been bigger if she'd known the part she'd played in Hector's actions.

Hector respected RosettaStone more than he respected anyone else. He craved Jason's friendship, but he *respected* her.

Her DNH "rule" resonated deeply with him. Which is why he created the kill switch. Jason had ordered him to get rid of it, and knowing that Hector always did what he wanted him to, Jason had never bothered to ask about it again.

But Hector couldn't understand why it bothered Jason so much. Jason didn't want people to get hurt, and those extra lines of code made sure of that. It gave Jason what he wanted. So Hector had left it in place.

Yet Jason's attitude led Hector to consider RosettaStone's warnings that Jason might be lying; he'd begun to really question it when she'd asked if he was sure about Jason. Though he'd given his standard "friends don't lie to each other" answer, he realized that he *didn't* know for sure. So he decided to ask. It hadn't escaped him that instead of a direct answer, Jason had answered a question with a question. In that moment, he knew Jason had lied to him.

Jason had violated what Hector had come to believe was doctrine in their relationship: Friend's don't lie to each other. But Jason had lied. Hector was devastated. He no longer had blind faith and utter trust in Jason.

This morning, Jason bullied him into giving the launch command.

But he'd done it knowing the kill switch would keep them from violating RosettaStone's #1 rule: DNH.

69

MOVING FORWARD AGAIN

Castillo didn't know why the truck stopped, and at the moment he didn't care. They'd get it all figured out, but right now he was glad that's *all* they had to figure out.

Then it happened. Castillo could not believe what he was seeing. The fucking truck was moving forward again!

Within seconds it was on the highway, headed for thousands of people.

70

I DIDN'T DO THIS

"Oh My God!" Melissa gasped, staring at Hector's laptop. "The truck's moving again!"

"No, I stopped it!" Hector protested. "With the kill switch!"

"Then what the hell is this!?" Dana grabbed him by the neck and shoved his faced toward the screen, more street cop than cybermarshal.

"I don't know. The kill switch should have stopped the truck. I didn't do this."

"Well who the fuck did!?" Dana was in full cop mode.

"I don't know. Ask Jason."

Jason! Dana had seen him off to the side when she came through the door, but in her race to stop Hector, she'd forgotten about him. Only now did it register that she'd allowed herself to ignore his presence because he vanished as she dove for Hector. She looked around, adrenalin pumping. "Where is he?"

71

WATCH THE FUN

Soldier grinned as he lay on the bed watching the live feed from his New York hotel room.

Seeing the truck stop at the ramp, only to restart and surge forward, he felt the same glow of satisfaction he did last night after rigging the truck. All it had taken for The Roc to jeopardize the mission was a few lines of code to create his oh-so-clever kill switch.

And that's all it took for Soldier to neutralize him. He could have deleted the kill switch altogether, but if Hector checked his code one last time he'd see it was missing. However, finding it safely in place, there'd be no reason to read beyond that.

If he did keep going, he'd discover Soldier's handiwork and delete it. But that was a chance Soldier had to take. It didn't matter—the C-4 would still be on the truck. And would very likely detonate when they towed the truck off the ramp.

His grin growing larger, Soldier sat back to watch the fun.

72

CAN'T FIRE THE MISSILE

112 seconds

As soon as the truck stopped, Castillo conference-called the Police Commissioner and the Office of Emergency Management. Just as he was reporting that the truck was no longer moving, it came back to life. Slamming the phone down, he called out the Commissioner's orders. "PC said any means necessary. Damage to property OK, but no casualties. Get me the RMP at the 4th Avenue exit!"

Seeing the truck start up again, Brown recalculated the time to impact and reset his clock: "One hundred and twelve seconds!"

93 seconds

Officer Dan Rodriguez was in his radio motor patrol car at the 4th Avenue exit ramp when Margolis's call came through. "Rodriguez, just listen," Castillo felt he couldn't talk fast enough. "Don't speak, or say 'yes sir.' Just do what I'm about to tell you. Put your car perpendicular to the roadway ASAP, blocking the entire center and parts of the left and right lanes. Safest place behind your car; shoot the tires of the truck coming your way. Got it?"

"Yes sir!"

When the truck's scanners picked up the patrol car, they would shift the truck from the center of the road to the left or right lane. The RMP couldn't block all three lanes, but the tighter fit would slow the truck and buy them a few precious seconds. It wasn't what Castillo needed, but he'd take what he could get.

"We're gonna have to take it out," he declared. "Where's the nearest armed bird?"

"Manhattan Bridge," Brown told him. "Four miles away." Gonna take one minute, at 240 mph, top speed."

"Get 'em goin'!" Castillo ordered, glad he'd insisted a few helicopters and drones be armed with missiles today for enhanced security.

61 seconds

The next half-minute was an eternity as they watched the truck bear down on Rodriguez's strategically-placed patrol car. Castillo's gambit paid off. The truck cut its speed, veered right, then slowed even more to maneuver between the police car and the cast-iron walls of the elevated highway.

Rodriguez shot at the tires until his pistol was empty. But his bullets had no effect on the hard rubber. And as soon as it was clear of the RMP, the truck returned to the center lane and began to pick up speed.

55 seconds

"How we lookin' on the missile?" Castillo asked Brown.

"Drone fires, it comes in at 600 mph, but locking on the truck will take at least three seconds."

"When they did this in Nice, they stopped the truck by shooting the driver," Margolis commented.

"There ain't no fucking driver here," Fields reminded him.

50 seconds

"Headwinds are slowing the drone," Brown told them. "We can't fire the missile. We'd hit runners and bring down the highway."

"Truck's picking up speed," Margolis shouted. "Fifty miles an hour!"

43 seconds

Castillo moved to his master console. As if reading his mind, Margolis said "It's at 60th." Castillo took control of the Roadway Zipper.

36 seconds

The RZ was programmed to move the median barrier on the Gowanus 12 feet with the push of a button. Castillo put it on manual control.

28 seconds

Someone seeing the RZ for the first time might think a large yellow RV had merged with a train. It rumbled along, an alien mechanized caterpillar ingesting the barrier through its front orifice and excreting it through its rear, leaving in its wake a new pattern. With the RZ in motion, the barrier was an articulated concrete snake bending and twisting according to the machine's whim.

The RZ moved at three feet per second. There was enough time for it to block the 36-foot-wide roadway by positioning the median barrier across the highway perpendicular to the truck's path, with the racers on the other side of the barrier. But at the truck's eventual speed, 60 mph, it would fly over the barrier and explode on impact, killing countless runners. Using the barrier to stop the truck was not an option.

Or was it?

15 seconds.

The Gowanus was closed to vehicles in both directions, but the runners used only half the roadway. The lanes in the opposite direction, on the other side of the barrier controlled by the RZ, were empty.

Seeing what Castillo was trying to do, Brown calculated the correct angle needed for the truck to hit the barrier and land in the closed lanes on the other side. "Thirty degrees," he told Castillo. But he knew that selecting an angle was not an RZ option, so he calculated the sine of 30 degrees and yelled out the hypotenuse: "42 feet!"

That was what Castillo needed to know. He steered the front of the RZ to a point 42 feet ahead and 36 feet to the left, so it would move the barrier where they needed it. If all went well, he'd have one second to spare. Castillo hadn't been to church in years. But he started praying now.

9 seconds

The truck was hurtling toward the runners, now at 60 mph, and now in a race with the RZ. Could the RZ move the barrier into place so the truck smashed into it instead of the people it was targeting?

1 second

Castillo pushed the RZ as hard as he could to wrestle the barrier into position.

With one second left on the clock, he got it almost directly in the truck's path.

The barrier caught the corner of the truck, sending it into the air at an angle that made it look like a marlin leaping out of the sea. It landed on its side, on the other half of the expressway. As it burst into flames, cheers erupted in the TMC.

Castillo slapped his hand to his forehead, muttering, "Fuck Me!"

The exhilarated staff knew nothing about the catastrophe they would have faced if the truck landed nose-first. There would be no inkling of that until a road crew arrived to tow the vehicle away and discovered "something weird" lying on the pavement. It was later determined that the C-4 detonator was knocked loose by the impact of the airborne truck's hard landing. The information was never made public. Privately, investigators dubbed it "the miracle of the marathon."

73

PROTECT AMERICANS' RIGHT TO DRIVE

Jason cursed as the Impala sped away from the apartment complex. He knew it! Hector's goddamn stupid "girlfriend" was a federal agent. Or Phoenix PD. Or an FBI informant.

His house was only minutes from the freeway and he'd soon be out of town, where he could really open it up. He wanted to be doing 90 now, but couldn't take the chance of being pulled over.

Glancing in the rear-view mirror, he saw flashing lights. Had he gone too fast after all?

No—a quick look at the speedometer told him he was doing only 60, five miles under the posted speed limit for this stretch of road.

But a police car was following him. Had to be her.

He could see that she was alone. And in a robo, which meant she'd be able to go only so fast. The speed of police robos in city limits was capped at 75 mph to prevent high-speed chases on the streets. With so much intelligent infrastructure everywhere, police departments now relied on data and video feeds to track and find vehicles they were pursuing. But it wouldn't work this time.

At 125 mph, his Impala could easily out-distance any robo, and he was headed for the cabin, an area where there were no cameras. He'd soon leave this meddlesome bitch and her hobbled robo far behind. He hit the gas and watched the speedometer crawl toward, then past, 85 mph.

Behind the wheel of the trailing robo, Dana screamed in frustration as the Impala took off.

Jason snickered as he watched the pursuing robo grow smaller behind him. It looked like it was standing still. In less than an hour he'd be at the cabin, where'd he'd hole up for as long as necessary.

He was now alone on the two-lane road he'd driven so often and knew so well. There was cross traffic every few miles, but so far no cars turning into or crossing the road. Even if there were, he had the right of way so there was no need to slow down. He nudged the speedometer higher.

Up ahead, a car was approaching in the oncoming lane. As he got closer, he saw it was a robo. When they were 200 feet apart, he dropped his wheels over the line, into the other lane. The robo immediately slowed and pulled toward the shoulder. Jason gave it the finger as he sped past.

Ten miles later, a robo-truck came toward him. When he dropped into the oncoming lane this time, he kept going until there was only 100 feet between them. As the robo swerved onto the shoulder, Jason jumped back to his own lane.

But he cut the wheels a little too sharply; for a few frantic seconds the Impala threatened to leave the road before he regained control and veered back onto asphalt.

OK, he thought. *No need for any more of that. Not the time to fuck with them. I can do that any time.* He'd just drive fast and straight to the cabin. He inched the speedometer toward 100 mph.

Approaching Seldon Way, he topped 100, heading toward 105. The sign indicating cross traffic flew past and he automatically glanced right and left to make sure there were no cars approaching.

A rise kept Jason from seeing the vintage station wagon on Seldon approaching Highway 87 from the right. Even if he had, he would not have seen the driver dialing a number on his cell phone, feeling free to do so because he was alone in the middle of nowhere.

The man behind the wheel of the station wagon never saw the STOP sign at the intersection with 87, never touched the brake as he crossed the highway.

Jason broadsided the car at 100 mph, instantly demolishing both vehicles and killing both drivers.

When the wreckage was cleared hours later, there was only one recognizable part of the Impala, and that would register only with someone who really knew the car: a piece of chrome in the shape of a sleek jet.

Somehow, the station wagon's rear bumper was left completely intact. On it was a bumper sticker: *Protect Americans' Right to Drive.*

Epilogue

A RIGHT WAY TO DO THIS

Two Months Later

Corby and Dana were enjoying their eighth dinner together. Both were still being cautious about a possible future together, but they were more relaxed about where they might be going. He wasn't a cop or soldier, but she'd tried that and it didn't work out.

Corby was now more comfortably moving on with his life. Tammy was gone, he'd grieved, and walling himself off was not going to bring her back.

Tonight, Dana was full of news. "The head of the Portland office is being bumped up to head Health and Human Services, which he knows zero about. But that's not my problem. The good news is, he's taking Kyle with him as a reward for his loyalty. Better good news: Guess who the new head of my office is? Not the head of the *unit*. The head of the *whole freaking office*!"

"You deserve it!"

"That's what I wanted to say when they told me. I restrained myself."

"Wise decision."

"Too bad they didn't keep Kyle. I'd be his boss!" Dana's eyes gleamed as she envisioned that reality. "But there's more," she raced on. "They know about Melissa. I pushed for no charges, but Kyle insisted. His final swipe at me. He wants her charged with hacking and anything else he can think of. He'd throw in kidnapping, homicide, and jaywalking if he could."

"Does she know?"

"Not yet. But it doesn't matter. The *new* head of the office has already interceded. All she's gonna get is a six-month suspended sentence. Then I'm gonna hire her to head our new anti-hacking unit."

Hector was sitting on a cold metal chair at a molded-plastic table in a featureless room, when someone who hadn't questioned him yet entered. He regarded this new person without registering his air of supreme authority. The newcomer didn't sit down, as the others had, as he presented a wallet holding a badge and ID that he didn't give Hector time to read.

"You've been indicted for hacking, property damage, and a raft of other offenses," he stated matter-of-factly. "Even with the judge's leniency because you tried to stop the attack in New York, you're still facing serious time in prison."

"I know."

"Or you can get counseling, five years of community service, and a job working for us."

"What would I do for you?"

"Let's say you'd be . . . a security analyst."

"Who would I be working for?"

"No one."

"You said I'd work for you."

"You will. But officially we don't exist."

"Then how can you give me a job?"

The man across the table was amused. He could already see

that Hector was a perfect candidate. "We'll work that out. You want the deal?"

Hector gazed down at the table for several seconds. Then he looked up at the man standing before him, who was waiting, endlessly patient, as if he had all the time in the world. "I'll do it," Hector said flatly. "But I won't hurt anyone."

The man smiled.

Six months later, an item appeared in the *New York Times:*

"Charles Larry Dawson has been charged with felony property damage and attempted murder in last month's aviation mishap that caused a small plane to crash into Lake Michigan. The pilot was able to bail out and was rescued unhurt by a passing fishing vessel.

Dawson had been under investigation for several months on suspicion that he was involved in a number of small-plane crashes, but he could not be tied to any of the incidents. Officials revealed they were able to link him to this crash—and a dozen others—with help from an unnamed source that hacked Dawson's computer."

Media attention led to the public outcry Corby had been fighting for, and Doris Richmond was able to ride that momentum to delay the pending federal regulations while her newly-approved committee held its hearings. Her press release promised that the committee would solicit public input.

One of Corby's now-frequent interviews with Sid Farrell happened to be scheduled for the day he was going to make an announcement of his own. He'd persuaded the heads of CAV-related companies to work with Washington to explore new ways of moving forward.

"There can be a Win-Win when industry cooperates with government instead of trying to game the system," he told Farrell. "There *is* a right way to do this."

Acknowledgments

A huge thank-you to Katrina Diaz-Arnold, the perfect editor, who generously went above and beyond, and gave me back a manuscript vastly improved from the one I gave her.

And to Laura, a true partner who is unerringly honest, nudges me to do things I'm reluctant to do but often should, saves me by seeing things that I miss, and is always there for me.

Cary Pepper

About the Authors

Sam Schwartz is a former New York City Traffic Commissioner and an award-winning and internationally-recognized transportation engineer. Mr. Schwartz, often referred to by his nom de plume "Gridlock Sam," released the word gridlock into the public lexicon during the 1980 NYC Transit strike. Currently, Schwartz is the Chair and Founder of the Transportation Research Program at Roosevelt House at Hunter College, where he teaches a course on urban transportation. He founded Sam Schwartz Engineering, a nation-wide transportation consultancy, and served as CEO from 1995–2021. He was the "Dear Abby" of NYC traffic with his Gridlock Sam column in the New York Daily News from 1990 to 2022. He started his transportation career in the late 1960s as a NYC cabbie and joined the Traffic Department as a junior engineer in 1971. Mr. Schwartz's most recent books, *No One at the Wheel: Driverless Cars and the Road of the Future* (2018) and *Street Smart: The Rise of Cities and The Fall of Cars* (2015), present a problem-solving recipe for cities faced with rapid changes in modes, automation, demographic shifts, and travelers' preferences. He obtained his Bachelor of Science degree in Physics at Brooklyn College and received a Master of Science degree in Civil Engineering from the University of Pennsylvania. He is a licensed Professional Engineer.

ABOUT THE AUTHORS

Cary Pepper is a playwright, novelist, and screenwriter. His plays have been presented throughout the United States and internationally. Among his one-act plays, *Small Things* won the Robert R. Lehan Playwriting Award and the Tennessee Williams/New Orleans Literary Festival 2006 One Act Play Contest, and has been airing on National Public Radio as part of the Playing on Air series. *Stealing Melissa* won the Doc Jim Martin Playwright Competition, and *The Walrus Said* won the Religious Arts Guild Playwriting Competition and *Party Favors* won the 2016 Goshen Peace Play Contest. Among his full-length plays, *How It Works* was given a staged reading at the Abingdon Theatre in New York City, was a Finalist at Dayton Playhouse's FutureFest 2010, and won the 2012 Ashland New Plays Festival. *Cufflinked* was a semifinalist in the 2014 Ashland New Plays Festival; *And Jonah Rose Up* was a semifinalist in the Dorothy Silver Playwriting Competition; *The Maltese Frenchman* was a Finalist for the National Play Award.

OPEN ROAD

INTEGRATED MEDIA

Find a full list of our authors and titles at www.openroadmedia.com

FOLLOW US

@OpenRoadMedia

EARLY BIRD BOOKS
FRESH DEALS, DELIVERED DAILY

Love to read?
Love great sales?

Get fantastic deals on bestselling ebooks delivered to your inbox every day!

Sign up today at
earlybirdbooks.com/book